I0557533

The

LISTENER

AND OTHER STORIES.

The

LISTENER

AND OTHER STORIES.

By ALGERNON BLACKWOOD

Edited by FINN J.D. JOHN

F.W. von Junzt
Dusseldorf - Stregoicavar - Corvallis
Bibliothekpreße

Published 2016 by F.W. von Junzt Bibliothekspreße

New material, book design, and layout copyright ©2016
by F.W. von Junzt Bibliothekspreße, with the exceptions
noted below:

Copyright protections on *The Listener and Other Stories* have
expired worldwide. In the spirit of good stewardship of the
public domain, no copyright claim is made over any of
Algernon Blackwood's original text as presented in this book,
including any and all corrections and style changes made
to the original text.

Original edition published in 1917
by Alfred A. Knopf, New York.

Softcover edition
ISBN: 978-1-63591-602-7

F.W. von Junzt Bibliothekspreße
c/o Pulp-Lit Productions
2323 Northwest Monroe Street
Post Office Box 77
Corvallis, Oregon

http://von-junzt.org
http://pulp-lit.com

CONTENTS.

The
LISTENER

AND OTHER STORIES.

The LISTENER.

SEPTEMBER 4. — I have hunted all over London for rooms suited to my income — £120 a year — and have at last found them. Two rooms, without modern conveniences, it is true, and in an old, ramshackle building, but within a stone's throw of P— Place and in an eminently respectable street. The rent is only £25 a year. I had begun to despair when at last I found them by chance.

The chance was a mere chance, and unworthy of record. I had to sign a lease for a year, and I did so willingly. The furniture from our old place in Hampshire, which has been stored so long, will just suit them.

OCTOBER 1. — Here I am in my two rooms, in the centre of London, and not far from the offices of the periodicals, where occasionally I dispose of an article or two. The building is at the end of a *cul-de-sac*. The alley is well paved and clean, and lined chiefly with the backs of sedate and institutional-looking buildings. There is a stable in it. My own house is dignified with the title of "Chambers." I feel as if one day the honour must prove too much for it, and it will swell with pride — and fall asunder. It is very old. The floor of my sitting-room has valleys and low hills on it, and the top of the door slants away from the ceiling with a glorious disregard of what is usual. They must have quarrelled — fifty years ago — and have been going apart ever since.

OCTOBER 2. — My landlady is old and thin, with a faded, dusty face. She is uncommunicative. The few words she utters seem to cost her pain. Probably her lungs are half choked with dust. She keeps my rooms as free from this commodity as possible, and has the assistance of a strong girl who brings up the breakfast and lights the fire. As I have said already, she is not communicative. In reply to pleasant efforts on my part she informed me briefly that I was the only occupant of the house at present. My rooms had not been occupied for some years. There had been other gentlemen upstairs, but they had left.

She never looks straight at me when she speaks, but fixes her dim eyes on my middle waistcoat button, till I get nervous and begin to think it isn't on straight, or is the wrong sort of button altogether.

OCTOBER 8. — My week's book is nicely kept, and so

far is reasonable. Milk and sugar 7d., bread 6d., butter 8d., marmalade 6d., eggs 1s. 8d., laundress 2s. 9d., oil 6d., attendance 5s.; total 12s. 2d.

The landlady has a son who, she told me, is "somethink on a homnibus." He comes occasionally to see her. I think he drinks, for he talks very loud, regardless of the hour of the day or night, and tumbles about over the furniture downstairs.

All the morning I sit indoors writing — articles; verses for the comic papers; a novel I've been "at" for three years, and concerning which I have dreams; a children's book, in which the imagination has free rein; and another book which is to last as long as myself, since it is an honest record of my soul's advance or retreat in the struggle of life. Besides these, I keep a book of poems which I use as a safety valve, and concerning which I have no dreams whatsoever.

Between the lot I am always occupied. In the afternoons I generally try to take a walk for my health's sake, through Regent's Park, into Kensington Gardens, or farther afield to Hampstead Heath.

OCTOBER 10. — Everything went wrong to-day. I have two eggs for breakfast. This morning one of them was bad. I rang the bell for Emily. When she came in I was reading the paper, and, without looking up, I said, "Egg's bad."

"Oh, is it, sir?" she said; "I'll get another one," and went out, taking the egg with her. I waited my breakfast for her return, which was in five minutes. She put the new egg on the table and went away. But, when I looked down, I saw that she had taken away the good egg and left the bad one — all green and yellow — in the slop basin. I rang again.

"You've taken the wrong egg," I said.

"Oh!" she exclaimed; "I thought the one I took down didn't smell so very bad." In due time she returned with the good egg, and I resumed my breakfast with two eggs, but less appetite. It was all very trivial, to be sure, but so stupid that I felt annoyed. The character of that egg influenced everything I did. I wrote a bad article, and tore it up. I got a bad headache. I used bad words — to myself. Everything was bad, so I "chucked" work and went for a long walk.

I dined at a cheap chop-house on my way back, and reached home about nine o'clock.

Rain was just beginning to fall as I came in, and the wind was rising. It promised an ugly night. The alley looked dismal and dreary, and the hall of the house, as I passed through it, felt chilly as a tomb. It was the first stormy night I had experienced in my new quarters. The draughts were awful. They came criss-cross, met in the middle of the room, and formed eddies and whirlpools and cold silent currents that almost lifted the hair of my head. I stuffed up the sashes of the windows with neckties and odd socks, and sat over the smoky fire to keep warm. First I tried to write, but found it too cold. My hand turned to ice on the paper.

What tricks the wind did play with the old place! It came rushing up the forsaken alley with a sound like the feet of a hurrying crowd of people who stopped suddenly at the door. I felt as if a lot of curious folk had arranged themselves just outside and were staring up at my windows. Then they took to their heels again and fled whispering and laughing down the lane, only, however, to return with the next gust of wind and repeat their impertinence. On the other side of my room a single square window opens into a sort of shaft, or well, that measures about six feet across to the back wall of another house. Down this funnel the wind dropped, and puffed and shouted. Such noises I never heard before. Between these two entertainments I sat over the fire in a great-coat, listening to the deep booming in the chimney. It was like being in a ship at sea, and I almost looked for the floor to rise in undulations and rock to and fro.

OCTOBER 12. — I wish I were not quite so lonely — and so poor. And yet I love both my loneliness and my poverty. The former makes me appreciate the companionship of the wind and rain, while the latter preserves my liver and prevents me wasting time in dancing attendance upon women. Poor, ill-dressed men are not acceptable "attendants."

My parents are dead, and my only sister is — no, not dead exactly, but married to a very rich man. They travel most of the time, he to find his health, she to lose herself. Through sheer neglect on her part she has long passed out of my life. The door closed when, after an absolute silence of five years, she sent me a cheque for £50 at Christmas. It was signed by her husband! I returned it to her in a thousand pieces and in an unstamped envelope. So at least I had the satisfaction of knowing that it cost her something! She wrote back with a broad quill pen that covered a whole page with three lines, "You are evidently as cracked as ever, and rude and ungrateful into the bargain." It had always been my special terror lest the insanity of my father's family should

leap across the generations and appear in me. This thought
haunted me, and she knew it. So after this little exchange
of civilities the door slammed, never to open again. I heard
the crash it made, and, with it, the falling from the walls of
my heart of many little bits of china with their own peculiar
value — rare china, some of it, that only needed dusting.
The same walls, too, carried mirrors in which I used sometimes to see reflected the misty lawns of childhood, the daisy
chains, the wind-torn blossoms scattered through the orchard
by warm rains, the robbers' cave in the long walk, and the
hidden store of apples in the hayloft. She was my inseparable
companion then — but, when the door slammed, the mirrors
cracked across their entire length, and the visions they held
vanished for ever. Now I am quite alone. At forty one cannot
begin all over again to build up careful friendships, and all
others are comparatively worthless.

OCTOBER 14. — My bedroom is 10 by 10. It is below
the level of the front room, and a step leads down into it.
Both rooms are very quiet on calm nights, for there is no
traffic down this forsaken alley-way. In spite of the occasional larks of the wind, it is a most sheltered strip. At its
upper end, below my windows, all the cats of the neighbourhood congregate as soon as darkness gathers. They lie
undisturbed on the long ledge of a blind window of the
opposite building, for after the postman has come and gone
at 9:30, no footsteps ever dare to interrupt their sinister
conclave, no step but my own, or sometimes the unsteady
footfall of the son who "is somethink on a homnibus."

OCTOBER 15. — I dined at an "A.B.C." shop on poached

eggs and coffee, and then went for a stroll round the outer edge of Regent's Park. It was ten o'clock when I got home. I counted no less than thirteen cats, all of a dark colour, crouching under the lee side of the alley walls. It was a cold night, and the stars shone like points of ice in a blue-black sky. The cats turned their heads and stared at me in silence as I passed. An odd sensation of shyness took possession of me under the glare of so many pairs of unblinking eyes. As I fumbled with the latch-key they jumped noiselessly down and pressed against my legs, as if anxious to be let in. But I slammed the door in their faces and ran quickly upstairs. The front room, as I entered to grope for the matches, felt as cold as a stone vault, and the air held an unusual dampness.

OCTOBER 17. — For several days I have been working on a ponderous article that allows no play for the fancy. My imagination requires a judicious rein; I am afraid to let it loose, for it carries me sometimes into appalling places beyond the stars and beneath the world. No one realises the danger more than I do. But what a foolish thing to write here — for there is no one to know, no one to realize! My mind of late has held unusual thoughts, thoughts I have never had before, about medicines and drugs and the treatment of strange illnesses. I cannot imagine their source.

At no time in my life have I dwelt upon such ideas as now constantly throng my brain. I have had no exercise lately, for the weather has been shocking; and all my afternoons have been spent in the reading-room of the British Museum, where I have a reader's ticket.

I have made an unpleasant discovery: there are rats in the house. At night from my bed I have heard them scampering across the hills and valleys of the front room, and my sleep has been a good deal disturbed in consequence.

OCTOBER 19.—The landlady, I find, has a little boy with her, probably her son's child. In fine weather he plays in the alley, and draws a wooden cart over the cobbles. One of the wheels is off, and it makes a most distracting noise. After putting up with it as long as possible, I found it was getting on my nerves, and I could not write. So I rang the bell. Emily answered it.

"Emily, will you ask the little fellow to make less noise? It's impossible to work."

The girl went downstairs, and soon afterwards the child was called in by the kitchen door. I felt rather a brute for spoiling his play. In a few minutes, however, the noise began again, and I felt that he was the brute. He dragged the broken toy with a string over the stones till the rattling noise jarred every nerve in my body. It became unbearable, and I rang the bell a second time.

"That noise *must* be put a stop to!" I said to the girl, with decision.

"Yes, sir," she grinned, "I know; but one of the wheels is hoff. The men in the stable offered to mend it for 'im, but he wouldn't let them. He says he likes it that way."

"I can't help what he likes. The noise must stop. I can't write."

"Yes, sir; I'll tell Mrs. Monson."

The noise stopped for the day then.

OCTOBER 23. — Every day for the past week that cart has rattled over the stones, till I have come to think of it as a huge carrier's van with four wheels and two horses; and every morning I have been obliged to ring the bell and have it stopped. The last time Mrs. Monson herself came up, and said she was sorry I had been annoyed; the sounds should not occur again. With rare discursiveness she went on to ask if I was comfortable, and how I liked the rooms. I replied cautiously. I mentioned the rats. She said they were mice. I spoke of the draughts. She said, "Yes, it were a draughty 'ouse." I referred to the cats, and she said they had been as long as she could remember. By way of conclusion, she informed me that the house was over two hundred years old, and that the last gentleman who had occupied my rooms was a painter who " 'ad real Jimmy Bueys and Raffles 'anging all hover the walls." It took me some moments to discern that Cimabue and Raphael were in the woman's mind.

OCTOBER 24. — Last night the son who is "somethink on a homnibus" came in. He had evidently been drinking, for I heard loud and angry voices below in the kitchen long after I had gone to bed. Once, too, I caught the singular words rising up to me through the floor, "Burning from top to bottom is the only thing that'll ever make this 'ouse right." I knocked on the floor, and the voices ceased suddenly, though later I again heard their clamour in my dreams.

These rooms are very quiet, almost too quiet sometimes. On windless nights they are silent as the grave, and the house might be miles in the country. The roar of London's traffic reaches me only in heavy, distant vibrations. It holds an ominous note sometimes, like that of an approaching army, or an immense tidal-wave very far away thundering in the night.

OCTOBER 27.—Mrs. Monson, though admirably silent, is a foolish, fussy woman. She does such stupid things. In dusting the room she puts all my things in the wrong places. The ash-trays, which should be on the writing-table, she sets in a silly row on the mantelpiece. The pen-tray, which should be beside the inkstand, she hides away cleverly among the books on my reading-desk.

My gloves she arranges daily in idiotic array upon a half-filled bookshelf, and I always have to rearrange them on the low table by the door. She places my armchair at impossible angles between the fire and the light, and the tablecloth—the one with Trinity Hall stains—she puts on the table in such a fashion that when I look at it I feel as if my tie and all my clothes were on crooked and awry. She exasperates me. Her very silence and meekness are irritating.

Sometimes I feel inclined to throw the inkstand at her, just to bring an expression into her watery eyes and a squeak from those colourless lips. Dear me! What violent expressions I am making use of! How very foolish of me! And yet it almost seems as if the words were not my own, but had been spoken into my ear—I mean, I never make use of such terms naturally.

OCTOBER 30.—I have been here a month. The place does not agree with me, I think. My headaches are more frequent and violent, and my nerves are a perpetual source of discomfort and annoyance.

I have conceived a great dislike for Mrs. Monson, a feeling I am certain she reciprocates.

Somehow, the impression comes frequently to me that there are goings on in this house of which I know nothing, and which she is careful to hide from me.

Last night her son slept in the house, and this morning as I was standing at the window I saw him go out. He glanced up and caught my eye. It was a loutish figure and a singularly repulsive face that I saw, and he gave me the benefit of a very unpleasant leer. At least, so I imagined.

Evidently I am getting absurdly sensitive to trifles, and I suppose it is my disordered nerves making themselves felt. In the British Museum this afternoon I noticed several people at the readers' table staring at me and watching every movement I made. Whenever I looked up from my books I found their eyes upon me. It seemed to me unnecessary and unpleasant, and I left earlier than was my custom. When I reached the door I threw back a last look into the room, and saw every head at the table turned in my direction. It annoyed me very much, and yet I know it is foolish to take note of such things. When I am well they pass me by. I must get more regular exercise. Of late I have had next to none.

NOVEMBER 2. — The utter stillness of this house is beginning to oppress me. I wish there were other fellows living upstairs. No footsteps ever sound overhead, and no tread ever passes my door to go up the next flight of stairs. I am beginning to feel some curiosity to go up myself and see what the upper rooms are like. I feel lonely here and isolated, swept into a deserted corner of the world and forgotten.... Once I actually caught myself gazing into the long, cracked mirrors, trying to see the sunlight dancing beneath the trees in the orchard. But only deep shadows seemed to congregate there now, and I soon desisted.

It has been very dark all day, and no wind stirring. The fogs have begun. I had to use a reading-lamp all this morning. There was no cart to be heard to-day. I actually missed it. This morning, in the gloom and silence, I think I could almost have welcomed it. After all, the sound is a very human one, and this empty house at the end of the alley holds other noises that are not quite so satisfactory. I have never once seen a policeman in the lane, and the postmen always hurry out with no evidence of a desire to loiter.

10 P.M. — As I write this I hear no sound but the deep murmur of the distant traffic and the low sighing of the wind. The two sounds melt into one another. Now and again a cat raises its shrill, uncanny cry upon the darkness. The cats are always there under my windows when the darkness falls. The wind is dropping into the funnel with a noise like the sudden sweeping of immense distant wings. It is a dreary night. I feel lost and forgotten.

NOVEMBER 3 — From my windows I can see arrivals. When anyone comes to the door I can just see the hat and shoulders and the hand on the bell. Only two fellows have been to see me since I came here two months ago. Both of them I saw from the window before they came up, and heard their voices asking if I was in. Neither of them ever came back.

I have finished the ponderous article. On reading it through, however, I was dissatisfied with it, and drew my pencil through almost every page. There were strange expressions and ideas in that I could not explain, and viewed with amazement, not to say alarm. They did not sound like my *very own*, and I could not remember having written them. Can it be that my memory is beginning to be affected?

My pens are never to be found. That stupid old woman puts them in a different place each day. I must give her due credit for finding so many new hiding places; such ingenuity is wonderful. I have told her repeatedly, but she always says, "I'll speak to Emily, sir." Emily always says, "I'll tell Mrs. Monson, sir." Their foolishness makes me irritable and scatters all my thoughts. I should like to stick the lost pens into them and turn them out, blind-eyed, to be scratched and mauled by those thousand hungry cats. Whew! What a ghastly thought! Where in the world did it come from? Such an idea is no more my own than it is the policeman's. Yet I felt I *had* to write it. It was like a voice singing in my head, and my pen wouldn't stop till the last word was finished. What ridiculous nonsense! I must and will restrain myself. I must take more regular exercise; my nerves and liver plague me horribly.

NOVEMBER 4. — I attended a curious lecture in the French quarter on "Death," but the room was so hot and I was so weary that I fell asleep. The only part I heard, however, touched my imagination vividly. Speaking of suicides, the lecturer said that self-murder was no escape from the miseries of the present, but only a preparation of greater sorrow for the future. Suicides, he declared, cannot shirk their responsibilities so easily. They must return to take up life exactly where they laid it so violently down, but with the added pain and punishment of their weakness. Many of them wander the earth in unspeakable misery till they can *reclothe* themselves in the body of someone else — generally a lunatic, or weak-minded person, who cannot resist the hideous obsession. This is their only means of escape. Surely a weird and horrible idea! I wish I had slept all the time and not heard it at all. My mind is morbid enough without such ghastly fancies. Such mischievous propaganda should be stopped by the police. I'll write to the *Times* and suggest it. Good idea.

I walked home through Greek Street, Soho, and imagined that a hundred years had slipped back into place and De Quincey was still there, haunting the night with invocations to his "just, subtle, and mighty" drug. His vast dreams seemed to hover not very far away. Once started in my brain, the pictures refused to go away; and I saw him sleeping in that cold, tenantless mansion with the strange little waif who was afraid of its ghosts, both together in the shadows under a single horseman's cloak; or wandering in the companionship of the spectral Anne; or, later still, on his way to the eternal rendezvous at the foot of Great Titchfield Street, the rendezvous she never was able to keep. What an unutterable gloom, what an untold horror of sorrow and suffering comes over me as I try to realise something of what that man — boy he then was — must have taken into his lonely heart.

As I came up the alley I saw a light in the top window, and a head and shoulders thrown in an exaggerated shadow upon the blind. I wondered what the son could be doing up there at such an hour.

NOVEMBER 5. — This morning, while writing, someone came up the creaking stairs and knocked cautiously at my door. Thinking it was the landlady, I said, "Come in!" The knock was repeated, and I cried louder, "Come in, come in!" But no one turned the handle, and I continued my writing with a vexed "Well, stay out, then!" under my breath. Went on writing? I tried to, but my thoughts had suddenly dried up at their source. I could not set down a single word. It was a dark, yellow-fog morning, and there was little enough inspiration in the air as it was, but that stupid woman standing just outside my door waiting to be told again to come in roused a spirit of vexation that filled my head to the exclusion of all else. At last I jumped up and opened the door myself.

"What do you want, and why in the world don't you come in?" I cried out. But the words dropped into empty air. There was no one there. The fog poured up the dingy staircase in deep yellow coils, but there was no sign of a human being anywhere.

I slammed the door, with imprecations upon the house and its noises, and went back to my work. A few minutes later Emily came in with a letter.

"Were you or Mrs. Monson outside a few minutes ago

knocking at my door?"

"No, sir."

"Are you sure?

"Mrs. Monson's gone to market, and there's no one but me and the child in the 'ole 'ouse, and I've been washing the dishes for the last hour, sir."

I fancied the girl's face turned a shade paler. She fidgeted towards the door with a glance over her shoulder.

"Wait, Emily," I said, and then told her what I had heard.

She stared stupidly at me, though her eyes shifted now and then over the articles in the room.

"Who was it?" I asked when I had come to the end.

"Mrs. Monson says it's honly mice," she said, as if repeating a learned lesson.

"Mice!" I exclaimed, "it's nothing of the sort. Someone was feeling about outside my door. Who was it? Is the son in the house?"

Her whole manner changed suddenly, and she became earnest instead of evasive. She seemed anxious to tell the truth.

"Oh no, sir; there's no one in the house at all but you and me and the child, and there couldn't 'ave been nobody at your door. As for them knocks — " She stopped abruptly, as though she had said too much.

"Well, what about the knocks?" I said more gently.

"Of course," she stammered, "the knocks isn't mice, nor the footsteps neither, but then — "

Again she came to a full halt.

"Anything wrong with the house?"

"Lor', no, sir; the drains is splendid!"

"I don't mean drains, girl. I mean, did anything — anything bad ever happen here?"

She flushed up to the roots of her hair, and then turned suddenly pale again. She was obviously in considerable distress, and there was something she was anxious, yet afraid to tell — some forbidden thing she was not allowed to mention.

"I don't mind what it was, only I should like to know," I said encouragingly.

Raising her frightened eyes to my face, she began to blurt out something about "that which 'appened once to a gentleman that lived hupstairs," when a shrill voice calling her name sounded below.

"Emily, Emily!" It was the returning landlady, and the girl tumbled downstairs as if pulled backwards by a rope, leaving me full of conjectures as to what in the world could have happened to a gentleman *upstairs* that could in so curious a manner affect my ears *downstairs*.

NOVEMBER 10. — I have done capital work; have finished the ponderous article and had it accepted for the — *Review,* and another one ordered. I feel well and cheerful, and have had regular exercise and good sleep; no headaches, no nerves, no liver! Those pills the chemist recommended are wonderful. I can watch the child playing with his cart and feel no annoyance; sometimes I almost feel inclined to join him. Even the grey-faced landlady rouses pity in me; I am sorry for her: so worn, so weary, so oddly put together, just like the building. She looks as if she had once suffered some shock of terror, and was momentarily dreading another. When I spoke to her to-day very gently about not putting the pens in the ash-tray and the gloves on the book-shelf she raised her faint eyes to mine for the first time, and said with the ghost of a smile, "I'll try and re-member, sir." I felt inclined to pat her on the back and say, "Come, cheer up and be jolly. Life's not so bad after all." Oh! I am much better. There's nothing like open air and success and good sleep. They build up as if by magic the portions of the heart eaten down by despair and unsatisfied yearnings. Even to the cats I feel friendly. When I came in at eleven o'clock to-night they followed me to the door in a stream, and I stooped down to stroke the one nearest to me.

Bah! The brute hissed and spat, and struck at me with her paws. The claw caught my hand and drew blood in a thin line. The others danced sideways into the darkness, screeching, as though I had done them an injury. I believe these cats really hate me. Perhaps they are only waiting to be reinforced. Then they will attack me. Ha, ha! In spite of the momentary annoyance, this fancy sent me laughing upstairs to my room.

The fire was out, and the room seemed unusually cold. As I groped my way over to the mantelpiece to find the matches I realised all at once that there was another person standing beside me in the darkness. I could, of course, see nothing, but my fingers, feeling along the ledge, came into forcible contact with something that was at once withdrawn. It was cold and moist. I could have sworn it was somebody's hand. My flesh began to creep instantly.

"Who's that?" I exclaimed in a loud voice.

My voice dropped into the silence like a pebble into a deep well. There was no answer, but at the same moment I heard someone moving away from me across the room in the direction of the door. It was a confused sort of footstep, and the sound of garments brushing the furniture on the way. The same second my hand stumbled upon the match-box, and I struck a light. I expected to see Mrs. Monson, or Emily, or perhaps the son who is something on an omnibus. But the flare of the gas-jet illumined an empty room; there was not a sign of a person anywhere. I felt the hair stir upon my head, and instinctively I backed up against the wall, lest something should approach me from behind. I was distinctly alarmed. But the next minute I recovered myself. The door was open on to the landing, and I crossed the room, not without some inward trepidation, and went out. The light from the room fell upon the stairs, but there was no one to be seen anywhere, nor was there any sound on the creaking wooden staircase to indicate a departing creature.

I was in the act of turning to go in again when a sound overhead caught my ear. It was a very faint sound, not unlike the sigh of wind; yet it could not have been the wind, for the night was still as the grave. Though it was not repeated, I resolved to go upstairs and see for myself what it all meant. Two senses had been affected — touch and hearing — and I could not believe that I had been deceived. So, with a lighted candle, I went stealthily forth on my unpleasant journey into the upper regions of this queer little old house.

On the first landing there was only one door, and it was locked. On the second there was also only one door, but when I turned the handle it opened. There came forth to meet me the chill musty air that is characteristic of a long unoccupied room. With it there came an indescribable odour. I use the adjective advisedly. Though very faint, diluted as it were, it was nevertheless an odour that made my gorge rise. I had never smelt anything like it before, and I cannot describe it.

The room was small and square, close under the roof, with a sloping ceiling and two tiny windows. It was cold as the grave, without a shred of carpet or a stick of furniture. The icy atmosphere and the nameless odour combined to make the room abominable to me, and, after lingering a moment to see that it contained no cupboards or corners into which a person might have crept for concealment, I made haste to shut the door, and went downstairs again to bed. Evidently I had been deceived after all as to the noise.

In the night I had a foolish but very vivid dream. I dreamed that the landlady and another person, dark and not properly visible, entered my room on all fours, followed by a horde of immense cats. They attacked me as I lay in bed, and murdered me, and then dragged my body upstairs and deposited it on the floor of that cold little square room under the roof.

NOVEMBER 11. — Since my talk with Emily — the unfinished talk — I have hardly once set eyes on her. Mrs. Monson now attends wholly to my wants. As usual, she does everything exactly as I don't like it done. It is all too utterly trivial to mention, but it is exceedingly irritating. Like small doses of morphine often repeated, she has finally a cumulative effect.

NOVEMBER 12. — This morning I woke early, and came into the front room to get a book, meaning to read in bed till it was time to get up. Emily was laying the fire.

"Good morning!" I said cheerfully. "Mind you make a good fire. It's very cold."

The girl turned and showed me a startled face. It was not Emily at all!

"Where's Emily?" I exclaimed.

"You mean the girl as was 'ere before me?"

"Has Emily left?"

"I came on the 6th," she replied sullenly, "and she'd gone then." I got my book and went back to bed. Emily must have been sent away almost immediately after our conversation. This reflection kept coming between me and the printed page. I was glad when it was time to get up. Such prompt energy, such merciless decision, seemed to argue something of importance — to somebody.

NOVEMBER 13. — The wound inflicted by the cat's claw has swollen, and causes me annoyance and some pain. It throbs and itches. I'm afraid my blood must be in poor condition, or it would have healed by now. I opened it with a penknife soaked in an antiseptic solution, and cleansed it thoroughly. I have heard unpleasant stories of the results of wounds inflicted by cats.

NOVEMBER 14. — In spite of the curious effect this house certainly exercises upon my nerves, I like it. It is lonely and deserted in the very heart of London, but it is also for that reason quiet to work in. I wonder why it is so cheap. Some people might he suspicious, but I did not even ask the reason. No answer is better than a lie. If only I could remove the cats from the outside and the rats from the inside. I feel that I shall grow accustomed more and more to its peculiarities, and shall die here. Ah, that expression reads queerly and gives a wrong impression: I meant *live and die* here. I shall renew the lease from year to year till one of us crumbles to pieces. From present indications the building will be the first to go.

NOVEMBER 16. — It is abominable the way my nerves go up and down with me — and rather discouraging. This morning I woke to find my clothes scattered about the room, and a cane chair overturned beside the bed. My coat and waistcoat looked just as if they had been *tried on* by someone in the night. I had horribly vivid dreams, too, in which someone covering his face with his hands kept coming close up to me, crying out as if in pain. "Where can I find covering? Oh, who will clothe me?" How silly, and yet it frightened me a little. It was so dreadfully real. It is now over a year since I last walked in my sleep and woke up with such a shock on the cold pavement of Earl's Court Road, where I then lived. I thought I was cured, but evidently not. This discovery has rather a disquieting effect upon me. To-night I shall resort to the old trick of tying my toe to the bed-post.

NOVEMBER 17.—Last night I was again troubled by most oppressive dreams. Someone seemed to be moving in the night up and down my room, sometimes passing into the front room, and then returning to stand beside the bed and stare intently down upon me. I was being watched by this person all night long. I never actually awoke, though I was often very near it. I suppose it was a nightmare from indigestion, for this morning I have one of my old vile headaches. Yet all my clothes lay about the floor when I awoke, where they had evidently been flung (had I so tossed them?) during the dark hours, and my trousers trailed over the step into the front room.

Worse than this, though—I fancied I noticed about the room in the morning that strange, fetid odour. Though very faint, its mere suggestion is foul and nauseating. What in the world can it be, I wonder?. . . In future I shall lock my door.

NOVEMBER 26.—I have accomplished a lot of good work during this past week, and have also managed to get regular exercise. I have felt well and in an equable state of mind. Only two things have occurred to disturb my equanimity. The first is trivial in itself, and no doubt to be easily explained. The upper window where I saw the light on the night of November 4, with the shadow of a large head and shoulders upon the blind, is one of the windows in the square room under the roof. In reality it has *no blind at all!*

Here is the other thing. I was coming home last night in a fresh fall of snow about eleven o'clock, my umbrella low down over my head. Half-way up the alley, where the snow was wholly untrodden, I saw a man's legs in front of me. The umbrella hid the rest of his figure, but on raising it I saw that he was tall and broad and was walking, as I was, towards the door of my house. He could not have been four feet ahead of me. I had thought the alley was empty when I entered it, but might of course have been mistaken very easily.

A sudden gust of wind compelled me to lower the umbrella, and when I raised it again, not half a minute later, there was no longer any man to be seen. With a few more steps I reached the door. It was closed as usual. I then noticed with a sudden sensation of dismay that the surface of the freshly fallen snow was *unbroken*. My own foot-marks were the only ones to be seen anywhere, and though I retraced my way to the point where I had first seen the man, I could find no slightest impression of any other boots. Feeling creepy and uncomfortable, I went upstairs, and was glad to get into bed.

NOVEMBER 28. — With the fastening of my bedroom door the disturbances ceased. I am convinced that I walked in my sleep. Probably I untied my toe and then tied it up again. The fancied security of the locked door would alone have been enough to restore sleep to my troubled spirit and enable me to rest quietly.

Last night, however, the annoyance was suddenly renewed in another and more aggressive form. I woke in the darkness with the impression that someone was standing outside my bedroom door *listening*. As I became more awake the impression grew into positive knowledge.

Though there was no appreciable sound of moving or breathing, I was so convinced of the propinquity of a listener that I crept out of bed and approached the door. As I did so there came faintly from the next room the unmistakable sound of someone retreating stealthily across the floor. Yet, as I heard it, it was neither the tread of a man nor a regular footstep, but rather, it seemed to me, a confused sort of crawling, almost as of someone on his hands and knees.

I unlocked the door in less than a second, and passed quickly into the front room, and I could feel, as by the subtlest imaginable vibrations upon my nerves, that the spot I was standing in had just that instant been vacated! The Listener had moved; he was now behind the other door, standing in the passage. Yet this door was also closed. I moved swiftly, and as silently as possible, across the floor, and turned the handle. A cold rush of air met me from the passage and sent shiver after shiver down my back. There was no one in the doorway; there was no one on the little landing; there was no one moving down the staircase. Yet I had been so quick that this midnight Listener could not be very far away, and I felt that if I persevered I should eventually come face to face with him. And the courage that came so opportunely to overcome my nervousness and horror seemed born of the unwelcome conviction that it was somehow necessary for my safety as well as my sanity that I should find this intruder and force his secret from him. For was it not the intent action of his mind upon my own, in concentrated listening, that had awakened me with such a vivid realisation of his presence?

Advancing across the narrow landing, I peered down

into the well of the little house. There was nothing to be seen; no one was moving in the darkness. How cold the oilcloth was to my bare feet.

I cannot say what it was that suddenly drew my eyes upwards. I only know that, without apparent reason, I looked up and saw a person about half-way up the next turn of the stairs, leaning forward over the balustrade and staring straight into my face. It was a man. He appeared to be clinging to the rail rather than standing on the stairs. The gloom made it impossible to see much beyond the general outline, but the head and shoulders were seemingly enormous, and stood sharply silhouetted against the skylight in the roof immediately above. The idea flashed into my brain in a moment that I was looking into the visage of something monstrous. The huge skull, the mane-like hair, the wide-humped shoulders, suggested, in a way I did not pause to analyse, that which was scarcely human; and for some seconds, fascinated by horror, I returned the gaze and stared into the dark, inscrutable countenance above me, without knowing exactly where I was or what I was doing.

Then I realised in quite a new way that I was face to face with the secret midnight Listener, and I steeled myself as best I could for what was about to come.

The source of the rash courage that came to me at this awful moment will ever be to me an inexplicable mystery. Though shivering with fear, and my forehead wet with an unholy dew, I resolved to advance. Twenty questions leaped to my lips: What are you? What do you want? Why do you listen and watch? Why do you come into my room? But none of them found articulate utterance.

I began forthwith to climb the stairs, and with the first signs of my advance *he* drew himself back into the shadows and began to move. He retreated as swiftly as I advanced. I heard the sound of his crawling motion a few steps ahead of me, ever maintaining the same distance. When I reached the landing he was half-way up the next flight, and when I was halfway up the next flight he had already arrived at the top landing. I then heard him open the door of the little square room under the roof and go in. Immediately, though the door did not close after him, the sound of his moving entirely ceased.

At this moment I longed for a light, or a stick, or any weapon whatsoever; but I had none of these things, and it was impossible to go back. So I marched steadily up the rest of the stairs, and in less than a minute found myself standing in the gloom face to face with the door through which this creature had just entered.

For a moment I hesitated. The door was about half-way open, and the Listener was standing evidently in his favourite attitude just behind it — listening. To search through that dark room for him seemed hopeless; to enter the same small space where he was seemed horrible. The very idea filled me with loathing, and I almost decided to turn back.

It is strange at such times how trivial things impinge on the consciousness with a shock as of something important and immense. Something — it may have been a beetle or a mouse — scuttled over the bare boards behind me. The door moved a quarter of an inch, closing. My decision came back with a sudden rush, as it were, and thrusting out a foot, I kicked the door so that it swung sharply back to its full extent, and permitted me to walk forward slowly into the aperture of profound blackness beyond. What a queer soft sound my bare feet made on the boards! How the blood sang and buzzed in my head!

I was inside. The darkness closed over me, hiding even the windows. I began to grope my way round the walls in a thorough search; but in order to prevent all possibility of the other's escape, I first of all *closed the door*.

There we were, we two, shut in together between four walls, within a few feet of one another.

But with what, with whom, was I thus momentarily imprisoned? A new light flashed suddenly over the affair with a swift, illuminating brilliance — and I knew I was a fool, an utter fool! I was wide awake at last, and the horror was evaporating. My cursed nerves again; a dream, a nightmare, and the old result — walking in my sleep. The figure was a dream-figure. Many a time before had the actors in my dreams stood before me for some moments after I was awake. . . .

There was a chance match in my pyjamas' pocket, and I struck it on the wall. The room was utterly empty. It held not even a shadow. I went quickly down to bed, cursing my wretched nerves and my foolish, vivid dreams. But as soon as ever I was asleep again, the same uncouth figure of a man crept back to my bedside, and bending over me with his immense head close to my ear, whispered repeatedly in my dreams, "I want your body; I want its covering. I'm waiting for it, and listening always." Words scarcely less foolish than the dream.

But I wonder what that queer odour was up in the

square room. I noticed it again, and stronger than ever before, and it seemed to be also in my bedroom when I woke this morning.

NOVEMBER 29. — Slowly, as moonbeams rise over a misty sea in June, the thought is entering my mind that my nerves and somnambulistic dreams do not adequately account for the influence this house exercises upon me. It holds me as with a fine, invisible net. I cannot escape if I would. It draws me, and it means to keep me.

NOVEMBER 30. — The post this morning brought me a letter from Aden, forwarded from my old rooms in Earl's Court. It was from Chapter, my former Trinity chum, who is on his way home from the East, and asks for my address. I sent it to him at the hotel he mentioned, "to await arrival."

As I have already said, my windows command a view of the alley, and I can see an arrival without difficulty. This morning, while I was busy writing, the sound of footsteps coming up the alley filled me with a sense of vague alarm that I could in no way account for. I went over to the window, and saw a man standing below waiting for the door to be opened. His shoulders were broad, his top-hat glossy, and his overcoat fitted beautifully round the collar. All this I could see, but no more. Presently the door was opened, and the shock to my nerves was unmistakable when I heard a man's voice ask, "Is Mr. — still here?" mentioning my name. I could not catch the answer, but it could only have been in the affirmative, for the man entered the hall and the door shut to behind him. But I waited in vain for the sound of his steps on the stairs. There was no sound of any kind. It seemed to me so strange that I opened my door and looked out. No one was anywhere to be seen. I walked across the narrow landing, and looked through the window that commands the whole length of the alley. There was no sign of a human being, coming or going.

The lane was deserted. Then I deliberately walked downstairs into the kitchen, and asked the grey-faced landlady if a gentleman had just that minute called for me. The answer, given with an odd, weary sort of smile, was *"No!"*

DECEMBER 1. — I feel genuinely alarmed and uneasy over the state of my nerves. Dreams are dreams, but never before have I had dreams in broad daylight.

I am looking forward very much to Chapter's arrival. He is a capital fellow, vigorous, healthy, with no nerves, and even less imagination; and he has £2,000 a year into the bargain.

Periodically he makes me offers — the last was to travel round the world with him as secretary, which was a delicate way of paying my expenses and giving me some pocket-money — offers, however, which I invariably decline. I prefer to keep his friendship. Women could not come between us; money might — therefore I give it no opportunity. Chapter always laughed at what he called my "fancies," being himself possessed only of that thin-blooded quality of imagination which is ever associated with the prosaic-minded man. Yet, if taunted with this obvious lack, his wrath is deeply stirred. His psychology is that of the crass materialist — always a rather funny article. It will afford

me genuine relief, none the less, to hear the cold judgment
his mind will have to pass upon the story of this house as
I shall have it to tell.

DECEMBER 2. — The strangest part of it all I have not
referred to in this brief diary. Truth to tell, I have been afraid
to set it down in black and white. I have kept it in the
background of my thoughts, preventing it as far as possible
from taking shape. In spite of my efforts, however, it has
continued to grow stronger.

Now that I come to face the issue squarely it is harder
to express than I imagined. Like a half-remembered melody
that trips in the head but vanishes the moment you try to
sing it, these thoughts form a group in the background of
my mind, *behind* my mind, as it were, and refuse to come
forward. They are crouching ready to spring, but the actual
leap never takes place.

In these rooms, except when my mind is strongly
concentrated on my own work, I find myself suddenly
dealing in thoughts and ideas that are not my own! New,
strange conceptions, wholly foreign to my temperament,
are forever cropping up in my head. What precisely they
are is of no particular importance. The point is that they
are entirely apart from the channel in which my thoughts
have hitherto been accustomed to flow. Especially they
come when my mind is at rest, unoccupied; when I'm
dreaming over the fire, or sitting with a book which fails
to hold my attention. Then these thoughts which are not
mine spring into life and make me feel exceedingly uncomfortable. Sometimes they are so strong that I almost feel as

if someone were in the room beside me, thinking aloud.

Evidently my nerves and liver are shockingly out of order. I must work harder and take more vigorous exercise. The horrid thoughts never come when my mind is much occupied. But they are always there — waiting and as it were *alive*.

What I have attempted to describe above came first upon me gradually after I had been some days in the house, and then grew steadily in strength. The other strange thing has come to me only twice in all these weeks. *It appals me.* It is the consciousness of the propinquity of some deadly and loathsome disease. It comes over me like a wave of fever heat, and then passes off, leaving me cold and trembling. The air seems for a few seconds to become tainted. So penetrating and convincing is the thought of this sickness, that on both occasions my brain has turned momentarily dizzy, and through my mind, like flames of white heat, have flashed the ominous names of all the dangerous illnesses I know. I can no more explain these visitations than I can fly, yet I know there is no dreaming about the clammy skin and palpitating heart which they always leave as witnesses of their brief visit.

Most strongly of all was I aware of this nearness of a mortal sickness when, on the night of the 28th, I went upstairs in pursuit of the listening figure. When we were shut in together in that little square room under the roof, I felt that I was face to face with the actual essence of this invisible and malignant disease. Such a feeling never entered my heart before, and I pray to God it never may again.

There! Now I have confessed. I have given some

expression at least to the feelings that so far I have been afraid to see in my own writing. For — since I can no longer deceive myself — the experiences of that night (28th) were no more a dream than my daily breakfast is a dream; and the trivial entry in this diary by which I sought to explain away an occurrence that caused me unutterable horror was due solely to my desire not to acknowledge in words what I really felt and believed to be true. The increase that would have accrued to my horror by so doing might have been more than I could stand.

DECEMBER 3. — I wish Chapter would come. My facts are all ready marshalled, and I can see his cool, grey eyes fixed incredulously on my face as I relate them: the knocking at my door, the well-dressed caller, the light in the upper window and the shadow upon the blind, the man who preceded me in the snow, the scattering of my clothes at night, Emily's arrested confession, the landlady's suspicious reticence, the midnight listener on the stairs, and those awful subsequent words in my sleep; and above all, and hardest to tell, the presence of the abominable sickness, and the stream of thoughts and ideas that are not my own.

I can see Chapter's face, and I can almost hear his deliberate words, "You've been at the tea again, and underfeeding, I expect, as usual. Better see my nerve doctor, and then come with me to the south of France." For this fellow, who knows nothing of disordered liver or high-strung nerves, goes regularly to a great nerve specialist with the periodical belief that his nervous system is beginning to decay.

DECEMBER 4. — Ever since the incident of the Listener, I have kept a night-light burning in my bedroom, and my sleep has been undisturbed. Last night, however, I was subjected to a far worse annoyance. I woke suddenly, and saw a man in front of the dressing-table regarding himself in the mirror. The door was locked, as usual. I knew at once it was the Listener, and the blood turned to ice in my veins. Such a wave of horror and dread swept over me that it seemed to turn me rigid in the bed, and I could neither move nor speak. I noted, however, that the odour I so abhorred was strong in the room.

The man seemed to be tall and broad. He was stooping forward over the mirror. His back was turned to me, but in the glass I saw the reflection of a huge head and face illumined fitfully by the flicker of the night-light. The spectral grey of very early morning stealing in round the edges of the curtains lent an additional horror to the picture, for it fell upon hair that was tawny and mane-like, hanging loosely about a face whose swollen, rugose features bore the once-seen-never-forgotten leonine expression of — I dare not write down that awful word. But, by way of corroborative proof, I saw in the faint mingling of the two lights that there were several bronze-coloured blotches on the cheeks which the man was evidently examining with great care in the glass. The lips were pale and very thick and large. One hand I could not see, but the other rested on the ivory back of my hairbrush. Its muscles were strangely contracted, the fingers thin to emaciation, the back of the hand closely puckered up. It was like a big grey spider crouching to spring, or the claw of a great bird.

The full realisation that I was alone in the room with this nameless creature, almost within arm's reach of him, overcame me to such a degree that, when he suddenly turned and regarded me with small beady eyes, wholly out of proportion to the grandeur of their massive setting, I sat bolt upright in bed, uttered a loud cry, and then fell back in a dead swoon of terror upon the bed.

DECEMBER 5. — . . . When I came to this morning, the first thing I noticed was that my clothes were strewn all over the floor. . . . I find it difficult to put my thoughts together, and have sudden accesses of violent trembling. I determined that I would go at once to Chapter's hotel and find out when he is expected. I cannot refer to what happened in the night; it is too awful, and I have to keep my thoughts rigorously away from it. I feel light-headed and queer, couldn't eat any breakfast, and have twice vomited with blood. While dressing to go out, a hansom rattled up noisily over the cobbles, and a minute later the door opened, and to my great joy in walked the very subject of my thoughts.

The sight of his strong face and quiet eyes had an immediate effect upon me, and I grew calmer again. His very handshake was a sort of tonic. But, as I listened eagerly to the deep tones of his reassuring voice, and the visions of the night-time paled a little, I began to realise how very hard it was going to be to tell him my wild intangible tale. Some men radiate an animal vigour that destroys the delicate woof of a vision and effectually prevents its reconstruction. Chapter was one of these men.

We talked of incidents that had filled the interval since

we last met, and he told me something of his travels. He talked and I listened. But, so full was I of the horrid thing I had to tell, that I made a poor listener. I was for ever watching my opportunity to leap in and explode it all under his nose.

Before very long, however, it was borne in upon me that he too was merely talking for time.

He too held something of importance in the background of his mind, something too weighty to let fall till the right moment presented itself. So that during the whole of the first half-hour we were both waiting for the psychological moment in which properly to release our respective bombs; and the intensity of our minds' action set up opposing forces that merely sufficed to hold one another in check — and nothing more. As soon as I realised this, therefore, I resolved to yield.

I renounced for the time my purpose of telling my story, and had the satisfaction of seeing that his mind, released from the restraint of my own, at once began to make preparations for the discharge of its momentous burden. The talk grew less and less magnetic; the interest waned; the descriptions of his travels became less alive. There were pauses between his sentences. Presently he repeated himself. His words clothed no living thoughts. The pauses grew longer. Then the interest dwindled altogether and went out like a candle in the wind. His voice ceased, and he looked up squarely into my face with serious and anxious eyes.

The psychological moment had come at last!

"I say —" he began, and then stopped short.

I made an unconscious gesture of encouragement, but

said no word. I dreaded the impending disclosure exceedingly. A dark shadow seemed to precede it.

"I say," he blurted out at last, "what in the world made
you ever come to this place — to these rooms, I mean?"

"They're cheap, for one thing," I began, "and central
and —"

"They're too cheap," he interrupted. "Didn't you ask
what made 'em so cheap?"

"It never occurred to me at the time."

There was a pause in which he avoided my eyes.

"For God's sake, go on, man, and tell it!" I cried, for the
suspense was getting more than I could stand in my nervous
condition.

"This was where Blount lived so long," he said quietly,
"and where he — died. You know, in the old days I often
used to come here and see him, and do what I could to
alleviate his —" He stuck fast again.

"Well!" I said with a great effort. "*Please* go on — faster."

"But," Chapter went on, turning his face to the window
with a perceptible shiver, "he finally got so terrible I simply
couldn't stand it, though I always thought I could stand
anything. It got on my nerves and made me dream, and
haunted me day and night."

I stared at him, and said nothing. I had never heard of
Blount in my life, and didn't know what he was talking
about. But, all the same, I was trembling, and my mouth
had become strangely dry.

"This is the first time I've been back here since," he said
almost in a whisper, "and, 'pon my word, it gives me the
creeps. I swear it isn't fit for a man to live in. I never saw

you look so bad, old man."

"I've got it for a year," I jerked out, with a forced laugh; "signed the lease and all. I thought it was rather a bargain."

Chapter shuddered, and buttoned his overcoat up to his neck. Then he spoke in a low voice, looking occasionally behind him as though he thought someone was listening. I too could have sworn someone else was in the room with us.

"He did it himself, you know, and no one blamed him a bit; his sufferings were awful. For the last two years he used to wear a veil when he went out, and even then it was always in a closed carriage. Even the attendant who had nursed him for so long was at length obliged to leave. The extremities of both the lower limbs were gone, dropped off, and he moved about the ground on all fours with a sort of crawling motion. The odour, too, was —"

I was obliged to interrupt him here. I could hear no more details of that sort. My skin was moist, I felt hot and cold by turns, for at last I was beginning to understand.

"Poor devil," Chapter went on; "I used to keep my eyes closed as much as possible. He always begged to be allowed to take his veil off, and asked if I minded very much. I used to stand by the open window. He never touched me, though. He rented the whole house. Nothing would induce him to leave it."

"Did he occupy — these very rooms?"

"No. He had the little room on the top floor, the square one just under the roof. He preferred it because it was dark. These rooms were too near the ground, and he was afraid people might see him through the windows. A crowd had been known to follow him up to the very door, and then stand below the windows in the hope of catching a glimpse of his face."

"But there were hospitals."

"He wouldn't go near one, and they didn't like to force him. You know, they say it's *not* contagious, so there was nothing to prevent his staying here if he wanted to. He spent all his time reading medical books, about drugs and so on. His head and face were something appalling, just like a lion's."

I held up my hand to arrest further description.

"He was a burden to the world, and he knew it. One night I suppose he realised it too keenly to wish to live. He had the free use of drugs — and in the morning he was found dead on the floor. Two years ago, that was, and they said then he had still several years to live."

"Then, in Heaven's name!" I cried, unable to bear the suspense any longer, "tell me what it was he had, and be quick about it."

"I thought you knew!" he exclaimed, with genuine surprise. "I thought you knew!"

He leaned forward and our eyes met. In a scarcely audible whisper I caught the words his lips seemed almost afraid to utter:

"He was a leper!"

MAX HENSING:

BACTERIOLOGIST AND MURDERER.

-A Story of New York-

I.

Besides the departmental men on the New York *Vulture*, there were about twenty reporters for general duty, and Williams had worked his way up till he stood easily among the first half-dozen; for, in addition to being accurate and painstaking, he was able to bring to his reports of common things that touch of imagination and humour which just lifted them out of the rut of mere faithful recording. Moreover, the city editor (*anglice* news editor) appreciated his powers, and always tried to give him assignments that did himself and the paper credit, and he was justified now in expecting to be relieved of the hack jobs that were usually allotted to new men.

He was therefore puzzled and a little disappointed one morning as he saw his inferiors summoned one after another to the news desk to receive the best assignments of the day, and when at length his turn came, and the city editor asked him to cover "the Hensig story," he gave a little start of vexation that almost betrayed him into asking what the devil "the Hensig story" was. For it is the duty of every morning newspaper man — in New York at least — to have made himself familiar with all the news of the day before he shows himself at the office, and though Williams had already done this, he could not recall either the name or the story.

"You can run to a hundred or a hundred and fifty, Mr. Williams. Cover the trial thoroughly, and get good interviews with Hensig and the lawyers. There'll be no night assignment for you till the case is over."

Williams was going to ask if there were any private "tips" from the District Attorney's office, but the editor was already speaking with Weekes, who wrote the daily "weather story," and he went back slowly to his desk, angry and disappointed, to read up the Hensig case and lay his plans for the day accordingly. At any rate, he reflected, it looked like "a soft job," and as there was to be no second assignment for him that night, he would get off by eight o'clock, and be able to dine and sleep for once like a civilised man. And that was something.

It took him some time, however, to discover that the Hensig case was only a murder story. And this increased his disgust. It was tucked away in the corners of most of the papers, and little importance was attached to it. A murder trial is not first-class news unless there are very special features connected with it, and Williams had already covered scores of them. There was a heavy sameness about them that made it difficult to report them interestingly, and as a rule they were left to the tender mercies of the "flimsy" men — the Press Associations — and no paper sent a special man unless the case was distinctly out of the usual. Moreover, a hundred and fifty meant a column and a half, and Williams, not being a space man, earned the same money whether he wrote a stickful or a page; so that he felt doubly aggrieved, and walked out into the sunny open spaces opposite Newspaper Row heaving a deep sigh and cursing the boredom of his trade.

Max Hensig, he found, was a German doctor accused of murdering his second wife by injecting arsenic. The woman had been buried several weeks when the suspicious relatives got the body exhumed, and a quantity of the poison had been found in her. Williams recalled something about the arrest, now he came to think of it; but he felt no special interest in it, for ordinary murder trials were no longer his legitimate work, and he scorned them. At first, of course, they had thrilled him horribly, and some of his interviews with the prisoners, especially just before execution, had deeply impressed his imagination and kept him awake at nights. Even now he could not enter the gloomy Tombs

Prison, or cross the Bridge of Sighs leading from it to the courts, without experiencing a real sensation, for its huge Egyptian columns and massive walls closed round him like death; and the first time he walked down Murderers' Row, and came in view of the cell doors, his throat was dry, and he had almost turned and run out of the building. The first time, too, that he covered the trial of a Negro and listened to the man's hysterical speech before sentence was pronounced, he was absorbed with interest, and his heart leaped. The wild appeals to the Deity, the long invented words, the ghastly pallor under the black skin, the rolling eyes, and the torrential sentences all seemed to him to be something tremendous to describe for his sensational sheet; and the stickfull that was eventually printed — written by the flimsy man too — had given him quite a new standard of the relative value of news and of the quality of the satiated public palate. He had reported the trials of a Chinaman, stolid as wood; of an Italian who had been too quick with his knife; and of a farm girl who had done both her parents to death in their beds, entering their room stark naked, so that no stains should betray her; and at the beginning these things haunted him for days.

But that was all months ago, when he first came to New York. Since then his work had been steadily in the criminal courts, and he had grown a second skin. An execution in the electric chair at Sing Sing could still unnerve him somewhat, but mere murder no longer thrilled or excited him, and he could be thoroughly depended on to write a good "murder story" — an account that his paper could print without blue pencil.

Accordingly he entered the Tombs Prison with nothing stronger than the feeling of vague oppression that gloomy structure always stirred in him, and certainly with no particular emotion connected with the prisoner he was about to interview; and when he reached the second iron door, where a warder peered at him through a small grating, he heard a voice behind him, and turned to find the *Chronicle* man at his heels.

"Hullo, Senator! What good trail are you following down here?" he cried, for the other got no small assignments, and never had less than a column on the *Chronicle* front page at space rates.

"Same as you, I guess — Hensig," was the reply.

"But there's no space in Hensig," said Williams with surprise. "Are you back on salary again?"

"Not much," laughed the Senator — no one knew his real name, but he was always called Senator. "But Hensig's good for two hundred easy. There's a whole list of murders behind him, we hear, and this is the first time he's been caught."

"Poison?"

The Senator nodded in reply, turning to ask the warder some question about another case, and Williams waited for him in the corridor, impatiently rather, for he loathed the musty prison odour. He watched the Senator as he talked, and was distinctly glad he had come. They were good friends: he had helped Williams when he first joined the small army of newspaper men and was not much welcomed, being an Englishman. Common origin and goodheartedness mixed themselves delightfully in his face, and he always made Williams think of a friendly, honest cart-horse — stolid, strong, with big and simple emotions.

"Get a hustle on, Senator," he said at length impatiently.

The two reporters followed the warder down the flagged corridor, past a row of dark cells, each with its occupant, until the man, swinging his keys in the direction indicated, stopped and pointed:

"Here's your gentleman," he said, and then moved on down the corridor, leaving them staring through the bars at a frail, slim young man, pacing to and fro. He had flaxen hair and very bright blue eyes; his skin was white, and his face wore so open and innocent an expression that one would have said he could not twist a kitten's tail without wincing.

"From the *Chronicle* and *Vulture*," explained Williams, by way of introduction, and the talk at once began in the usual way.

The man in the cell ceased his restless pacing up and down, and stopped opposite the bars to examine them. He stared straight into Williams's eyes for a moment, and the reporter noted a very different expression from the one he had first seen. It actually made him shift his position and stand a little to one side. But the movement was wholly instinctive. He could not have explained why he did it.

"Guess you vish me to say I did it, and then egsplain to you *how* I did it," the young doctor said coolly, with a marked German accent. "But I haf no copy to gif you shust now. You see at the trial it is nothing but spite — and shealosy of another woman. I lofed my vife. I vould not haf gilled her for anything in the vorld — "

"Oh, of course, of course, Dr. Hensig," broke in the Senator, who was more experienced in the ways of difficult interviewing. "We quite understand that. But, you know, in New York the newspapers try a man as much as the courts, and we thought you might like to make a statement to the public which we should be very glad to print for you. It may help your case — "

"Nothing can help my case in this tamned country where shustice is to be pought mit tollars!" cried the prisoner, with a sudden anger and an expression of face still further belying the first one; "nothing except a lot of money. But I tell you now two things you may write for your public: One is, no motive can be shown for the murder, because I lofed Zinka and vished her to live alvays. And the other is — " He stopped a moment and stared steadily at Williams making shorthand notes — "that with my knowledge — my egceptional knowledge — of poisons and pacteriology I could have done it in a dozen ways without pumping arsenic into her body. That is a fool's way of killing. It is clumsy and childish and sure of discofery! See?"

He turned away, as though to signify that the interview was over, and sat down on his wooden bench.

"Seems to have taken a fancy to you," laughed the Senator, as they went off to get further interviews with the lawyers. "He never looked at me once."

"He's got a bad face — the face of a devil. I don't feel complimented," said Williams shortly. "I'd hate to be in his power."

"Same here," returned the other. "Let's go into Silver

Dollars and wash the dirty taste out."

So, after the custom of reporters, they made their way up the Bowery and went into a saloon that had gained a certain degree of fame because the Tammany owner had let a silver dollar into each stone of the floor. Here they washed away most of the "dirty taste" left by the Tombs atmosphere and Hensig, and then went on to Steve Brodie's, another saloon a little higher up the same street.

"There'll be others there," said the Senator, meaning drinks as well as reporters, and Williams, still thinking over their interview, silently agreed.

Brodie was a character; there was always something lively going on in his place. He had the reputation of having once jumped from the Brooklyn Bridge and reached the water alive. No one could actually deny it, and no one could prove that it really happened: and anyhow, he had enough imagination and personality to make the myth live and to sell much bad liquor on the strength of it. The walls of his saloon were plastered with lurid oil-paintings of the bridge, the height enormously magnified, and Steve's body in midair, an expression of a happy puppy on his face.

Here, as expected, they found "Whitey" Fife, of the *Recorder*, and Galusha Owen, of the *World*. "Whitey," as his nickname implied, was an albino, and clever. He wrote the daily "weather story" for his paper, and the way he spun a column out of rain, wind, and temperature was the envy of everyone except the Weather Clerk, who objected to being described as "Farmer Dunne, cleaning his rat-tail file," and to having his dignified office referred to in the public press as "a down-country farm." But the public liked it, and laughed, and "Whitey" was never really spiteful.

Owen, too, when sober, was a good man who had long passed the rubicon of hack assignments. Yet both these men were also on the Hensig story. And Williams, who had already taken an instinctive dislike to the case, was sorry to see this, for it meant frequent interviewing and the possession, more or less, of his mind and imagination. Clearly, he would have much to do with this German doctor. Already, even at this stage, he began to hate him.

The four reporters spent an hour drinking and talking. They fell at length to discussing the last time they had chanced to meet on the same assignment — a private lunatic asylum owned by an incompetent quack without a licence, and where most of the inmates, not mad in the first instance, and all heavily paid for by relatives who wished them out of the way, had gone mad from ill-treatment. The place had been surrounded before dawn by the Board of Health officers, and the quasi-doctor arrested as he opened his front door. It was a splendid newspaper "story," of course.

"My space bill ran to sixty dollars a day for nearly a week," said Whitey Fife thickly, and the others laughed, because Whitey wrote most of his stuff by cribbing it from the evening papers.

"A dead cinch," said Galusha Owen, his dirty flannel collar poking up through his long hair almost to his ears. "I 'faked' the whole of the second day without going down there at all."

He pledged Whitey for the tenth time that morning, and the albino leered happily across the table at him, and passed him a thick compliment before emptying his glass.

"Hensig's going to be good, too," broke in the Senator, ordering a round of gin-fizzes, and Williams gave a little start of annoyance to hear the name brought up again. "He'll make good stuff at the trial. I never saw a cooler hand. You should've heard him talk about poisons and bacteriology, and boasting he could kill in a dozen ways without fear of being caught. I guess he was telling the truth right enough!"

"That so?" cried Galusha and Whitey in the same breath, not having done a stroke of work so far on the case.

"Run down to the Tombsh an'getaninerview," added Whitey, turning with a sudden burst of enthusiasm to his companion. His white eyebrows and pink eyes fairly shone against the purple of his tipsy face.

"No, no," cried the Senator; "don't spoil a good story. You're both as full as ticks. I'll match with Williams which of us goes. Hensig knows us already, and we'll all 'give up' in this story right along. No 'beats.' "

So they decided to divide news till the case was finished, and to keep no exclusive items to themselves; and Williams, having lost the toss, swallowed his gin-fizz and went back to the Tombs to get a further talk with the prisoner on his knowledge of expert poisoning and bacteriology.

Meanwhile his thoughts were very busy elsewhere.

He had taken no part in the noisy conversation in the barroom, because something lay at the back of his mind, bothering him, and claiming attention with great persistence. Something was at work in his deeper consciousness, something that had impressed him with a vague sense of unpleasantness and nascent fear, reaching below that second skin he had grown.

And, as he walked slowly through the malodorous slum streets that lay between the Bowery and the Tombs, dodging the pullers-in outside the Jew clothing stores, and nibbling at a bag of peanuts he caught up off an Italian push-cart en route, this "something" rose a little higher out of its obscurity, and began to play with the roots of the ideas floating higgledypiggledy on the surface of his mind. He thought he knew what it was, but could not make quite sure. From the roots of his thoughts it rose a little higher, so that he clearly felt it as something disagreeable. Then, with a sudden rush, it came to the surface, and poked its face before him so that he fully recognised it.

The blond visage of Dr. Max Hensig rose before him, cool, smiling, and implacable.

Somehow, he had expected it would prove to be Hensig — this unpleasant thought that was troubling him. He was not really surprised to have labelled it, because the man's personality had made an unwelcome impression upon him at the very start. He stopped nervously in the Street, and looked round. He did not expect to see anything out of the way, or to find that he was being followed. It was not that exactly. The act of turning was merely the outward expression of a sudden inner discomfort, and a man with better nerves, or nerves more under control, would not have turned at all.

But what caused this tremor of the nerves? Williams probed and searched within himself. It came, he felt, from some part of his inner being he did not understand; there had been an intrusion, an incongruous intrusion, into the stream of his normal consciousness. Messages from this region always gave him pause; and in this particular case he saw no reason why he should think specially of Dr. Hensig with alarm — this light-haired stripling with blue eyes and drooping moustache. The faces of other murderers had haunted him once or twice because they were more than ordinarily bad, or because their case possessed unusual features of horror. But there was nothing so very much out of the way about Hensig — at least, if there was, the reporter could not seize and analyse it. There seemed no adequate reason to explain his emotion. Certainly, it had nothing to do with the fact that he was merely a murderer, for that stirred no thrill in him at all, except a kind of pity, and a wonder how the man would meet his execution. It must, he argued, be something to do with the *personality* of the man, apart from any particular deed or characteristic.

Puzzled, and still a little nervous, he stood in the road, hesitating. In front of him the dark walls of the Tombs rose in massive steps of granite. Overhead white summer clouds sailed across a deep blue sky; the wind sang cheerfully among the wires and chimney-pots, making him think of fields and trees; and down the Street surged the usual cosmopolitan New York crowd of laughing Italians, surly Negroes, hebrews chattering Yiddish, tough-looking hooligans with that fighting lurch of the shoulders peculiar to New York roughs, Chinamen, taking little steps like boys — and every other sort of nondescript imaginable. It was early June, and there were faint odours of the sea and of sea-beaches in the air. Williams caught himself shivering a little with delight at the sight of the sky and scent of the wind.

Then he looked back at the great prison, rightly named the Tombs, and the sudden change of thought from the fields to the cells, from life to death, somehow landed him straight into the discovery of what caused this attack of nervousness:

Hensig was no ordinary murderer! That was it.

There was something quite out of the ordinary about him. The man was a horror, pure and simple, standing apart from normal humanity. The knowledge of this rushed over him like a revelation, bringing unalterable conviction in its train. Something of it had reached him in that first brief interview, but without explaining itself sufficiently to be recognised, and since then it had been working in his system, like a poison, and was now causing a disturbance, not having been assimilated. A quicker temperament would have labelled it long before.

Now, Williams knew well that he drank too much, and had more than a passing acquaintance with drugs; his nerves were shaky at the best of times. His life on the newspapers afforded no opportunity of cultivating pleasant social relations, but brought him all the time into contact with the seamy side of life — the criminal, the abnormal, the unwholesome in human nature. He knew, too, that strange thoughts, *idées fixes* and what not, grew readily in such a soil as this, and, not wanting these, he had formed a habit — peculiar to himself — of deliberately sweeping his mind clean once a week of all that had haunted, obsessed, or teased him, of the horrible or unclean, during his work; and his eighth day, his holiday, he invariably spent in the woods, walking, building fires, cooking a meal in the open, and getting all the country air and the exercise he possibly could. He had in this way kept his mind free from many unpleasant pictures that might otherwise have lodged there abidingly, and the habit of thus cleansing his imagination had proved more than once of real value to him.

So now he laughed to himself, and turned on those whizzing brooms of his, trying to forget these first impressions of Hensig, and simply going in, as he did a hundred other times, to get an ordinary interview with an ordinary prisoner. This habit, being nothing more nor less than the practice of suggestion, was more successful sometimes than others. This time — since fear is less susceptible to suggestion than other emotions — it was less so.

Williams got his interview, and came away fairly creeping with horror. Hensig was all that he had felt, and more besides. He belonged, the reporter felt convinced, to that rare type of deliberate murderer, coldblooded and calculating, who kills for a song, delights in killing, and gives its whole intellect to the consideration of each detail, glorying in evading detection and revelling in the notoriety of the trial, if caught. At first he had answered reluctantly, but as Williams plied his questions intelligently, the young doctor warmed up and became enthusiastic with a sort of cold intellectual enthusiasm, till at last he held forth like a lecturer, pacing his cell, gesticulating, explaining with admirable exposition how easy murder could be to a man who knew his business.

And *he* did know his business! No man, in these days of inquests and post-mortem examination, would inject poisons that might be found weeks afterwards in the viscera of the victim. No man who knew his business!

"What is more easy," he said, holding the bars with his long white fingers and gazing into the reporter's eyes, "than to take a disease germ" (cherm,' he pronounced it) "of typhus, plague, or any cherm you blease, and make so virulent a culture that no medicine in the world could counteract it; a really powerful microbe — and then scratch the skin of your victim with a pin? And who could drace it to you, or accuse you of murder?"

Williams, as he watched and heard, was glad the bars were between them; but, even so, something invisible seemed to pass from the prisoner's atmosphere and lay an icy finger on his heart. He had come into contact with every possible kind of crime and criminal, and had interviewed scores of men who, for jealousy, greed, passion or other comprehensible emotion, had killed and paid the penalty of killing. He understood that. Any man with strong passions was a potential killer. But never before had he met a man who in cold blood, deliberately, under no emotion greater than boredom, would destroy a human life and then boast of his ability to do it. Yet this, he felt sure, was what Hensig had done, and what his vile words shadowed forth and betrayed. Here was something outside humanity, something terrible, monstrous; and it made him shudder. This young doctor, he felt, was a fiend incarnate, a man who thought less of human life than the lives of flies in summer, and who would kill with as steady a hand and cool a brain as though he were performing a common operation in the hospital.

Thus the reporter left the prison gates with a vivid impression in his mind, though exactly how his conclusion was reached was more than he could tell. This time the mental brooms failed to act. The horror of it remained.

On the way out into the street he ran against Policeman Dowling of the ninth precinct, with whom he had been fast friends since the day he wrote a glowing account of Dowling's capture of a "greengoods-man," when Dowling had been so drunk that he nearly lost his prisoner altogether. The policeman had never forgotten the good turn; it had promoted him to plain clothes; and he was always ready to give the reporter any news he had.

"Know of anything good today?" he asked by way of habit.

"Bet your bottom dollar I do," replied the coarsefaced Irish policeman; "one of the best, too. I've got Hensig!"

Dowling spoke with pride and affection. He was mighty pleased, too, because his name would be in the paper every day for a week or more, and a big case helped the chances of promotion.

Williams cursed inwardly. Apparently there was no escape from this man Hensig.

"Not much of a case, is it?" he asked.

"It's a jim dandy, that's what it is," replied the other, a little offended. "Hensig may miss the Chair because the evidence is weak, but he's the worst I've ever met. Why, he'd poison you as soon as spit in your eye, and if he's got a heart at all he keeps it on ice."

"What makes you think that?"

"Oh, they talk pretty freely to us sometimes," the policeman said, with a significant wink.

"Can't be used against them at the trial, and it kind o' relieves their mind, I guess. But I'd just as soon not have heard most of what that guy told me — see? Come in," he added, looking round cautiously; "I'll set 'em up and tell you a bit."

Williams entered the side-door of a saloon with him, but not too willingly.

"A glarss of Scotch for the Englishman," ordered the officer facetiously, "and I'll take a horse's collar with a dash of peach bitters in it — just what you'd notice, no more." He flung down a half-dollar, and the bar-tender winked and pushed it back to him across the counter.

"What's yours, Mike?" he asked him.

"I'll take a cigar," said the bar-tender, pocketing the proffered dime and putting a cheap cigar in his waistcoat pocket, and then moving off to allow the two men elbow-room to talk in.

They talked in low voices with heads close together for fifteen minutes, and then the reporter set up another round of drinks. The bar-tender took *his* money. Then they talked a bit longer, Williams rather white about the gills and the policeman very much in earnest.

"The boys are waiting for me up at Brodie's," said Williams at length. "I must be off."

"That's so," said Dowling, straightening up. "We'll just liquor up again to show there's no ill-feeling. And mind you see me every morning before the case is called.

Trial begins tomorrow."

They swallowed their drinks, and again the bartender took a ten-cent piece and pocketed a cheap cigar.

"Don't print what I've told you, and don't give it up to the other reporters," said Dowling as they separated. "And if you want confirmation jest take the cars and run down to Amityville, Long Island, and you'll find what I've said is O.K. every time."

Williams went back to Steve Brodie's, his thoughts whizzing about him like bees in a swarm. What he had heard increased tenfold his horror of the man. Of course, Dowling may have lied or exaggerated, but he thought not. It was probably all true, and the newspaper offices knew something about it when they sent good men to cover the case. Williams wished to Heaven he had nothing to do with the thing; but meanwhile he could not write what he had heard, and all the other reporters wanted was the result of his interview. That was good for half a column, even expurgated.

He found the Senator in the middle of a story to Galusha, while Whitey Fife was knocking cocktail glasses off the edge of the table and catching them just before they reached the floor, pretending they were Steve Brodie jumping from the Brooklyn Bridge. He had promised to set up the drinks for the whole bar if he missed, and just as Williams entered a glass smashed to atoms on the stones, and a roar of laughter went up from the room. Five or six men moved up to the bar and took their liquor, Williams included, and soon after Whitey and Galusha went off to get some lunch and sober up, having first arranged to meet

Williams later in the evening and get the "story" from him.

"Get much?" asked the Senator.

"More than I care about," replied the other, and then told his friend the story.

The Senator listened with intense interest, making occasional notes from time to time, and asking a few questions. Then, when Williams had finished, he said quietly:

"I guess Dowling's right. Let's jump on a car and go down to Amityville, and see what they think about him down there."

Amityville was a scattered village some twenty miles away on Long Island, where Dr. Hensig had lived and practised for the last year or two, and where Mrs. Hensig No. 2 had come to her suspicious death. The neighbours would be sure to have plenty to say, and though it might not prove of great value, it would be certainly interesting. So the two reporters went down there, and interviewed anyone and everyone they could find, from the man in the drug-store to the parson and the undertaker, and the stories they heard would fill a book.

"Good stuff," said the Senator, as they journeyed back to New York on the steamer, "but nothing we can use, I guess." His face was very grave, and he seemed troubled in his mind.

"Nothing the District Attorney can use either at the trial," observed Williams.

"It's simply a devil — not a man at all," the other continued, as if talking to himself. "Utterly unmoral! I swear I'll make MacSweater put me to another job." For the stories they had heard showed Dr. Hensig as a man who openly boasted that he could kill without detection; that no enemy of his lived long; that, as a doctor, he had, or ought to have, the right over life and death; and that if a person was a nuisance, or a trouble to him, there was no reason he should not put them away, provided he did it without rousing suspicion. Of course he had not shouted these views aloud in the market-place, but he had let people know that he held them, and held them seriously. They had fallen from him in conversation, in unguarded moments, and were clearly the natural expression of his mind and views. And many people in the village evidently had no doubt that he had put them into practice more than once.

"There's nothing to give up to Whitey or Galusha, though," said the Senator decisively, "and there's hardly anything we can use in our story."

"I don't think I should care to use it anyhow," Williams said, with rather a forced laugh.

The Senator looked round sharply by way of question.

"Hensig *may be acquitted and get out*," added Williams.

"Same here. I guess you're dead right," he said slowly, and then added more cheerfully, "Let's go and have dinner in Chinatown, and write our copy together."

So they went down Pell Street, and turned up some dark wooden stairs into a Chinese restaurant, smelling strongly of opium and of cooking not Western. Here at a little table on the sanded floor they ordered chou chop suey and chou om dong in brown bowls, and washed it down with frequent doses of the fiery white whisky, and then moved into a corner and began to cover their paper with pencil writing for the consumption of the great American public in the morning.

"There's not much to choose between Hensig and *that*," said the Senator, as one of the degraded white women who frequent Chinatown entered the room and sat down at an empty table to order whisky. For, with four thousand Chinamen in the quarter, there is not a single Chinese woman.

"All the difference in the world," replied Williams, following his glance across the smoky room. "She's been decent once, and may be again some day, but that damned doctor has never been anything but what he is — a soulless, intellectual devil. He doesn't belong to humanity at all. I've got a horrid idea that — "

"How do you spell 'bacteriology', two r's or one?" asked the Senator, going on with his scrawly writing of a story that would be read with interest by thousands next day.

"Two r's and one k," laughed the other. And they wrote on for another hour, and then went to turn it into their respective offices in Park Row.

II.

The trial of Max Hensig lasted two weeks, for his relations supplied money, and he got good lawyers and all manner of delays. From a newspaper point of view it fell utterly flat, and before the end of the fourth day most of the papers had shunted their big men on to other jobs more worthy of their powers.

From Williams's point of view, however, it did not fall flat, and he was kept on it till the end. A reporter, of course, has no right to indulge in editorial remarks, especially when a case is still *sub judice*, but in New York journalism and the dignity of the law have a standard all their own, and into his daily reports there crept the distinct flavour of his own conclusions. Now that new men, with whom he had no agreement to "give up," were covering the story for the other papers, he felt free to use any special knowledge in his possession, and a good deal of what he had heard at Amityville and from officer Dowling somehow managed to creep into his writing.

Something of the horror and loathing he felt for this doctor also betrayed itself, more by inference than actual statement, and no one who read his daily column could come to any other conclusion than that Hensig was a calculating, cool-headed murderer of the most dangerous type.

This was a little awkward for the reporter, because it was his duty every morning to interview the prisoner in his cell, and get his views on the conduct of the case in general and on his chances of escaping the Chair in particular.

Yet Hensig showed no embarrassment. All the newspapers were supplied to him, and he evidently read every word that Williams wrote. He must have known what the reporter thought about him, at least so far as his guilt or innocence was concerned, but he expressed no opinion as to the fairness of the articles, and talked freely of his chances of ultimate escape. The very way in which he glorified in being the central figure of a matter that bulked so large in the public eye seemed to the reporter an additional proof of the man's perversity. His vanity was immense. He made most careful toilets, appearing every day in a clean shirt and a new tie, and never wearing the same suit on two consecutive days. He noted the descriptions of his personal appearance in the Press, and was quite offended if his clothes and bearing in court were not referred to in detail. And he was unusually delighted and pleased when any of the papers stated that he looked smart and self-possessed, or showed great self-control — which some of them did.

"They make a hero of me," he said one morning when Williams went to see him as usual before court opened, "and if I go to the Chair — which I tink I not do, you know — you shall see something fine. Berhaps they electrocute a corpse only!"

And then, with dreadful callousness, he began to chaff the reporter about the tone of his articles — for the first time.

"I only report what is said and done in court," stammered Williams, horribly uncomfortable, "and I am always ready to write anything you care to say — "

"I haf no fault to find," answered Hensig, his cold blue eyes fixed on the reporter's face through the bars, "none at all. You tink I haf killed, and you show it in all your sendences. Haf you ever seen a man in the Chair, I ask you?"

Williams was obliged to say he had.

"*Ach was!* You haf indeed!" said the doctor coolly.

"It's instantaneous, though," the other added quickly, "and must be quite painless." This was not exactly what he thought, but what else could he say to the poor devil who might presently be strapped down into it with that horrid band across his shaved head!

Hensig laughed, and turned away to walk up and down the narrow cell. Suddenly he made a quick movement and sprang like a panther close up to the bars, pressing his face between them with an expression that was entirely new. Williams started back a pace in spite of himself.

"There are worse ways of dying than that," he said in a low voice, with a diabolical look in his eyes: "slower ways that are bainful much more. I shall get oudt. I shall not be conficted. I shall get oudt, and then perhaps I come and tell you apout them."

The hatred in his voice and expression was unmistakable, but almost at once the face changed back to the cold pallor it usually wore, and the extraordinary doctor was laughing again and quietly discussing his lawyers and their good or bad points. After all, then, that skin of indifference was only assumed, and the man really resented bitterly the tone of his articles. He liked the publicity, but was furious with Williams for having come to a conclusion and for letting that conclusion show through his reports.

The reporter was relieved to get out into the fresh air. He walked briskly up the stone steps to the courtroom, still haunted by the memory of that odious white face pressing between the bars and the dreadful look in the eyes that had come and gone so swiftly. And what did those words mean exactly? Had he heard them right? Were they a threat?

"There are slower and more painful ways of dying, and if I get out I shall perhaps come and tell you about them."

The work of reporting the evidence helped to chase the disagreeable vision, and the compliments of the city editor on the excellence of his "story," with its suggestion of a possible increase of salary, gave his mind quite a different turn; yet always at the back of his consciousness there remained the vague, unpleasant memory that he had roused the bitter hatred of this man, and, as he thought, of a man who was a veritable monster. There may have been something hypnotic, a little perhaps, in this obsessing and haunting idea of the man's steely wickedness, intellectual and horribly skilful, moving freely through life with something like a god's power and with a list of unproved and unprovable murders behind him. Certainly it impressed his imagination with very vivid force, and he could not think of this doctor, young, with unusual knowledge and out-of-the-way skill, yet utterly unmoral, free to work his will on men and women who displeased him, and almost safe from detection — he could not think of it all without a shudder and a crawling of the skin. He was exceedingly glad when the last day of the trial was reached and he no longer was obliged to seek the daily interview in the cell, or to sit all day in the crowded court watching the detestable white face of the prisoner in the dock and listening to the web of evidence closing round him, but just failing to hold him tight enough for the Chair. For Hensig was acquitted, though the jury sat up all night to come to a decision, and the final interview Williams had with the man immediately before his release into the street was the pleasantest and yet the most disagreeable of all.

"I knew I get oudt all right," said Hensig with a slight laugh, but without showing the real relief he must have felt. "No one peliefed me guilty but my vife's family and yourself, Mr. *Vulture* reporter. I read efery day your repordts. You chumped to a conglusion too quickly, I tink — "

"Oh, we write what we're told to write — "

"Berhaps some day you write anozzer story, or berhaps you read the story someone else write of your own trial. Then you understand better what you make me feel."

Williams hurried on to ask the doctor for his opinion

of the conduct of the trial, and then inquired what his plans were for the future. The answer to the question caused him genuine relief.

"Ach! I return of course to Chermany," he said. "People here are now afraid of me a liddle. The newspapers haf killed me instead of the Chair. Goot-bye, Mr. *Vulture* reporter, goot-bye!"

And Williams wrote out his last interview with as great a relief, probably, as Hensig felt when he heard the foreman of the jury utter the words "Not guilty"; but the line that gave him most pleasure was the one announcing the intended departure of the acquitted man for Germany.

III.

The New York public want sensational reading in their daily life, and they get it, for the newspaper that refused to furnish it would fail in a week, and New York newspaper proprietors do not pose as philanthropists. Horror succeeds horror, and the public interest is never for one instant allowed to faint by the way.

Like any other reporter who betrayed the smallest powers of description, Williams realised this fact with his very first week on the *Vulture*. His daily work became simply a series of sensational reports of sensational happenings; he lived in a perpetual whirl of exciting arrests, murder trials, cases of blackmail, divorce, forgery, arson, corruption, and every other kind of wickedness imaginable. Each case thrilled him a little less than the preceding one; excess of sensation had simply numbed him; he became, not callous, but irresponsive, and had long since reached the stage when excitement ceases to betray judgment, as with inexperienced reporters it was apt to do.

The Hensig case, however, for a long time lived in his imagination and haunted him. The bald facts were buried in the police files at Mulberry Street headquarters and in the newspaper office "morgues," while the public, thrilled daily by fresh horrors, forgot the very existence of the evil doctor a couple of days after the acquittal of the central figure. But for Williams it was otherwise. The personality of the heartless and calculating murderer — the intellectual poisoner, as he called him — had made a deep impression on his imaginations and for many weeks his memory kept him alive as a moving and actual horror in his life. The words he had heard him titter, with their covert threats and ill-concealed animosity, helped, no doubt, to vivify the recollection and to explain why Hensig stayed in his thoughts and haunted his dreams with a persistence that reminded him of his very earliest cases on the paper. With time, however, even Hensig began to fade away into the confused background of piled up memories of prisoners and prison scenes, and at length the memory became so deeply buried that it no longer troubled him at all.

The summer passed, and Williams came back from his hard-earned holiday of two weeks in the Maine backwoods. New York was at its best, and the thousands who had been forced to stay and face its torrid summer heats were beginning to revive under the spell of the brilliant autumn days. Cool sea breezes swept over its burnt streets from the Lower Bay, and across the splendid flood of the Hudson River the woods on the Palisades of New Jersey had turned to crimson and gold. The air was electric, sharp, sparkling, and the life of the city began to pulse anew with its restless and impetuous energy. Bronzed faces from sea and mountains thronged the streets, health and light-heartedness showed in every eye, for autumn in New York wields a potent magic not to be denied, and even the East Side slums, where the unfortunates crowd in their squalid thousands, had the appearance of having been swept and cleansed. Along the water-fronts especially the powers of sea and sun and scented winds combined to work an irresistible fever in the hearts of all who chafed within their prison walls.

And in Williams, perhaps more than in most, there was something that responded vigorously to the influences of hope and cheerfulness everywhere abroad. Fresh with the vigour of his holiday and full of good resolutions for the coming winter he felt released from the evil spell of irregular living, and as he crossed one October morning to Staten Island in the big double-ender ferry-boat, his heart was light, and his eye wandered to the blue waters and the hazy line of woods beyond with feelings of pure gladness and delight.

He was on his way to Quarantine to meet an incoming liner for the *Vulture*. A Jew-baiting member of the German Reichstag was coming to deliver a series of lectures in New York on his favourite subject, and the newspapers who deemed him worthy of notice at all were sending him fair warning that his mission would be tolerated perhaps, but not welcomed. The Jews were good citizens and America a "free country" and his meetings in the Cooper Union Hall would meet with derision certainly, and violence possibly.

The assignment was a pleasant one, and Williams had instructions to poke fun at the officious and interfering German, and advise him to return to Bremen by the next steamer without venturing among flying eggs and dead cats on the platform. He entered fully into the spirit of the job and was telling the Quarantine doctor about it as they steamed down the bay in the little tug to meet the huge liner just anchoring inside Sandy Hook.

The decks of the ship were crowded with passengers watching the arrival of the puffing tug, and just as they drew alongside in the shadow Williams suddenly felt his eyes drawn away from the swinging rope ladder to some point about half-way down the length of the vessel. There, among the intermediate passengers on the lower deck, he saw a face staring at him with fixed intentness. The eyes were bright blue, and the skin, in that row of bronzed passengers, showed remarkably white. At once, and with a violent rush of blood from the heart, he recognised Hensig.

In a moment everything about him changed: the blue waters of the bay turned black, the light seemed to leave the sun, and all the old sensations of fear and loathing came over him again like the memory of some great pain. He shook himself, and clutched the rope ladder to swing up after the Health Officer, angry, and yet genuinely alarmed at the same time, to realise that the return of this man could so affect him. His interview with the Jew-baiter was of the briefest possible description, and he hurried through to catch the Quarantine tug back to Staten Island, instead of steaming up the bay with the great liner into dock, as the other reporters did. He had caught no second glimpse of the hated German, and he even went so far as to harbour a faint hope that he might have been deceived, and that some trick of resemblance in another face had caused a sort of subjective hallucination. At any rate, the days passed into weeks, and October slipped into November, and there was no recurrence of the distressing vision. Perhaps, after all, it was a stranger only; or, if it was Hensig, then he had forgotten all about the reporter, and his return had no connection necessarily with the idea of revenge.

None the less, however, Williams felt uneasy. He told his friend Dowling, the policeman.

"Old news," laughed the Irishman. "Headquarters are keeping an eye on him as a suspect. Berlin wants a man for two murders — goes by the name of Brunner — and from their description we think it's this feller Hensig. Nothing certain yet, but we're on his trail. *I'm* on his trail," he added proudly, "and don't you forget it! I'll let you know anything when the time comes, but mum's the word just now!"

One night, not long after this meeting, Williams and the Senator were covering a big fire on the West Side docks. They were standing on the outskirts of the crowd watching the immense flames that a shouting wind seemed to carry half-way across the river. The surrounding shipping was brilliantly lit up and the roar was magnificent. The Senator, having come out with none of his own, borrowed his friend's overcoat for a moment to protect him from spray and flying cinders while he went inside the fire lines for the latest information obtainable. It was after midnight, and the main story had been telephoned to the office; all they had now to do was to send in the latest details and corrections to be written up at the news desk.

"I'll wait for you over at the corner!" shouted Williams, in moving off through a scene of indescribable confusion and taking off his fire badge as he went.

This conspicuous brass badge, issued to reporters by the Fire Department, gave them the right to pass within the police cordon in the pursuit of information, and at their own risk. Hardly had he unpinned it from his coat when a hand dashed out of the crowd surging up against him and made a determined grab at it. He turned to trace the owner, but at that instant a great lurching of the mob nearly carried him off his feet, and he only just succeeded in seeing the arm withdrawn, having failed of its object, before he was landed with a violent push upon the pavement he had been aiming for.

The incident did not strike him as particularly odd, for in such a crowd there are many who covet the privilege of getting closer to the blaze. He simply laughed and put the badge safely in his pocket, and then stood to watch the dying flames until his friend came to join him with the latest details.

Yet, though time was pressing and the Senator had little enough to do, it was fully half an hour before he came lumbering up through the darkness. Williams recognised him some distance away by the check ulster he wore — his own.

But *was* it the Senator, after all? The figure moved oddly and with a limp, as though injured. A few feet off it stopped and peered at Williams through the darkness.

"That you, Williams?" asked a gruff voice.

"I thought you were someone else for a moment," answered the reporter, relieved to recognise his friend, and moving forward to meet him. "But what's wrong? Are you hurt?"

The Senator looked ghastly in the lurid glow of the fire. His face was white, and there was a little trickle of blood on the forehead.

"Some fellow nearly did for me," he said; "deliberately pushed me clean off the edge of the dock. If I hadn't fallen on to a broken pile and found a boat, I'd have been drowned sure as God made little apples. Think I know who it was, too. *Think!* I mean I *know*, because I saw his damned white face and heard what he said."

"Who in the world was it? What did he want?" stammered the other.

The Senator took his arm, and lurched into the saloon behind them for some brandy. As he did so he kept looking over his shoulder.

"Quicker we're off from this dirty neighbourhood, the better," he said.

Then he turned to Williams, looking oddly at him over the glass, and answering his questions.

"Who was it? — why, it was Hensig! And what did he want? — well, he wanted *you!*"

"Me! Hensig!" gasped the other.

"Guess he mistook me for you," went on the Senator, looking behind him at the door. "The crowd was so thick I cut across by the edge of the dock. It was quite dark. There wasn't a soul near me. I was running. Suddenly what I thought was a stump got up in front of me, and, Gee whiz, man! I tell you it was Hensig, or I'm a drunken Dutchman. I looked bang into his face. 'Good-pye, Mr. *Vulture* reporter,' he said, with a damned laugh, and gave me a push that sent me backwards clean over the edge."

The Senator paused for breath, and to empty his second glass.

"*My* overcoat!" exclaimed Williams faintly.

"Oh, he'd been following you right enough, I guess."

The Senator was not really injured, and the two men walked back towards Broadway to find a telephone, passing through a region of dimly-lighted streets known as Little Africa, where the negroes lived, and where it was safer to keep the middle of the road, thus avoiding sundry dark alley-ways opening off the side. They talked hard all the way.

"He's after you, no doubt," repeated the Senator. "I guess he never forgot your report of his trial. Better keep your eye peeled!" he added with a laugh.

But Williams didn't feel a bit inclined to laugh, and the thought that it certainly *was* Hensig he had seen on the steamer, and that he was following him so closely as to mark his check ulster and make an attempt on his life, made him feel horribly uncomfortable, to say the least. To be stalked by such a man was terrible. To realise that he was marked down by that white-faced, cruel wretch, merciless and implacable, skilled in the manifold ways of killing by stealth — that somewhere in the crowds of the great city he was watched and waited for, hunted, observed: here was an obsession really to torment and become dangerous. Those light-blue eyes, that keen intelligence, that mind charged with revenge, had been watching him ever since the trial, even from across the sea. The idea terrified him. It brought death into his thoughts for the first time with a vivid sense of nearness and reality — far greater than anything he had experienced when watching others die.

That night, in his dingy little room in the East Nineteenth Street boarding-house, Williams went to bed in a blue funk, and for days afterwards he went about his business in a continuation of the same blue funk. It was useless to deny it. He kept his eyes everywhere, thinking he was being watched and followed. A new face in the office, at the boarding-house table, or anywhere on his usual beat, made him jump. His daily work was haunted; his dreams were all nightmares; he forgot all his good resolutions, and plunged into the old indulgences that helped him to forget his distress. It took twice as much liquor to make him jolly, and four times as much to make him reckless. Not that he really was a drunkard, or cared to drink for its own sake, but he moved in a thirsty world of reporters, policemen, reckless and loose-living men and women, whose form of greeting was "What'll you take?" and method of reproach "Oh, he's sworn off!" Only now he was more careful how much he took, counting the cocktails and fizzes poured into him during the course of his day's work, and was anxious never to lose control of himself. He must be on the watch. He changed his eating and drinking haunts, and altered any habits that could give a clue to the devil on his trail. He even went so far as to change his boardinghouse. His emotion — the emotion of fear — changed everything. It tinged the outer world with gloom, draping it in darker colours, stealing something from the sunlight, reducing enthusiasm, and acting as a heavy drag, as it were, upon all the normal functions of life.

The effect upon his imagination, already diseased by alcohol and drugs, was, of course, exceedingly strong. The doctor's words about developing a germ until it became too powerful to be touched by any medicine, and then letting it into the victim's system by means of a pin-scratch — this possessed him more than anything else. The idea dominated his thoughts; it seemed so clever, so cruel, so devilish. The "accident" at the fire had been, of course, a real accident, conceived on the spur of the moment — the result of a chance meeting and a foolish mistake. Hensig had no need to resort to such clumsy methods. When the right moment came he would adopt a far simpler, *safer* plan.

Finally, he became so obsessed by the idea that Hensig was following him, waiting for his opportunity, that one day he told the news editor the whole story. His nerves were so shaken that he could not do his work properly.

"That's a good story. Make two hundred of it," said the editor at once. "Fake the name, of course. Mustn't mention Hensig, or there'll be a libel suit." But Williams was in earnest, and insisted so forcibly that Treherne, though busy as ever, took him aside into his room with the glass door.

"Now, see here, Williams, you're drinking too much," he said; "that's about the size of it. Steady up a bit on the wash, and Hensig's face will disappear."

He spoke kindly, but sharply. He was young himself, awfully keen, with much knowledge of human nature and a rare "nose for news." He understood the abilities of his small army of men with intuitive judgment. That they drank was nothing to him, provided they did their work. Everybody in that world drank, and the man who didn't was looked upon with suspicion.

Williams explained rather savagely that the face was no mere symptom of delirium tremens and the editor spared him another two minutes before rushing out to tackle the crowd of men waiting for him at the news desk.

"That so? You don't say!" he asked, with more interest. "Well, I guess Hensig's simply trying to razzle-dazzle you. You tried to kill him by your reports, and he wants to scare you by way of revenge. But he'll never dare *do* anything. Throw him a good bluff, and he'll give in like a baby. Everything's pretence in this world. But I rather like the idea of the germs. That's original!"

Williams, a little angry at the other's flippancy, told the story of the Senator's adventure and the changed overcoat.

"May be, may be," replied the hurried editor; "but the Senator drinks Chinese whisky, and a man who does that might imagine anything on God's earth. Take a tip, Williams, from an old hand, and let up a bit on the liquor. Drop cocktails and keep to straight whisky, and never drink on an empty stomach. Above all, *don't mix!*"

He gave him a keen look and was off. "Next time you see this German," cried Treherne from the door, "go up and ask him for an interview on what it feels like to escape from the Chair — just to show him you don't care a red cent. Talk about having him watched and followed — suspected man — and all that sort of flim-flam. Pretend to warn him. It'll turn the tables and make him digest a bit. See?"

Williams sauntered out into the street to report a meeting of the Rapid Transit Commissioners, and the first person he met as he ran down the office steps was — Max Hensig.

Before he could stop, or swerve aside, they were face to face. His head swam for a moment and he began to tremble. Then some measure of self-possession returned, and he tried instinctively to act on the editor's advice. No other plan was ready, so he drew on the last force that had occupied his mind. It was that — or running.

Hensig, he noticed, looked prosperous; he wore a fur overcoat and cap. His face was whiter than ever, and his blue eyes burned like coals.

"Why! Dr. Hensig, you're back in New York!" he exclaimed. "When did you arrive? I'm glad — I suppose — I mean — er — will you come and have a drink?" he concluded desperately. It was very foolish, but for the life of him he could think of nothing else to say. And the last thing in the world he wished was that his enemy should know that he was afraid.

"I tink not, Mr. *Vulture* reporder, tanks," he answered

coolly; "but I sit py and vatch you drink."

His self-possession was as perfect, as it always was. But Williams, more himself now, seized on the refusal and moved on, saying something about having a meeting to go to.

"I walk a liddle way with you, berhaps," Hensig said, following him down the pavement.

It was impossible to prevent him, and they started side by side across City Hall Park towards Broadway. It was after four o'clock: the dusk was falling: the little park was thronged with people walking in all directions, everyone in a terrific hurry as usual. Only Hensig seemed calm and unmoved among that racing, tearing life about them. He carried an atmosphere of ice about with him: it was his voice and manner that produced this impression; his mind was alert, watchful, determined, always sure of itself. Williams wanted to run. He reviewed swiftly in his mind a dozen ways of getting rid of him quickly, yet knowing well they were all futile. He put his hands in his overcoat pockets — the check ulster — and watched sideways every movement of his companion.

"Living in New York again, aren't you?" he began.

"Not as a doctor any more," was the reply. "I now teach and study. Also I write sciendific books a liddle — "

"What about?"

"Cherms," said the other, looking at him and laughing. "Disease cherms, their culture and development." He put the accent on the "op."

Williams walked more quickly. With a great effort he tried to put Treherne's advice into practice. "You care to give me an interview any time — on your special subjects?" he asked, as naturally as he could.

"Oh yes; with much bleasure. I lif in Harlem now, if you will call von day — "

"Our office is best," interrupted the reporter. "Paper, desks, library, all handy for use, you know."

"If you're afraid — " began Hensig. Then, without finishing the sentence, he added with a laugh, "I haf no arsenic there. You not tink me any more a pungling boisoner? You haf changed your mind about all dat?"

Williams felt his flesh beginning to creep. How could he speak of such a matter! His own wife, too!

He turned quickly and faced him, standing still for a moment so that the throng of people deflected into two streams past them. He felt it absolutely imperative upon him to say something that should convince the German he was not afraid.

"I suppose you are aware, Dr. Hensig, that the police know you have returned, and that you are being watched probably?" he said in a low voice, forcing himself to meet the odious blue eyes.

"And why not, bray?" he asked imperturbably.

"They may suspect something — "

"Susbected — already again? *Ach was!*" said the German.

"I only wished to warn you — " stammered Williams, who always found it difficult to remain self-possessed under the other's dreadful stare.

"No boliceman see what I do — or catch me again," he laughed quite horribly. "But I tank you all the same."

Williams turned to catch a Broadway car going at full

speed. He could not stand another minute with this man, who affected him so disagreeably.

"I call at the office one day to gif you interview!" Hensig shouted as he dashed off, and the next minute he was swallowed up in the crowd, and Williams, with mixed feelings and a strange inner trembling, went to cover the meeting of the Rapid Transit Board.

But, while he reported the proceedings mechanically, his mind was busy with quite other thoughts. Hensig was at his side the whole time. He felt quite sure, however unlikely it seemed, that there was no fancy in his fears, and that he had judged the German correctly. Hensig hated him, and would put him out of the way if he could. He would do it in such a way that detection would be almost impossible. He would not shoot or poison in the ordinary way, or resort to any clumsy method. He would simply follow, watch, wait his opportunity, and then act with utter callousness and remorseless determination. And Williams already felt pretty certain of the means that would be employed: *"Cherms!"*

This meant proximity. He must watch everyone who came close to him in trains, cars, restaurants — anywhere and everywhere. It could be done in a second: only a slight scratch would be necessary, and the disease would be in his blood with such strength that the chances of recovery would be slight. And what could he do? He could not have Hensig watched or arrested. He had no story to tell to a magistrate, or to the police, for no one would listen to such a tale. And, if he were stricken down by sudden illness, what was more likely than to say he had caught the fever in the ordinary course of his work, since he was always frequenting noisome dens and the haunts of the very poor, the foreign and filthy slums of the East Side, and the hospitals, morgues, and cells of all sorts and conditions of men? No; it was a disagreeable situation, and Williams, young, shaken in nerve, and easily impressionable as he was, could not prevent its obsession of his mind and imagination.

"If I get suddenly ill," he told the Senator, his only friend in the whole city, "and send for you, look carefully for a scratch on my body. Tell Dowling, and tell the doctor the story."

"You think Hensig goes about with a little bottle of plague germs in his vest pockets," laughed the other reporter, "ready to scratch you with a pin?"

"Some damned scheme like that, I'm sure."

"Nothing could be proved anyway. He wouldn't keep the evidence in his pocket till he was arrested, would he?"

During the next week or two Williams ran against Hensig twice — accidentally. The first time it happened just outside his own boarding-house — the new one. Hensig had his foot on the stone steps as if just about to come up, but quick as a flash he turned his face away and moved on down the Street. This was about eight o'clock in the evening, and the hall light fell through the opened door upon his face. The second time it was not so clear: the reporter was covering a case in the courts, a case of suspicious death in which a woman was chief prisoner, and he thought he saw the doctor's white visage watching him from among the crowd at the back of the court-room. When he looked a second time, however, the face had disappeared, and there was no sign afterwards of its owner in the lobby or corridor.

That same day he met Dowling in the building; he was promoted now, and was always in plain clothes. The detective drew him aside into a corner. The talk at once turned upon the German.

"We're watching him too," he said. "Nothing you can use yet, but he's changed his name again, and never stops at the same address for more than a week or two. I guess he's Brunner right enough, the man Berlin's looking for. He's a holy terror if ever there was one."

Dowling was happy as a schoolboy to be in touch with such a promising case.

"What's he up to now in particular?" asked the other.

"Something pretty black," said the detective. "But I can't tell you yet awhile. He calls himself Schmidt now, and he's dropped the 'Doctor.' We may take him any day — just waiting for advices from Germany."

Williams told his story of the overcoat adventure with the Senator, and his belief that Hensig was waiting for a suitable opportunity to catch him alone.

"That's dead likely too," said Dowling, and added carelessly, "I guess we'll have to make some kind of a case against him anyway, just to get him out of the way. He's dangerous to be around huntin' on the loose."

IV.

So gradual sometimes are the approaches of fear that the processes by which it takes possession of a man's soul are often too insidious to be recognised, much less to be dealt with, until their object has been finally accomplished and the victim has lost the power to act. And by this time the reporter, who had again plunged into excess, felt so nerveless that, if he met Hensig face to face, he could not answer for what he might do. He might assault his tormentor violently — one result of terror — or he might find himself powerless to do anything at all but yield, like a bird fascinated before a snake.

He was always thinking now of the moment when they would meet, and of what would happen; for he was just as certain that they must meet eventually, and that Hensig would try to kill him, as that his next birthday would find him twenty-five years old. That meeting, he well knew, could be delayed only, not prevented, and his changing again to another boarding-house, or moving altogether to a different city, could only postpone the final accounting between them. It was bound to come.

A reporter on a New York newspaper has one day in seven to himself. Williams's day off was Monday, and he was always glad when it came. Sunday was especially arduous for him, because in addition to the unsatisfactory nature of the day's assignments, involving private interviewing which the citizens pretended to resent on their day of rest, he had the task in the evening of reporting a difficult sermon in a Brooklyn church. Having only a column and a half at his disposal, he had to condense as he went along, and the speaker was so rapid, and so fond of lengthy quotations, that the reporter found his shorthand only just equal to the task. It was usually after halfpast nine o'clock when he left the church, and there was still the labour of transcribing his notes in the office against time.

The Sunday following the glimpse of his tormentor's face in the court-room he was busily condensing the wearisome periods of the preacher, sitting at a little table immediately under the pulpit, when he glanced up during a brief pause and let his eye wander over the congregation and up to the crowded galleries. Nothing was farther at the moment from his much-occupied brain than the doctor of Amityville, and it was such an unexpected shock to encounter his fixed stare up there among the occupants of the front row, watching him with an evil smile, that his senses temporarily deserted him. The next sentence of the preacher was wholly lost, and his shorthand during the brief remainder of the sermon was quite illegible, he found, when he came to transcribe it at the office.

It was after one o'clock in the morning when he finished, and he went out feeling exhausted and rather shaky. In the all-night drug-store at the corner he indulged accordingly in several more glasses of whisky than usual, and talked a long time with the man who guarded the back room and served liquor to the few who knew the pass-word, since the shop had really no licence at all. The true reason for this delay he recognised quite plainly: he was afraid of the journey home along the dark and emptying streets. The lower end of New York is practically deserted after ten o'clock: it has no residences, no theatres, no *cafés*, and only a few travellers from late ferries share it with reporters, a sprinkling of policemen, and the ubiquitous ne'er-do-wells who haunt the saloon doors. The newspaper world of Park Row was, of course, alive with light and movement, but once outside that narrow zone and the night descended with an effect of general darkness.

Williams thought of spending three dollars on a cab, but dismissed the idea because of its extravagance. Presently Galusha Owens came in — too drunk to be of any use, though, as a companion. Besides, he lived in Harlem, which was miles beyond Nineteenth Street, where Williams had to go. He took another rye whisky — his fourth — and looked cautiously through the coloured glass windows into the Street. No one was visible. Then he screwed up his nerves another twist or two, and made a bolt for it, taking the steps in a sort of flying leap — and running full tilt into a man whose figure seemed almost to have risen out of the very pavement.

He gave a cry and raised his fists to strike.

"Where's your hurry?" laughed a familiar voice. "Is the Prince of Wales dead?" It was the Senator, most welcome of all possible appearances.

"Come in and have a horn," said Williams, "and then I'll walk home with you." He was immensely glad to see him, for only a few streets separated their respective boarding-houses.

"But he'd never sit out a long sermon just for the pleasure of watching you," observed the Senator after hearing his friend's excited account.

"That man'll take any trouble in the world to gain his end," said the other with conviction. "He's making a study of all my movements and habits. He's not the sort to take chances when it's a matter of life and death. I'll bet he's not far away at this moment."

"Rats!" exclaimed the Senator, laughing in rather a forced way. "You're getting the jumps with your Hensig and death. Have another rye." They finished their drinks and went out together, crossing City Hall Park diagonally towards Broadway, and then turning north. They crossed Canal and Grand Streets, deserted and badly lighted. Only a few drunken loiterers passed them. Occasionally a policeman on the corner, always close to the side-door of a saloon, of course, recognised one or other of them and called good night. Otherwise there was no one, and they seemed to have this part of Manhattan Island pretty well to themselves. The presence of the Senator, ever cheery and kind, keeping close to his friend all the way, the effect of the half-dozen whiskies, and the sight of the guardians of the law, combined to raise the reporter's spirits somewhat: and when they reached Fourteenth Street, with its better light and greater traffic, and saw Union Square lying just beyond, close to his own street, he felt a distinct increase of courage and no objection to going on alone. "Good night!" cried the Senator cheerily. "Get home safe; I turn off here anyway." He hesitated a moment before turning down the street, and then added, "You feel O.K., don't you?"

"You may get double rates for an exclusive bit of news if you come on and see me assaulted," Williams replied, laughing aloud, and then waiting to see the last of his friend. But the moment the Senator was gone the laughter disappeared. He went on alone, crossing the square among the trees and walking very quickly.

Once or twice he turned to see if anybody were following him, and his eyes scanned carefully as he passed every occupant of the park benches where a certain number of homeless loafers always find their night's lodging. But there was nothing apparently to cause him alarm, and in a few minutes more he would be safe in the little back bedroom of his own house. Over the way he saw the lights of Burbacher's saloon, where respectable Germans drank Rhine wine and played chess till all hours. He thought of going in for a night-cap, hesitating for a moment, but finally going on. When he got to the end of the square, however, and saw the dark opening of East Eighteenth Street, he thought after all he would go back and have another drink.

He hovered for a moment on the kerbstone and then turned; his will often slipped a cog now in this way.

It was only when he was on his way back that he realised the truth: that his real reason for turning back and avoiding the dark open mouth of the street was because he was afraid of something its shadows might conceal. This dawned upon him quite suddenly. If there had been a light at the corner of the street he would never have turned back at all. And as this passed through his mind, already somewhat fuddled with what he had drunk, he became aware that the figure of a man had slipped forward out of the dark space he had just refused to enter, and was following him down the street. The man was pressing, too, close into the houses, using any protection of shadow or railing that would enable him to move unseen.

But the moment Williams entered the bright section of pavement opposite the wine-room windows he knew that this man had come close up behind him, with a little silent run, and he turned at once to face him. He saw a slim man with dark hair and blue eyes, and recognised him instantly.

"It's very late to be coming home," said the man at once. "I thought I recognised my reporder friend from the *Vulture*." These were the actual words, and the voice was meant to be pleasant, but what Williams thought he heard, spoken in tones of ice, was something like, "At last I've caught you! You are in a state of collapse nervously, and you are exhausted. I can do what I please with you." For the face and the voice were those of Hensig the Tormentor, and the dyed hair only served to emphasise rather grotesquely the man's features and make the pallor of the skin greater by contrast.

His first instinct was to turn and run, his second to fly at the man and strike him. A terror beyond death seized him. A pistol held to his head, or a waving bludgeon, he could easily have faced; but this odious creature, slim, limp, and white of face, with his terrible suggestion of cruelty, literally appalled him so that he could think of nothing intelligent to do or to say. This accurate knowledge of his movements, too, added to his distress — this waiting for him at night when he was tired and foolish from excess. At that moment he knew all the sensations of the criminal a few hours before his execution: the bursts of hysterical terror, the inability to realise his position, to hold his thoughts steady, the helplessness of it all.

Yet, in the end, the reporter heard his own voice speaking with a rather weak and unnatural kind of tone and accompanied by a gulp of forced laughter — heard himself stammering the ever-ready formula: "I was going to have a drink before turning in — will you join me?"

The invitation, he realised afterwards, was prompted by the one fact that stood forth clearly in his mind at the moment — the thought, namely, that whatever he did or said, he must never let Hensig for one instant imagine that he felt afraid and was so helpless a victim.

Side by side they moved down the street, for Hensig had acquiesced in the suggestion, and Williams already felt dazed by the strong, persistent will of his companion. His thoughts seemed to be flying about somewhere outside his brain, beyond control, scattering wildly. He could think of nothing further to say, and had the smallest diversion furnished the opportunity he would have turned and run for his life through the deserted streets.

"A glass of lager," he heard the German say, "I take berhaps that with you. You know me in spite of—" he added, indicating by a movement the changed colour of his hair and moustache. "Also, I gif you now the interview you asked for, if you like."

The reporter agreed feebly, finding nothing adequate to reply. He turned helplessly and looked into his face with something of the sensations a bird may feel when it runs at last straight into the jaws of the reptile that has fascinated it. The fear of weeks settled down upon him, focussing about his heart. It was, of course, an effect of hypnotism, he remembered thinking vaguely through the befuddlement of his drink — this culminating effect of an evil and remorseless personality acting upon one that was diseased and extra receptive. And while he made the suggestion and heard the other's acceptance of it, he knew perfectly well that he was falling in with the plan of the doctor's own making, a plan that would end in an assault upon his person, perhaps a technical assault only — a mere touch — still, an assault that would be at the same time an attempt at murder. The alcohol buzzed in his ears. He felt strangely powerless. He walked steadily to his doom, side by side with his executioner.

Any attempt to analyse the psychology of the situation was utterly beyond him. But, amid the whirl of emotion and the excitement of the whisky, he dimly grasped the importance of two fundamental things.

And the first was that, though he was now muddled and frantic, yet a moment would come when his will would be capable of one supreme effort to escape, and that therefore it would be wiser for the present to waste no atom of volition on temporary half-measures. He would play dead dog. The fear that now paralysed him would accumulate till it reached the point of saturation: that would be the time to strike for his life. For just as the coward may reach a stage where he is capable of a sort of frenzied heroism that no ordinarily brave man could compass, so the victim of fear, at a point varying with his balance of imagination and physical vigour, will reach a state where fear leaves him and he becomes numb to its effect from sheer excess of feeling it. It is the point of saturation. He may then turn suddenly calm and act with a judgment and precision that simply bewilder the object of the attack. It is, of course, the inevitable swing of the pendulum, the law of equal action and reaction.

Hazily, tipsily perhaps, Williams was conscious of this potential power deep within him, below the superficial layers of smaller emotions — could he but be sufficiently terrified to reach it and bring it to the surface where it must result in action.

And, as a consequence of this foresight of his sober subliminal self, he offered no opposition to the least suggestion of his tormentor, but made up his mind instinctively to agree to all that he proposed. Thus he lost no atom of the force he might eventually call upon, by friction over details which in any case he would yield in the end. And at the same time he felt intuitively that his utter weakness might even deceive his enemy a little and increase the chances of his single effort to escape when the right moment arrived.

That Williams was able to "imagine" this true psychology, yet wholly unable to analyse it, simply showed that on occasion he could be psychically active. His deeper subliminal self, stirred by the alcohol and the stress of emotion, was guiding him, and would continue to guide him in proportion as he let his fuddled normal self slip into the background without attempt to interfere.

And the second fundamental thing he grasped — due even more than the first to psychic intuition — was the certainty that he could drink more, up to a certain point, with distinct advantage to his power and lucidity — but up to a given point only. After that would come unconscious-ness, a single sip too much and he would cross the fron-tier — a very narrow one. It was as though he knew intuitively that "the drunken consciousness is one bit of the mystic consciousness." At present he was only fuddled and fearful, but additional stimulant would inhibit the effects of the other emotions, give him unbounded confidence, clarify his judgment and increase his capacity to a stage far beyond the normal. Only — he must stop in time.

His chances of escape, therefore, so far as he could understand, depended on these two things: he must drink till he became self-confident and arrived at the abnormally clear-minded stage of drunkenness; and he must wait for the moment when Hensig had so filled him up with fear that he no longer could react to it. Then would be the time to strike. Then his will would be free and have judgment behind it. These were the two things standing up clearly somewhere behind that great confused turmoil of mingled fear and alcohol.

Thus for the moment, though with scattered forces and rather wildly feeble thoughts, he moved down the street beside the man who hated him and meant to kill him. He had no purpose at all but to agree and to wait. Any attempt he made now could end only in failure.

They talked a little as they went, the German calm, chatting as though he were merely an agreeable acquaintance, but behaving with the obvious knowledge that he held his victim secure, and that his struggles would prove simply rather amusing. He even laughed about his dyed hair, saying by way of explanation that he had done it to please a woman who told him it would make him look younger. Williams knew this was a lie, and that the police had more to do with the change than a woman; but the man's vanity showed through the explanation, and was a vivid little self-revelation.

He objected to entering Burbacher's, saying that he (Burbacher) paid no blackmail to the police, and might be raided for keeping open after hours.

"I know a nice quiet blace on T"ird Avenue. We go there," he said.

Williams, walking unsteadily and shaking inwardly, still groping, too, feebly after a way of escape, turned down the side street with him. He thought of the men he had watched walking down the short corridor from the cell to the "Chair" at Sing Sing, and wondered if they felt as he did. It was like going to his own execution.

"I haf a new disgovery in bacteriology — in cherms,"

the doctor went on, "and it will make me famous, for it is very imbortant. I gif it you egsclusive for the *Vulture*, as you are a friend." He became technical, and the reporter's mind lost itself among such words as "toxins," "alkaloids," and the like. But he realised clearly enough that Hensig was playing with him and felt absolutely sure of his victim. When he lurched badly, as he did more than once, the German took his arm by way of support, and at the vile touch of the man it was all Williams could do not to scream or strike out blindly.

They turned up Third Avenue and stopped at the side door of a cheap saloon. He noticed the name of Schumacher over the porch, but all lights were out except a feeble glow that came through the glass fanlight. A man pushed his face cautiously round the half-opened door, and after a brief examination let them in with a whispered remark to be quiet. It was the usual formula of the Tammany saloon-keeper, who paid so much a month to the police to be allowed to keep open all night, provided there was no noise or fighting. It was now well after one o'clock in the morning, and the streets were deserted.

The reporter was quite at home in the sort of place they had entered; otherwise the sinister aspect of a drinking "joint" after hours, with its gloom and general air of suspicion, might have caused him some extra alarm. A dozen men, unpleasant of countenance, were standing at the bar, where a single lamp gave just enough light to enable them to see their glasses. The bar-tender gave Hensig a swift glance of recognition as they walked along the sanded floor.

"Come," whispered the German; "we go to the back

room. I know the bass-word," he laughed, leading the way.

They walked to the far end of the bar and opened a door into a brightly lit room with about a dozen tables in it, at most of which men sat drinking with highly painted women, talking loudly, quarrelling, singing, and the air thick with smoke. No one took any notice of them as they went down the room to a table in the corner farthest from the door — Hensig chose it; and when the single waiter came up with "Was nehmen die Herren?" and a moment later brought the rye whisky they both asked for, Williams swallowed his own without the "chaser" of soda water, and ordered another on the spot.

"It'sh awfully watered," he said rather thickly to his companion, "and I'm tired."

"Cocaine, under the circumstances, would help you quicker, berhaps!" replied the German with an expression of amusement. Good God! Was there nothing about him the man had not found out? He must have been shadowing him for days; it was at least a week since Williams had been to the First Avenue drug store to get the wicked bottle refilled. Had he been on his trail every night when he left the office to go home? This idea of remorseless persistence made him shudder.

"Then we finish quickly if you are tired," the doctor continued, "and tomorrow you can show me your repordt for gorrections if you make any misdakes berhaps. I gif you the address to-night pefore we leave."

The increased ugliness of his speech and accent betrayed his growing excitement. Williams drank his whisky, again without water, and called for yet another, clinking glasses with the murderer opposite, and swallowing half of this last glass, too, while Hensig merely tasted his own, looking straight at him over the performance with his evil eyes.

"I can write shorthand," began the reporter, trying to appear at his ease.

"*Ach*, I know, of course."

There was a mirror behind the table, and he took a quick glance round the room while the other began searching in his coat pocket for the papers he had with him. Williams lost no single detail of his movements, but at the same time managed swiftly to get the "note" of the other occupants of the tables.

Degraded and besotted faces he saw, almost without exception, and not one to whom he could appeal for help with any prospect of success. It was a further shock, too, to realise that he preferred the more or less bestial countenances round him to the intellectual and ascetic face opposite. They were at least human, whereas *he* was something quite outside the pale; and this preference for the low creatures, otherwise loathsome to him, brought his mind by sharp contrast to a new and vivid realisation of the personality before him. He gulped down his drink, and again ordered it to be refilled.

But meanwhile the alcohol was beginning to key him up out of the dazed and negative state into which his first libations and his accumulations of fear had plunged him. His brain became a shade clearer. There was even a faint stirring of the will. He had already drunk enough under normal circumstances to be simply reeling, but to-night the emotion of fear inhibited the effects of the alcohol, keeping him singularly steady. Provided he did not exceed a given point, he could go on drinking till he reached the moment of high power when he could combine all his forces into the single consummate act of cleverly calculated escape. If he missed this psychological moment he would collapse.

A sudden crash made him jump. It was behind him against the other wall. In the mirror he saw that a middle-aged man had lost his balance and fallen off his chair, foolishly intoxicated, and that two women were ostensibly trying to lift him up, but really were going swiftly through his pockets as he lay in a heap on the floor. A big man who had been asleep the whole evening in the corner stopped snoring and woke up to look and laugh, but no one interfered. A man must take care of himself in such a place and with such company, or accept the consequences. The big man composed himself again for sleep, sipping his glass a little first, and the noise of the room continued as before. It was a case of "knock-out drops" in the whisky, put in by the women, however, rather than by the saloon-keeper. Williams remembered thinking he had nothing to fear of that kind. Hensig's method would be far more subtle and clever — *cherms!* A scratch with a pin and a germ!

"I haf zome notes here of my disgovery," he went on, smiling significantly at the interruption, and taking some papers out of an inner pocket. "But they are written in Cherman, so I dranslate for you. You haf paper and benzil?"

The reporter produced the sheaf of office copy paper he always carried about with him, and prepared to write. The rattle of the elevated trains outside and the noisy buzz of drunken conversation inside formed the background against which he heard the German's steely insistent voice going on ceaselessly with the "dranslation and egsplanation."

From time to time people left the room, and new customers reeled in. When the clatter of incipient fighting and smashed glasses became too loud, Hensig waited till it was quiet again. He watched every new arrival keenly. They were very few now, for the night had passed into early morning and the room was gradually emptying. The waiter took snatches of sleep in his chair by the door; the big man still snored heavily in the angle of the wall and window. When he was the only one left, the proprietor would certainly close up. He had not ordered a drink for an hour at least. Williams, however, drank on steadily, always aiming at the point when he would be at the top of his power, full of confidence and decision. That moment was undoubtedly coming nearer all the time. Yes, but so was the moment Hensig was waiting for. He, too, felt absolutely confident, encouraging his companion to drink more, and watching his gradual collapse with unmasked glee. He betrayed his gloating quite plainly now: he held his victim too securely to feel anxious; when the big man reeled out they would be alone for a brief minute or two unobserved — and meanwhile he allowed himself to become a little too careless from over-confidence. And Williams noted that too.

For slowly the will of the reporter began to assert itself, and with this increase of intelligence he of course appreciated his awful position more keenly, and therefore, *felt more fear*. The two main things he was waiting for were coming perceptibly within reach: to reach the saturation point of terror and the culminating moment of the alcohol. Then, action and escape!

Gradually, thus, as he listened and wrote, he passed from the stage of stupid, negative terror into that of active, positive terror. The alcohol kept driving hotly at those hidden centres of imagination within, which, once touched, begin to reveal: in other words, he became observant, critical, alert. Swiftly the power grew. His lucidity increased till he became almost conscious of the workings of the other man's mind, and it was like sitting opposite a clock whose wheels and needles he could just hear clicking. His eyes seemed to spread their power of vision all over his skin; he could see what was going on without actually looking. In the same way he heard all that passed in the room without turning his head. Every moment he became clearer in mind. He almost touched clairvoyance. The presentiment earlier in the evening that this stage would come was at last being actually fulfilled.

From time to time he sipped his whisky, but more cautiously than at first, for he knew that this keen psychical activity was the forerunner of helpless collapse. Only for a minute or two would he be at the top of his power. The frontier was a dreadfully narrow one, and already he had lost control of his fingers, and was scrawling a shorthand that bore no resemblance to the original system of its inventor. As the white light of this abnormal perceptiveness increased, the horror of his position became likewise more and more vivid. He knew that he was fighting for his life with a soulless and malefic being who was next door to a devil. The sense of fear was being magnified now with every minute that passed. Presently the power of *perceiving* would pass into *doing*; he would strike the blow for his life, whatever form that blow might take.

Already he was sufficiently master of himself to act — to act in the sense of deceiving. He exaggerated his drunken writing and thickness of speech, his general condition of collapse: and this power of *hearing* the workings of the other man's mind showed him that he was successful. Hensig was a little deceived. He proved this by increased carelessness, and by allowing the expression of his face to become plainly exultant.

Williams's faculties were so concentrated upon the causes operating in the terrible personality opposite to him, that he could spare no part of his brain for the explanations and sentences that came from his lips. He did not hear or understand a hundredth part of what the doctor was saying, but occasionally he caught up the end of a phrase and managed to ask a blundering question out of it; and Hensig, obviously pleased with his increasing obfuscation, always answered at some length, quietly watching with pleasure the reporter's foolish hieroglyphics upon the paper.

The whole thing, of course, was an utter blind.

Hensig had no discovery at all. He was talking scientific jargon, knowing full well that those shorthand notes would never be transcribed, and that he himself would be out of harm's way long before his victim's senses had cleared sufficiently to tell him that he was in the grasp of a deadly sickness which no medicines could prevent ending in death.

Williams saw and felt all this clearly. It somehow came to him, rising up in that clear depth of his mind that was stirred by the alcohol, and yet beyond the reach, so far, of its deadly confusion. He understood perfectly well that Hensig was waiting for a moment to act; that he would do nothing violent, but would carry out his murderous intention in such an innocent way that the victim would have no suspicions at the moment, and would only realise later that he had been poisoned and —

Hark! What was that? There was a change.

Something had happened. It was like the sound of a gong, and the reporter's fear suddenly doubled. Hensig's scheme had moved forward a step. There was no sound actually, but his senses seemed grouped together into one, and for some reason his perception of the change came by way of audition. Fear brimmed up perilously near the breaking-point. But the moment for action had not quite come yet, and he luckily saved himself by the help of another and contrary emotion. He emptied his glass, spilling half of it purposely over his coat, and burst out laughing in Hensig's face. The vivid picture rose before him of Whitey Fife catching cocktail glasses off the edge of Steve Brodie's table.

The laugh was admirably careless and drunken, but the German was startled and looked up suspiciously. He had not expected this, and through lowered eyelids Williams observed an expression of momentary uncertainty on his features, as though he felt he was not absolutely master of the situation after all, as he imagined.

"Su'nly thought of Whitey Fife knocking Stevebrodie off'sh Brooklyn Bridsh in a cocock'tail glashh — " Williams explained in a voice hopelessly out of control. "You know

Whhhiteyfife, of coursh, don't you? — ha, ha, ha!"

Nothing could have helped him more in putting Hensig off the scent. His face resumed its expression of certainty and cold purpose. The waiter, wakened by the noise, stirred uneasily in his chair, and the big man in the corner indulged in a gulp that threatened to choke him as he sat with his head sunk upon his chest. But otherwise the empty room became quiet again. The German resumed his confident command of the situation. Williams, he saw, was drunk enough to bring him easily into his net.

None the less, the reporter's perception had not been at fault. There *was* a change. Hensig was about to do something, and his mind was buzzing with preparations. The victim, now within measuring distance of his supreme moment — the point where terror would release his will, and alcohol would inspire him beyond possibility of error — saw everything as in the clear light of day. Small things led him to the climax: the emptied room; the knowledge that shortly the saloon would close; the grey light of day stealing under the chinks of door and shutter; the increased vileness of the face gleaming at him opposite in the paling gas glare. Ugh! How the air reeked of stale spirits, the fumes of cigar smoke, and the cheap scents of the vanished women. The floor was strewn with sheets of paper, absurdly scrawled over. The table had patches of wet, and cigarette ash lay over everything. His hands and feet were icy, his eyes burning hot. His heart thumped like a soft hammer. Hensig was speaking in quite a changed voice now. He had been leading up to this point for hours. No one was there to see, even if anything was to be seen — which was unlikely. The big man still snored; the waiter was asleep too. There was silence in the outer room, and between the walls of the inner there was — *Death*.

"Now, Mr. *Vulture* reporder, I *show* you what I mean all this time to egsplain," he was saying in his most metallic voice.

He drew a blank sheet of the reporter's paper towards him across the little table, avoiding carefully the wet splashes.

"Lend me your bencil von moment, please. Yes?" Williams, simulating almost total collapse, dropped the pencil and shoved it over the polished wood as though the movement was about all he could manage. With his head sunk forward upon his chest he watched stupidly. Hensig began to draw some kind of outline; his touch was firm, and there was a smile on his lips.

"Here, you see, is the human arm," he said, sketching rapidly; "and here are the main nerves, and here the artery. Now, my discovery, as I haf peen egsplaining to you, is simply — " He dropped into a torrent of meaningless scientific phrases, during which the other purposely allowed his hand to lie relaxed upon the table, knowing perfectly well that in a moment Hensig would seize it — for the purposes of illustration.

His terror was so intense that, for the first time this awful night, he was within an ace of action. The point of saturation had been almost reached. Though apparently sodden drunk, his mind was really at the highest degree of clear perception and judgment, and in another moment — the moment Hensig actually began his final assault — the terror would provide the reporter with the extra vigour and decision necessary to strike his one blow. Exactly how he would do it, or what precise form it would take, he had no idea; that could be left to the inspiration of the moment; he only knew that his strength would last just long enough to bring this about, and that then he would collapse in utter intoxication upon the floor.

Hensig dropped the pencil suddenly: it clattered away to a corner of the room, showing it had been propelled with force, not merely allowed to fall, and he made no attempt to pick it up. Williams, to test his intention, made a pretended movement to stoop after it, and the other, as he imagined he would, stopped him in a second.

"I haf another," he said quickly, diving into his inner pocket and producing a long dark pencil. Williams saw in a flash, through his half-closed eyes, that it was sharpened at one end, while the other end was covered by a little protective cap of transparent substance like glass, a third of an inch long. He heard it click as it struck a button of the coat, and also saw that by a very swift motion of the fingers, impossible to be observed by a drunken man, Hensig removed the cap so that the end was free. Something gleamed there for a moment, something like a point of shining metal — the point of a pin.

"Gif me your hand von minute and I drace the nerve up the arm I speak apout," the doctor continued in that steely voice that showed no sign of nervousness, though he was on the edge of murder. "So, I show you much petter vot I mean."

Without a second's hesitation — for the moment for

action had not quite come — he lurched forward and stretched his arm clumsily across the table. Hensig seized the fingers in his own and turned the palm uppermost. With his other hand he pointed the pencil at the wrist, and began moving it a little up towards the elbow, pushing the sleeve back for the purpose. His touch was the touch of death. On the point of the black pin, engrafted into the other end of the pencil, Williams knew there clung the germs of some deadly disease, germs unusually powerful from special culture; and that within the next few seconds the pencil would turn and the pin would *accidentally* scratch his wrist and let the virulent poison into his blood.

He knew this, yet at the same time he managed to remain master of himself. For he also realised that at last, just in the nick of time, the moment he had been waiting for all through these terrible hours had actually arrived, and he was ready to act.

And the little unimportant detail that furnished the extra quota of fear necessary to bring him to the point was — *touch*. It was the touch of Hensig's hand that did it, setting every nerve a-quiver to its utmost capacity, filling him with a black horror that reached the limits of sensation.

In that moment Williams regained his self-control and became absolutely sober. Terror removed its paralysing inhibitions, having led him to the point where numbness succeeds upon excess, and sensation ceases to register in the brain. The emotion of fear was dead, and he was ready to act with all the force of his being — that force, too, raised to a higher power after long repression.

Moreover, he could make no mistake, for at the same time be had reached the culminating effect of the alcohol, and a sort of white light filled his mind, showing him clearly what to do and how to do it. He felt master of himself, confident, capable of anything. He followed blindly that inner guidance he had been dimly conscious of the whole night, and what he did he did instinctively, as it were, without deliberate plan.

He was *waiting for the pencil to turn* so that the pin pointed at his vein. Then, when Hensig was wholly concentrated upon the act of murder, and thus oblivious of all else, he would find his opportunity. For at this supreme moment the German's mind would be focussed on the one thing. He would notice nothing else round him. He would be open to successful attack. But this — supreme moment would hardly last more than five seconds at most!

The reporter raised his eyes and stared for the first time steadily into his opponent's eyes, till the room faded out and he saw only the white skin in a blaze of its own light. Thus staring, he caught in himself the full stream of venom, hatred, and revenge that had been pouring at him across the table for so long — caught and held it for one instant, and then returned it into the other's brain with all its original force and the added impetus of his own recovered will behind it.

Hensig felt this, and for a moment seemed to waver; he was surprised out of himself by the sudden change in his victim's attitude. The same instant, availing himself of a diversion caused by the big man in the corner waking noisily and trying to rise, he slowly *turned the pencil round* so that the point of the pin was directed at the hand lying in his. The sleepy waiter was helping the drunken man to cross to the door, and the diversion was all in his favour.

But Williams knew what he was doing. He did not even tremble.

"When that pin scratches me," he said aloud in a firm, sober voice, "it means — death."

The German could not conceal his surprise on hearing the change of voice, but he still felt sure of his victim, and clearly wished to enjoy his revenge thoroughly. After a moment's hesitation he replied, speaking very low:

"You tried, I tink, to get me conficted, and now I punish you, dat is all."

His fingers moved, and the point of the pin descended a little lower. Williams felt the faintest imaginable prick on his skin — or thought he did. The German had lowered his head again to direct the movement of the pin properly. But the moment of Hensig's concentration was also the moment of his own attack. And it had come.

"But the alcohol will counteract it!" he burst out, with a loud and startling laugh that threw the other completely off his guard. The doctor lifted his face in amazement. That same instant the hand that lay so helplessly and tipsily in his turned like a flash of lightning, and, before he knew what had happened, their positions were reversed. Williams held his wrist, pencil and all, in a grasp of iron. And from the reporter's other hand the German received a terrific smashing blow in the face that broke his glasses and dashed him back with a howl of pain against the wall.

There was a brief passage of scramble and wild blows,

during which both table and chairs were sent flying, and then Williams was aware that a figure behind him had stretched forth an arm and was holding a bright silvery thing close to Hensig's bleeding face. Another glance showed him that it was a pistol, and that the man holding it was the big drunken man who had apparently slept all night in the corner of the room. Then, in a flash, he recognised him as Dowling's partner — a headquarters detective. The reporter stepped back, his head swimming again. He was very unsteady on his feet.

"I've been watching your game all the evening," he heard the headquarters man saying as he slipped the handcuffs over the German's unresisting wrists. "We have been on your trail for weeks, and I might jest as soon have taken you when you left the Brooklyn church a few hours ago, only I wanted to see what you were up to — see? You're wanted in Berlin for one or two little dirty tricks, but our advices only came last night. Come along now."

"You'll get nozzing," Hensig replied very quietly, wiping his bloody face with the corner of his sleeve. "See, I have scratched myself!"

The detective took no notice of this remark, not understanding it, probably, but Williams noticed the direction of the eyes, and saw a scratch on his wrist, slightly bleeding. Then he understood that in the struggle the pin had accidentally found another destination than the one intended for it. But he remembered nothing more after that, for the reaction set in with a rush. The strain of that awful night left him utterly limp, and the accumulated effect of the alcohol, now that all was past, overwhelmed him like a wave, and he sank in a heap upon the floor, unconscious.

T he illness that followed was simply "nerves," and he got over it in a week or two, and returned to his work on the paper. He at once made inquiries, and found that Hensig's arrest had hardly been noticed by the papers. There was no interesting feature about it, and New York was already in the throes of a new horror. But Dowling, that enterprising Irishman — always with an eye to promotion and the main chance — Dowling had something to say about it.

"No luck, Mr. English," he said ruefully, "no luck at all. It would have been a mighty good story, but it never got in the papers. That damned German, Schmidt, alias Brunner, alias Hensig, died in the prison hospital before we could even get him remanded for further inquiries — "

"What did be die of?" interrupted the reporter quickly.

"Black typhus. I think they call it. But it was terribly swift, and he was dead in four days. The doctor said he'd never known such a case."

"I'm glad he's out of the way," observed Williams.

"Well, yes," Dowling said hesitatingly; "but it was a jim dandy of a story, an' he might have waited a little bit longer jest so as I got something out of it for meself."

The WILLOWS.

I.

After leaving Vienna, and long before you come to Budapest, the Danube enters a region of singular loneliness and desolation, where its waters spread away on all sides regardless of a main channel, and the country becomes a swamp for miles upon miles, covered by a vast sea of low willow-bushes. On the big maps this deserted area is painted in a fluffy blue, growing fainter in color as it leaves the banks, and across it may be seen in large straggling letters the word *Sumpfe*, meaning marshes.

In high flood this great acreage of sand, shingle-beds, and willow-grown islands is almost topped by the water, but in normal seasons the bushes bend and rustle in the free winds, showing their silver leaves to the sunshine in an ever-moving plain of bewildering beauty. These willows never attain to the dignity of trees; they have no rigid trunks; they remain humble bushes, with rounded tops and soft outline, swaying on slender stems that answer to the least pressure of the wind; supple as grasses, and so continually shifting that they somehow give the impression that the entire plain is moving and alive. For the wind sends waves rising and falling over the whole surface, waves of leaves instead of waves of water, green swells like the sea, too, until the branches turn and lift, and then silvery white as their underside turns to the sun.

Happy to slip beyond the control of the stern banks, the Danube here wanders about at will among the intricate network of channels intersecting the islands everywhere with broad avenues down which the waters pour with a shouting sound; making whirlpools, eddies, and foaming rapids; tearing at the sandy banks; carrying away masses of shore and willow-clumps; and forming new islands innumerably which shift daily in size and shape and possess at best an impermanent life, since the flood-time obliterates their very existence.

Properly speaking, this fascinating part of the river's life begins soon after leaving Pressburg, and we, in our Canadian canoe, with gipsy tent and frying-pan on board, reached it on the crest of a rising flood about mid-July. That very same morning, when the sky was reddening before sunrise, we had slipped swiftly through still-sleeping Vienna, leaving it a couple of hours later a mere patch of smoke against the blue hills of the Wienerwald on the horizon; we had breakfasted below Fischeramend under a grove of birch trees roaring in the wind; and had then swept on the tearing current past Orth, Hainburg, Petronell (the old Roman Carnuntum of Marcus Aurelius), and so under the frowning heights of Thelsen on a spur of the Carpathians, where the March steals in quietly from the left and the frontier is crossed between Austria and Hungary.

Racing along at twelve kilometers an hour soon took us well into Hungary, and the muddy waters — sure sign of flood — sent us aground on many a shingle-bed, and twisted us like a cork in many a sudden belching whirlpool before the towers of Pressburg (Hungarian, Poszony) showed against the sky; and then the canoe, leaping like a spirited horse, flew at top speed under the grey walls, negotiated safely the sunken chain of the Fliegende Brucke ferry, turned the corner sharply to the left, and plunged on yellow foam into the wilderness of islands, sandbanks, and swamp-land beyond — the land of the willows.

The change came suddenly, as when a series of bioscope pictures snaps down on the streets of a town and shifts without warning into the scenery of lake and forest. We entered the land of desolation on wings, and in less than half an hour there was neither boat nor fishing-hut nor red roof, nor any single sign of human habitation and civilization within sight. The sense of remoteness from the world of humankind, the utter isolation, the fascination of this singular world of willows, winds, and waters, instantly laid its spell upon us both, so that we allowed laughingly to one another that we ought by rights to have held some special kind of passport to admit us, and that we had, somewhat audaciously, come without asking leave into a separate little kingdom of wonder and magic — a kingdom that was reserved for the use of others who had a right to it, with everywhere unwritten warnings to trespassers for those who had the imagination to discover them.

Though still early in the afternoon, the ceaseless buffetings of a most tempestuous wind made us feel weary, and we at once began casting about for a suitable camping-ground for the night. But the bewildering character of the islands made landing difficult; the swirling flood carried us in shore and then swept us out again; the willow branches tore our hands as we seized them to stop the canoe, and we pulled many a yard of sandy bank into the water before at length we shot with a great sideways blow from the wind into a backwater and managed to beach the bows in a cloud of spray. Then we lay panting and laughing after our exertions on the hot yellow sand, sheltered from the wind, and in the full blaze of a scorching sun, a cloudless blue sky above, and an immense army of dancing, shouting willow bushes, closing in from all sides, shining with spray and clapping their thousand little hands as though to applaud the success of our efforts.

"What a river!" I said to my companion, thinking of all the way we had traveled from the source in the Black Forest, and how he had often been obliged to wade and push in the upper shallows at the beginning of June.

"Won't stand much nonsense now, will it?" he said, pulling the canoe a little farther into safety up the sand, and then composing himself for a nap.

I lay by his side, happy and peaceful in the bath of the elements — water, wind, sand, and the great fire of the sun — thinking of the long journey that lay behind us, and of the great stretch before us to the Black Sea, and how lucky I was to have such a delightful and charming traveling companion as my friend, the Swede.

We had made many similar journeys together, but the Danube, more than any other river I knew, impressed us from the very beginning with its *aliveness*. From its tiny bubbling entry into the world among the pinewood gardens of Donaueschingen, until this moment when it began to play the great river-game of losing itself among the deserted swamps, unobserved, unrestrained, it had seemed to us like following the growing of some living creature. Sleepy at first, but later developing violent desires as it became conscious of its deep soul, it rolled, like some huge fluid being, through all the countries we had passed, holding our little craft on its mighty shoulders, playing roughly with us sometimes, yet always friendly and well-meaning, till at length we had come inevitably to regard it as a Great Personage.

How, indeed, could it be otherwise, since it told us so much of its secret life? At night we heard it singing to the moon as we lay in our tent, uttering that odd sibilant note peculiar to itself and said to be caused by the rapid tearing of the pebbles along its bed, so great is its hurrying speed. We knew, too, the voice of its gurgling whirlpools, suddenly bubbling up on a surface previously quite calm; the roar of its shallows and swift rapids; its constant steady thundering below all mere surface sounds; and that ceaseless tearing of its icy waters at the banks. How it stood up and shouted when the rains fell flat upon its face! And how its laughter roared out when the wind blew up-stream and tried to stop its growing speed! We knew all its sounds and voices, its tumblings and foamings, its unnecessary splashing against the bridges; that self-conscious chatter when there were hills to look on; the affected dignity of its speech when it passed through the little towns, far too important to laugh; and all these faint, sweet whisperings when the sun caught it fairly in some slow curve and poured down upon it till the steam rose.

It was full of tricks, too, in its early life before the great world knew it. There were places in the upper reaches among the Swabian forests, when yet the first whispers of its destiny had not reached it, where it elected to disappear through holes in the ground, to appear again on the other side of the porous limestone hills and start a new river with another name; leaving, too, so little water in its own bed that we had to climb out and wade and push the canoe through miles of shallows.

And a chief pleasure, in those early days of its irresponsible youth, was to lie low, like Br'er Fox, just before the little turbulent tributaries came to join it from the Alps, and to refuse to acknowledge them when in, but to run for miles side by side, the dividing line well marked, the very levels different, the Danube utterly declining to recognize the newcomer. Below Passau, however, it gave up this particular trick, for there the Inn comes in with a thundering power impossible to ignore, and so pushes and incommodes the parent river that there is hardly room for them in the long twisting gorge that follows, and the Danube is shoved this way and that against the cliffs, and forced to hurry itself with great waves and much dashing to and fro in order to get through in time. And during the fight our canoe slipped down from its shoulder to its breast, and had the time of its life among the struggling waves. But the Inn taught the old river a lesson, and after Passau it no longer pretended to ignore new arrivals.

This was many days back, of course, and since then we had come to know other aspects of the great creature, and across the Bavarian wheat plain of Straubing she wandered so slowly under the blazing June sun that we could well imagine only the surface inches were water, while below there moved, concealed as by a silken mantle, a whole army of Undines, passing silently and unseen down to the sea, and very leisurely too, lest they be discovered.

Much, too, we forgave her because of her friendliness to the birds and animals that haunted the shores. Cormorants lined the banks in lonely places in rows like short black pilings; grey crows crowded the shingle-beds; storks stood fishing in the vistas of shallower water that opened up between the islands, and hawks, swans, and marsh birds of all sorts filled the air with glinting wings and singing, petulant cries. It was impossible to feel annoyed with the river's vagaries after seeing a deer leap with a splash into the water at sunrise and swim past the bows of the canoe; and often we saw fawns peering at us from the underbrush, or looked straight into the brown eyes of a stag as we charged full tilt round a corner and entered another reach of the river. Foxes, too, everywhere haunted the banks, tripping daintily among the driftwood and disappearing so suddenly that it was impossible to see how they managed it.

But now, after leaving Pressburg, everything changed a little, and the Danube became more serious. It ceased trifling. It was half-way to the Black Sea, within scenting distance almost of other, stranger countries where no tricks would be permitted or understood. It became suddenly grown-up, and claimed our respect and even our awe. It broke out into three arms, for one thing, that only met again a hundred kilometers farther down, and for a canoe there were no indications which one was intended to be followed.

"If you take a side channel," said the Hungarian officer we met in the Pressburg shop while buying provisions, "you may find yourselves, when the flood subsides, forty miles from anywhere, high and dry, and you may easily starve. There are no people, no farms, no fishermen. I warn you not to continue. The river, too, is still rising, and this wind will increase."

The rising river did not alarm us in the least, but the matter of being left high and dry by a sudden subsidence of the waters might be serious, and we had consequently laid in an extra stock of provisions. For the rest, the officer's prophecy held true, and the wind, blowing down a perfectly clear sky, increased steadily till it reached the dignity of a westerly gale.

It was earlier than usual when we camped, for the sun was a good hour or two from the horizon, and leaving my friend still asleep on the hot sand, I wandered about in desultory examination of our hotel. The island, I found, was less than an acre in extent, a mere sandy bank standing some two or three feet above the level of the river. The far end, pointing into the sunset, was covered with flying spray which the tremendous wind drove off the crests of the broken waves. It was triangular in shape, with the apex up stream.

I stood there for several minutes, watching the impetuous crimson flood bearing down with a shouting roar, dashing in waves against the bank as though to sweep it bodily away, and then swirling by in two foaming streams on either side. The ground seemed to shake with the shock and rush, while the furious movement of the willow bushes as the wind poured over them increased the curious illusion that the island itself actually moved. Above, for a mile or two, I could see the great river descending upon me; it was like looking up the slope of a sliding hill, white with foam, and leaping up everywhere to show itself to the sun.

The rest of the island was too thickly grown with willows to make walking pleasant, but I made the tour, nevertheless. From the lower end the light, of course, changed, and the river looked dark and angry. Only the backs of the flying waves were visible, streaked with foam, and pushed forcibly by the great puffs of wind that fell upon them from behind. For a short mile it was visible, pouring in and out among the islands, and then disappearing with a huge sweep into the willows, which closed about it like a herd of monstrous antediluvian creatures crowding down to drink. They made me think of gigantic sponge-like growths that sucked the river up into themselves. They caused it to vanish from sight. They herded there together in such overpowering numbers.

Altogether it was an impressive scene, with its utter loneliness, its bizarre suggestion; and as I gazed, long and curiously, a singular emotion began to stir somewhere in the depths of me. Midway in my delight of the wild beauty, there crept, unbidden and unexplained, a curious feeling of disquietude, almost of alarm.

A rising river, perhaps, always suggests something of the ominous; many of the little islands I saw before me would probably have been swept away by the morning; this resistless, thundering flood of water touched the sense of awe. Yet I was aware that my uneasiness lay deeper far than the emotions of awe and wonder. It was not that I felt. Nor had it directly to do with the power of the driving wind — this shouting hurricane that might almost carry up a few acres of willows into the air and scatter them like so much chaff over the landscape. The wind was simply enjoying itself, for nothing rose out of the flat landscape to stop it, and I was conscious of sharing its great game with a kind of pleasurable excitement. Yet this novel emotion had nothing to do with the wind. Indeed, so vague was the sense of distress I experienced, that it was impossible to trace it to its source and deal with it accordingly, though I was aware somehow that it had to do with my realization of our utter insignificance before this unrestrained power of the elements about me. The huge-grown river had something to do with it too — a vague, unpleasant idea that we had somehow trifled with these great elemental forces in whose power we lay helpless every hour of the day and night. For here, indeed, they were gigantically at play together, and the sight appealed to the imagination.

But my emotion, so far as I could understand it, seemed to attach itself more particularly to the willow bushes, to these acres and acres of willows, crowding, so thickly growing there, swarming everywhere the eye could reach, pressing upon the river as though to suffocate it, standing in dense array mile after mile beneath the sky, watching, waiting, listening. And, apart quite from the elements, the willows connected themselves subtly with my malaise, attacking the mind insidiously somehow by reason of their vast numbers, and contriving in some way or other to represent to the imagination a new and mighty power, a power, moreover, not altogether friendly to us.

Great revelations of nature, of course, never fail to impress in one way or another, and I was no stranger to moods of the kind. Mountains overawe and oceans terrify, while the mystery of great forests exercises a spell peculiarly its own. But all these, at one point or another, somewhere link on intimately with human life and human experience. They stir comprehensible, even if alarming, emotions. They tend on the whole to exalt.

With this multitude of willows, however, it was something far different, I felt. Some essence emanated from them that besieged the heart. A sense of awe awakened, true, but of awe touched somewhere by a vague terror. Their serried ranks, growing everywhere darker about me as the shadows deepened, moving furiously yet softly in the wind, woke in me the curious and unwelcome suggestion that we had trespassed here upon the borders of an alien world, a world where we were intruders, a world where we were not wanted or invited to remain — where we ran grave risks perhaps!

The feeling, however, though it refused to yield its meaning entirely to analysis, did not at the time trouble me by passing into menace. Yet it never left me quite, even during the very practical business of putting up the tent in a hurricane of wind and building a fire for the stew-pot. It remained, just enough to bother and perplex, and to rob a most delightful camping-ground of a good portion of its charm. To my companion, however, I said nothing, for he was a man I considered devoid of imagination. In the first place, I could never have explained to him what I meant, and in the second, he would have laughed stupidly at me if I had.

There was a slight depression in the center of the island, and here we pitched the tent. The surrounding willows broke the wind a bit.

"A poor camp," observed the imperturbable Swede when at last the tent stood upright, "no stones and precious little firewood. I'm for moving on early tomorrow — eh? This sand won't hold anything."

But the experience of a collapsing tent at midnight had taught us many devices, and we made the cozy gipsy house as safe as possible, and then set about collecting a store of wood to last till bed-time. Willow bushes drop no branches, and driftwood was our only source of supply. We hunted the shores pretty thoroughly. Everywhere the banks were crumbling as the rising flood tore at them and carried away great portions with a splash and a gurgle.

"The island's much smaller than when we landed," said the accurate Swede. "It won't last long at this rate. We'd better drag the canoe close to the tent, and be ready to start at a moment's notice. I shall sleep in my clothes."

He was a little distance off, climbing along the bank, and I heard his rather jolly laugh as he spoke.

"By Jove!" I heard him call, a moment later, and turned to see what had caused his exclamation. But for the moment he was hidden by the willows, and I could not find him.

"What in the world's this?" I heard him cry again, and this time his voice had become serious.

I ran up quickly and joined him on the bank. He was looking over the river, pointing at something in the water.

"Good heavens, it's a man's body!" he cried excitedly. "Look!"

A black thing, turning over and over in the foaming waves, swept rapidly past. It kept disappearing and coming up to the surface again. It was about twenty feet from the shore, and just as it was opposite to where we stood it lurched round and looked straight at us. We saw its eyes reflecting the sunset, and gleaming an odd yellow as the body turned over. Then it gave a swift, gulping plunge, and dived out of sight in a flash.

"An otter, by gad!" we exclaimed in the same breath, laughing.

It *was* an otter, alive, and out on the hunt; yet it had looked exactly like the body of a drowned man turning helplessly in the current. Far below it came to the surface once again, and we saw its black skin, wet and shining in the sunlight.

Then, too, just as we turned back, our arms full of driftwood, another thing happened to recall us to the river bank. This time it really was a man, and what was more, a man in a boat. Now a small boat on the Danube was an unusual sight at any time, but here in this deserted region, and at flood time, it was so unexpected as to constitute a real event. We stood and stared.

Whether it was due to the slanting sunlight, or the refraction from the wonderfully illumined water, I cannot say, but, whatever the cause, I found it difficult to focus my sight properly upon the flying apparition. It seemed, however, to be a man standing upright in a sort of flat-bottomed boat, steering with a long oar, and being carried down the opposite shore at a tremendous pace. He apparently was looking across in our direction, but the distance was too great and the light too uncertain for us to make out very plainly what he was about. It seemed to me that he was gesticulating and making signs at us. His voice came across the water to us shouting something furiously, but the wind drowned it so that no single word was audible. There was something curious about the whole appearance — man, boat, signs, voice — that made an impression on me out of all proportion to its cause.

"He's crossing himself!" I cried. "Look, he's making the sign of the Cross!"

"I believe you're right," the Swede said, shading his eyes with his hand and watching the man out of sight. He seemed to be gone in a moment, melting away down there into the sea of willows where the sun caught them in the bend of the river and turned them into a great crimson wall of beauty. Mist, too, had begun to ruse, so that the air was hazy.

"But what in the world is he doing at nightfall on this flooded river?" I said, half to myself. "Where is he going at such a time, and what did he mean by his signs and shouting? D'you think he wished to warn us about something?"

"He saw our smoke, and thought we were spirits probably," laughed my companion. "These Hungarians believe in all sorts of rubbish; you remember the shopwoman at Pressburg warning us that no one ever landed here because it belonged to some sort of beings outside man's world! I suppose they believe in fairies and elementals, possibly demons, too. That peasant in the boat saw people on the islands for the first time in his life," he added, after a slight pause, "and it scared him, that's all."

The Swede's tone of voice was not convincing, and his manner lacked something that was usually there. I noted the change instantly while he talked, though without being able to label it precisely.

"If they had enough imagination," I laughed loudly — I remember trying to make as much noise as I could — "they might well people a place like this with the old gods of antiquity. The Romans must have haunted all this region more or less with their shrines and sacred groves and elemental deities."

The subject dropped and we returned to our stew-pot, for my friend was not given to imaginative conversation as a rule. Moreover, just then I remember feeling distinctly glad that he was not imaginative; his stolid, practical nature suddenly seemed to me welcome and comforting. It was an admirable temperament, I felt; he could steer down rapids like a red Indian, shoot dangerous bridges and whirl-pools better than any white man I ever saw in a canoe. He was a grand fellow for an adventurous trip, a tower of strength when untoward things happened. I looked at his strong face and light curly hair as he staggered along under his pile of driftwood (twice the size of mine!), and I experienced a feeling of relief. Yes, I was distinctly glad just then that the Swede was — what he was, and that he never made remarks that suggested more than they said.

"The river's still rising, though," he added, as if following out some thoughts of his own, and dropping his load with a gasp. "This island will be under water in two days if it goes on."

"I wish the *wind* would go down," I said. "I don't care a fig for the river."

The flood, indeed, had no terrors for us; we could get off at ten minutes' notice, and the more water the better we liked it. It meant an increasing current and the obliteration of the treacherous shingle-beds that so often threatened to tear the bottom out of our canoe.

Contrary to our expectations, the wind did not go down with the sun. It seemed to increase with the darkness, howling overhead and shaking the willows round us like straws. Curious sounds accompanied it sometimes, like the explosion of heavy guns, and it fell upon the water and the island in great flat blows of immense power. It made me think of the sounds a planet must make, could we only hear it, driving along through space.

But the sky kept wholly clear of clouds, and soon after supper the full moon rose up in the east and covered the river and the plain of shouting willows with a light like the day.

We lay on the sandy patch beside the fire, smoking, listening to the noises of the night round us, and talking happily of the journey we had already made, and of our plans ahead. The map lay spread in the door of the tent, but the high wind made it hard to study, and presently we lowered the curtain and extinguished the lantern. The firelight was enough to smoke and see each other's faces by, and the sparks flew about overhead like fireworks. A few yards beyond, the river gurgled and hissed, and from time to time a heavy splash announced the falling away of further portions of the bank.

Our talk, I noticed, had to do with the faraway scenes and incidents of our first camps in the Black Forest, or of other subjects altogether remote from the present setting, for neither of us spoke of the actual moment more than was necessary — almost as though we had agreed tacitly to avoid discussion of the camp and its incidents. Neither the otter nor the boatman, for instance, received the honor of a single mention, though ordinarily these would have furnished discussion for the greater part of the evening. They were, of course, distinct events in such a place.

The scarcity of wood made it a business to keep the fire going, for the wind, that drove the smoke in our faces wherever we sat, helped at the same time to make a forced draught. We took it in turn to make some foraging expeditions into the darkness, and the quantity the Swede brought back always made me feel that he took an absurdly long time finding it; for the fact was I did not care much about being left alone, and yet it always seemed to be my turn to grub about among the bushes or scramble along the slippery banks in the moonlight. The long day's battle with wind and water — such wind and such water! — had tired us both, and an early bed was the obvious program. Yet neither of us made the move for the tent. We lay there, tending the fire, talking in desultory fashion, peering about us into the dense willow bushes, and listening to the thunder of wind and river. The loneliness of the place had entered our very bones, and silence seemed natural, for after a bit the sound of our voices became a trifle unreal and forced; whispering would have been the fitting mode of communication, I felt, and the human voice, always rather absurd amid the roar of the elements, now carried with it something almost illegitimate. It was like talking out loud in church, or in some place where it was not lawful, perhaps not quite *safe*, to be overheard.

The eeriness of this lonely island, set among a million willows, swept by a hurricane, and surrounded by hurrying deep waters, touched us both, I fancy. Untrodden by man, almost unknown to man, it lay there beneath the moon, remote from human influence, on the frontier of another world, an alien world, a world tenanted by willows only and the souls of willows. And we, in our rashness, had dared to invade it, even to make use of it! Something more than the power of its mystery stirred in me as I lay on the sand, feet to fire, and peered up through the leaves at the stars. For the last time I rose to get firewood.

"When this has burnt up," I said firmly, "I shall turn in," and my companion watched me lazily as I moved off into the surrounding shadows.

For an unimaginative man I thought he seemed unusually receptive that night, unusually open to suggestion of things other than sensory. He too was touched by the beauty and loneliness of the place. I was not altogether pleased, I remember, to recognize this slight change in him, and instead of immediately collecting sticks, I made my way to the far point of the island where the moonlight on plain and river could be seen to better advantage. The desire to be alone had come suddenly upon me; my former dread returned in force; there was a vague feeling in me I wished to face and probe to the bottom.

When I reached the point of sand jutting out among the waves, the spell of the place descended upon me with a positive shock. No mere "scenery" could have produced such an effect. There was something more here, something to alarm.

I gazed across the waste of wild waters; I watched the whispering willows; I heard the ceaseless beating of the tireless wind; and, one and all, each in its own way, stirred in me this sensation of a strange distress. But the *willows* especially; for ever they went on chattering and talking among themselves, laughing a little, shrilly crying out, sometimes sighing — but what it was they made so much to-do about belonged to the secret life of the great plain they inhabited. And it was utterly alien to the world I knew, or to that of the wild yet kindly elements. They made me think of a host of beings from another plane of life, another evolution altogether, perhaps, all discussing a mystery known only to themselves. I watched them moving busily together, oddly shaking their big bushy heads, twirling their myriad leaves even when there was no wind. They moved of their own will as though alive, and they touched, by some incalculable method, my own keen sense of the *horrible*.

There they stood in the moonlight, like a vast army surrounding our camp, shaking their innumerable silver spears defiantly, formed all ready for an attack.

The psychology of places, for some imaginations at least, is very vivid; for the wanderer, especially, camps have their "note" either of welcome or rejection. At first it may not always be apparent, because the busy preparations of tent and cooking prevent, but with the first pause — after supper usually — it comes and announces itself. And the note of this willow-camp now became unmistakably plain to me; we were interlopers, trespassers; we were not welcomed. The sense of unfamiliarity grew upon me as I stood there watching. We touched the frontier of a region where our presence was resented. For a night's lodging we might perhaps be tolerated; but for a prolonged and inquisitive stay — no! by all the gods of the trees and wilderness, no! We were the first human influences upon this island, and we were not wanted. *The willows were against us.*

Strange thoughts like these, bizarre fancies, borne I know not whence, found lodgment in my mind as I stood listening. What, I thought, if, after all, these crouching willows proved to be alive; if suddenly they should rise up, like a swarm of living creatures, marshaled by the gods whose territory we had invaded, sweep towards us off the vast swamps, booming overhead in the night — and then *settle down!* As I looked it was so easy to imagine they actually moved, crept nearer, retreated a little, huddled together in masses, hostile, waiting for the great wind that should finally start them a-running. I could have sworn their aspect changed a little, and their ranks deepened and pressed more closely together.

The melancholy shrill cry of a night-bird sounded overhead, and suddenly I nearly lost my balance as the piece of bank I stood upon fell with a great splash into the river, undermined by the flood. I stepped back just in time, and went on hunting for firewood again, half laughing at the odd fancies that crowded so thickly into my mind and cast their spell upon me. I recalled the Swede's remark about moving on next day, and I was just thinking that I fully agreed with him, when I turned with a start and saw the subject of my thoughts standing immediately in front of me. He was quite close. The roar of the elements had covered his approach.

"You've been gone so long," he shouted above the wind, "I thought something must have happened to you."

But there was that in his tone, and a certain look in his face as well, that conveyed to me more than his usual words, and in a flash I understood the real reason for his coming. It was because the spell of the place had entered his soul too, and he did not like being alone.

"River still rising," he cried, pointing to the flood in the moonlight, "and the wind's simply awful."

He always said the same things, but it was the cry for companionship that gave the real importance to his words.

"Lucky," I cried back, "our tent's in the hollow. I think

it'll hold all right." I added something about the difficulty of finding wood, in order to explain my absence, but the wind caught my words and flung them across the river, so that he did not hear, but just looked at me through the branches, nodding his head.

"Lucky if we get away without disaster!" he shouted, or words to that effect; and I remember feeling half angry with him for putting the thought into words, for it was exactly what I felt myself. There was disaster impending somewhere, and the sense of presentiment lay unpleasantly upon me.

We went back to the fire and made a final blaze, poking it up with our feet. We took a last look round. But for the wind the heat would have been unpleasant. I put this thought into words, and I remember my friend's reply struck me oddly: that he would rather have the heat, the ordinary July weather, than this "diabolical wind."

Everything was snug for the night; the canoe lying turned over beside the tent, with both yellow paddles beneath her; the provision sack hanging from a willow-stem, and the washed-up dishes removed to a safe distance from the fire, all ready for the morning meal.

We smothered the embers of the fire with sand, and then turned in. The flap of the tent door was up, and I saw the branches and the stars and the white moonlight. The shaking willows and the heavy buffetings of the wind against our taut little house were the last things I remembered as sleep came down and covered all with its soft and delicious forgetfulness.

II.

Suddenly I found myself lying awake, peering from my sandy mattress through the door of the tent. I looked at my watch pinned against the canvas, and saw by the bright moonlight that it was past twelve o'clock — the threshold of a new day — and I had therefore slept a couple of hours. The Swede was asleep still beside me; the wind howled as before; something plucked at my heart and made me feel afraid. There was a sense of disturbance in my immediate neighborhood.

I sat up quickly and looked out. The trees were swaying violently to and fro as the gusts smote them, but our little bit of green canvas lay snugly safe in the hollow, for the wind passed over it without meeting enough resistance to make it vicious. The feeling of disquietude did not pass, however, and I crawled quietly out of the tent to see if our belongings were safe. I moved carefully so as not to waken my companion. A curious excitement was on me.

I was half-way out, kneeling on all fours, when my eye first took in that the tops of the bushes opposite, with their moving tracery of leaves, made shapes against the sky. I sat back on my haunches and stared. It was incredible, surely, but there, opposite and slightly above me, were shapes of some indeterminate sort among the willows, and as the branches swayed in the wind they seemed to group them-selves about these shapes, forming a series of monstrous outlines that shifted rapidly beneath the moon. Close, about fifty feet in front of me, I saw these things.

My first instinct was to waken my companion, that he too might see them, but something made me hesitate — the sudden realization, probably, that I should not welcome corroboration; and meanwhile I crouched there staring in amazement with smarting eyes. I was wide awake. I remember saying to myself that I was *not* dreaming.

They first became properly visible, these huge figures, just within the tops of the bushes — immense, bronze-col-ored, moving, and wholly independent of the swaying of the branches. I saw them plainly and noted, now I came to examine them more calmly, that they were very much larger than human, and indeed that something in their appearance proclaimed them to be *not human* at all. Certainly they were not merely the moving tracery of the branches against the moonlight. They shifted independently. They rose upwards in a continuous stream from earth to sky, vanishing utterly as soon as they reached the dark of the sky. They were interlaced one with another, making a great column, and I saw their limbs and huge bodies melting in and out of each other, forming this serpentine line that bent and swayed and twisted spirally with the contortions of the wind-tossed trees. They were nude, fluid shapes, passing up the bushes, *within* the leaves almost — rising up in a living column into the heavens. Their faces I never could see. Unceasingly they poured upwards, swaying in great bending curves, with a hue of dull bronze upon their skins.

I stared, trying to force every atom of vision from my eyes. For a long time I thought they *must* every moment disappear and resolve themselves into the movements of the branches and prove to be an optical illusion. I searched everywhere for a proof of reality, when all the while I understood quite well that the standard of reality had changed. For the longer I looked the more certain I became that these figures were real and living, though perhaps not according to the standards that the camera and the biologist would insist upon.

Far from feeling fear, I was possessed with a sense of awe and wonder such as I have never known. I seemed to be gazing at the personified elemental forces of this haunted and primeval region. Our intrusion had stirred the powers of the place into activity. It was we who were the cause of the disturbance, and my brain filled to bursting with stories and legends of the spirits and deities of places that have been acknowledged and worshipped by men in all ages of the world's history. But, before I could arrive at any possible explanation, something impelled me to go farther out, and I crept forward on the sand and stood upright. I felt the ground still warm under my bare feet; the wind tore at my hair and face; and the sound of the river burst upon my ears with a sudden roar. These things, I knew, were real, and proved that my senses were acting normally. Yet the figures still rose from earth to heaven, silent, majestically, in a great spiral of grace and strength that overwhelmed me at length with a genuine deep emotion of worship. I felt that I must fall down and worship — absolutely worship.

Perhaps in another minute I might have done so, when a gust of wind swept against me with such force that it blew me sideways, and I nearly stumbled and fell. It seemed to shake the dream violently out of me. At least it gave me another point of view somehow. The figures still remained, still ascended into heaven from the heart of the night, but my reason at last began to assert itself. It must be a subjective experience, I argued — none the less real for that, but still subjective. The moonlight and the branches combined to work out these pictures upon the mirror of my imagination, and for some reason I projected them outwards and made them appear objective. I knew this must be the case, of course. I took courage, and began to move forward across the open patches of sand. By Jove, though, was it all hallucination? Was it merely subjective? Did not my reason argue in the old futile way from the little standard of the known?

I only know that great column of figures ascended darkly into the sky for what seemed a very long period of time, and with a very complete measure of reality as most men are accustomed to gauge reality. Then suddenly they were gone!

And, once they were gone and the immediate wonder

of their great presence had passed, fear came down upon me with a cold rush. The esoteric meaning of this lonely and haunted region suddenly flamed up within me, and I began to tremble dreadfully. I took a quick look round — a look of horror that came near to panic — calculating vainly ways of escape; and then, realizing how helpless I was to achieve anything really effective, I crept back silently into the tent and lay down again upon my sandy mattress, first lowering the door-curtain to shut out the sight of the willows in the moonlight, and then burying my head as deeply as possible beneath the blankets to deaden the sound of the terrifying wind.

III.

As though further to convince me that I had not been dreaming, I remember that it was a long time before I fell again into a troubled and restless sleep; and even then only the upper crust of me slept, and underneath there was something that never quite lost consciousness, but lay alert and on the watch.

But this second time I jumped up with a genuine start of terror. It was neither the wind nor the river that woke me, but the slow approach of something that caused the sleeping portion of me to grow smaller and smaller till at last it vanished altogether, and I found myself sitting bolt upright — listening.

Outside there was a sound of multitudinous little patterings. They had been coming, I was aware, for a long time, and in my sleep they had first become audible. I sat there nervously wide awake as though I had not slept at all. It seemed to me that my breathing came with difficulty, and that there was a great weight upon the surface of my body. In spite of the hot night, I felt clammy with cold and shivered. Something surely was pressing steadily against the sides of the tent and weighing down upon it from above. Was it the body of the wind? Was this the pattering rain, the dripping of the leaves? The spray blown from the river by the wind and gathering in big drops? I thought quickly of a dozen things.

Then suddenly the explanation leaped into my mind: a bough from the poplar, the only large tree on the island, had fallen with the wind. Still half caught by the other branches, it would fall with the next gust and crush us, and meanwhile its leaves brushed and tapped upon the tight canvas surface of the tent. I raised a loose flap and rushed out, calling to the Swede to follow.

But when I got out and stood upright I saw that the tent was free. There was no hanging bough; there was no rain or spray; nothing approached.

A cold, grey light filtered down through the bushes and lay on the faintly gleaming sand. Stars still crowded the sky directly overhead, and the wind howled magnificently, but the fire no longer gave out any glow, and I saw the east reddening in streaks through the trees. Several hours must have passed since I stood there before watching the ascending figures, and the memory of it now came back to me horribly, like an evil dream. Oh, how tired it made me feel, that ceaseless raging wind! Yet, though the deep lassitude of a sleepless night was on me, my nerves were tingling with the activity of an equally tireless apprehension, and all idea of repose was out of the question. The river I saw had risen further. Its thunder filled the air, and a fine spray made itself felt through my thin sleeping shirt.

Yet nowhere did I discover the slightest evidence of anything to cause alarm. This deep, prolonged disturbance in my heart remained wholly unaccounted-for.

My companion had not stirred when I called him, and there was no need to waken him now. I looked about me carefully, noting everything; the turned-over canoe; the yellow paddles — two of them, I'm certain; the provision sack and the extra lantern hanging together from the tree; and, crowding everywhere about me, enveloping all, the willows, those endless, shaking willows. A bird uttered its morning cry, and a string of ducks passed with whirring flight overhead in the twilight. The sand whirled, dry and stinging, about my bare feet in the wind.

I walked round the tent and then went out a little way into the bush, so that I could see across the river to the farther landscape, and the same profound yet indefinable emotion of distress seized upon me again as I saw the interminable sea of bushes stretching to the horizon, looking ghostly and unreal in the wan light of dawn. I walked softly here and there, still puzzling over that odd sound of infinite pattering, and of that pressure upon the tent that had wakened me. It *must* have been the wind, I reflected — the wind bearing upon the loose, hot sand, driving the dry particles smartly against the taut canvas — the wind dropping heavily upon our fragile roof.

Yet all the time my nervousness and malaise increased appreciably.

I crossed over to the farther shore and noted how the coast-line had altered in the night, and what masses of sand the river had torn away. I dipped my hands and feet into the cool current, and bathed my forehead. Already there was a glow of sunrise in the sky and the exquisite freshness of coming day. On my way back I passed purposely beneath the very bushes where I had seen the column of figures rising into the air, and midway among the clumps I suddenly found myself overtaken by a sense of vast terror. From the shadows a large figure went swiftly by. Someone passed me, as sure as ever man did. . . .

It was a great staggering blow from the wind that helped me forward again, and once out in the more open space, the sense of terror diminished strangely. The winds were about and walking, I remember saying to myself, for the winds often move like great presences under the trees. And altogether the fear that hovered about me was such an unknown and immense kind of fear, so unlike anything I had ever felt before, that it woke a sense of awe and wonder in me that did much to counteract its worst effects; and when I reached a high point in the middle of the island from which I could see the wide stretch of river, crimson in the sunrise, the whole magical beauty of it all was so overpowering that a sort of wild yearning woke in me and almost brought a cry up into the throat.

But this cry found no expression, for as my eyes wandered from the plain beyond to the island round me and noted our little tent half hidden among the willows, a dreadful discovery leaped out at me, compared to which my terror of the walking winds seemed as nothing at all.

For a change, I thought, had somehow come about in the arrangement of the landscape. It was not that my point of vantage gave me a different view, but that an alteration had apparently been effected in the relation of the tent to the willows, and of the willows to the tent. Surely the bushes now crowded much closer — unnecessarily, unpleasantly close. *They had moved nearer.*

Creeping with silent feet over the shifting sands, drawing imperceptibly nearer by soft, unhurried movements, the willows had come closer during the night. But had the wind moved them, or had they moved of themselves? I recalled the sound of infinite small patterings and the pressure upon the tent and upon my own heart that caused me to wake in terror. I swayed for a moment in the wind like a tree, finding it hard to keep my upright position on the sandy hillock. There was a suggestion here of personal agency, of deliberate intention, of aggressive hostility, and it terrified me into a sort of rigidity.

Then the reaction followed quickly. The idea was so bizarre, so absurd, that I felt inclined to laugh. But the laughter came no more readily than the cry, for the knowledge that my mind was so receptive to such dangerous imaginings brought the additional terror that it was through our minds and not through our physical bodies that the attack would come, and was coming.

The wind buffeted me about, and, very quickly it seemed, the sun came up over the horizon, for it was after four o'clock, and I must have stood on that little pinnacle of sand longer than I knew, afraid to come down to close quarters with the willows. I returned quietly, creepily, to the tent, first taking another exhaustive look round and — yes, I confess it — making a few measurements. I paced out on the warm sand the distances between the willows and the tent, making a note of the shortest distance particularly.

I crawled stealthily into my blankets. My companion, to all appearances, still slept soundly, and I was glad that this was so. Provided my experiences were not corroborated, I could find strength somehow to deny them, perhaps. With the daylight I could persuade myself that it was all a subjective hallucination, a fantasy of the night, a projection of the excited imagination.

Nothing further came in to disturb me, and I fell asleep almost at once, utterly exhausted, yet still in dread of hearing again that weird sound of multitudinous pattering, or of feeling the pressure upon my heart that had made it difficult to breathe.

IV.

The sun was high in the heavens when my companion woke me from a heavy sleep and announced that the porridge was cooked and there was just time to bathe. The grateful smell of frizzling bacon entered the tent door.

"River still rising," he said, "and several islands out in mid-stream have disappeared altogether. Our own island's much smaller."

"Any wood left?" I asked sleepily.

"The wood and the island will finish tomorrow in a dead heat," he laughed, "but there's enough to last us till then."

I plunged in from the point of the island, which had indeed altered a lot in size and shape during the night, and was swept down in a moment to the landing-place opposite the tent. The water was icy, and the banks flew by like the country from an express train. Bathing under such conditions was an exhilarating operation, and the terror of the night seemed cleansed out of me by a process of evaporation in the brain. The sun was blazing hot; not a cloud showed itself anywhere; the wind, however, had not abated one little jot.

Quite suddenly then the implied meaning of the Swede's words flashed across me, showing that he no longer wished to leave post-haste, and had changed his mind. "Enough to last till tomorrow" — he assumed we should stay on the island another night. It struck me as odd. The night before he was so positive the other way. How had the change come about?

Great crumblings of the banks occurred at breakfast, with heavy splashings and clouds of spray which the wind brought into our frying-pan, and my fellow-traveler talked incessantly about the difficulty the Vienna-Pesth steamers must have to find the channel in flood. But the state of his mind interested and impressed me far more than the state of the river or the difficulties of the steamers. He had changed somehow since the evening before. His manner was different — a trifle excited, a trifle shy, with a sort of suspicion about his voice and gestures. I hardly know how to describe it now in cold blood, but at the time I remember being quite certain of one thing — that he had become frightened!

He ate very little breakfast, and for once omitted to smoke his pipe. He had the map spread open beside him, and kept studying its markings.

"We'd better get off sharp in an hour," I said presently, feeling for an opening that must bring him indirectly to a partial confession at any rate. And his answer puzzled me uncomfortably: "Rather! If they'll let us."

"Who'll let us? The elements?" I asked quickly, with affected indifference.

"The powers of this awful place, whoever they are," he replied, keeping his eyes on the map. "The gods are here, if they are anywhere at all in the world."

"The elements are always the true immortals," I replied, laughing as naturally as I could manage, yet knowing quite well that my face reflected my true feelings when he looked up gravely at me and spoke across the smoke:

"We shall be fortunate if we get away without further disaster."

This was exactly what I had dreaded, and I screwed myself up to the point of the direct question. It was like agreeing to allow the dentist to extract the tooth; it *had* to come anyhow in the long run, and the rest was all pretence.

"Further disaster! Why, what's happened?"

"For one thing — the steering paddle's gone," he said quietly.

"The steering paddle gone!" I repeated, greatly excited, for this was our rudder, and the Danube in flood without a rudder was suicide. "But what — "

"And there's a tear in the bottom of the canoe," he added, with a genuine little tremor in his voice.

I continued staring at him, able only to repeat the words in his face somewhat foolishly. There, in the heat of the sun, and on this burning sand, I was aware of a freezing atmosphere descending round us. I got up to follow him, for he merely nodded his head gravely and led the way towards the tent a few yards on the other side of the fire-place. The canoe still lay there as I had last seen her in the night, ribs uppermost, the paddles, or rather, *the* paddle, on the sand beside her.

"There's only one," he said, stooping to pick it up. "And here's the rent in the base-board."

It was on the tip of my tongue to tell him that I had clearly noticed two paddles a few hours before, but a second impulse made me think better of it, and I said nothing. I approached to see.

There was a long, finely made tear in the bottom of the canoe where a little slither of wood had been neatly taken clean out; it looked as if the tooth of a sharp rock or snag had eaten down her length, and investigation showed that the hole went through. Had we launched out in her without observing it we must inevitably have foundered. At first the water would have made the wood swell so as to close the hole, but once out in mid-stream the water must have poured in, and the canoe, never more than two inches above the surface, would have filled and sunk very rapidly.

"There, you see an attempt to prepare a victim for the sacrifice," I heard him saying, more to himself than to me, "two victims rather," he added as he bent over and ran his fingers along the slit.

I began to whistle — a thing I always do unconsciously when utterly nonplussed — and purposely paid no attention to his words. I was determined to consider them foolish.

"It wasn't there last night," he said presently, straightening up from his examination and looking anywhere but at me.

"We must have scratched her in landing, of course," I stopped whistling to say. "The stones are very sharp."

I stopped abruptly, for at that moment he turned round and met my eye squarely. I knew just as well as he did how impossible my explanation was. There were no stones, to begin with.

"And then there's this to explain too," he added quietly, handing me the paddle and pointing to the blade.

A new and curious emotion spread freezingly over me as I took and examined it. The blade was scraped down all over, beautifully scraped, as though someone had sand-papered it with care, making it so thin that the first vigorous stroke must have snapped it off at the elbow.

"One of us walked in his sleep and did this thing," I said feebly, "or — or it has been filed by the constant stream of sand particles blown against it by the wind, perhaps."

"Ah," said the Swede, turning away, laughing a little, "you can explain everything."

"The same wind that caught the steering paddle and flung it so near the bank that it fell in with the next lump that crumbled," I called out after him, absolutely determined to find an explanation for everything he showed me.

"I see," he shouted back, turning his head to look at me before disappearing among the willow bushes.

Once alone with these perplexing evidences of personal agency, I think my first thoughts took the form of "One of us must have done this thing, and it certainly was not I."

But my second thought decided how impossible it was to suppose, under all the circumstances, that either of us had done it. That my companion, the trusted friend of a dozen similar expeditions, could have knowingly had a hand in it, was a suggestion not to be entertained for a moment. Equally absurd seemed the explanation that this imperturbable and densely practical nature had suddenly become insane and was busied with insane purposes.

Yet the fact remained that what disturbed me most, and kept my fear actively alive even in this blaze of sunshine and wild beauty, was the clear certainty that some curious alteration had come about in his *mind*— that he was nervous, timid, suspicious, aware of goings on he did not speak about, watching a series of secret and hitherto unmentionable events — waiting, in a word, for a climax that he expected, and, I thought, expected very soon. This grew up in my mind intuitively — I hardly knew how.

I made a hurried examination of the tent and its surroundings, but the measurements of the night remained the same. There were deep hollows formed in the sand I now noticed for the first time, basin-shaped and of various depths and sizes, varying from that of a tea-cup to a large bowl. The wind, no doubt, was responsible for these miniature craters, just as it was for lifting the paddle and tossing it towards the water. The rent in the canoe was the only thing that seemed quite inexplicable; and, after all, it *was* conceivable that a sharp point had caught it when we landed. The examination I made of the shore did not assist this theory, but all the same I clung to it with that diminishing portion of my intelligence which I called my "reason." An explanation of some kind was an absolute necessity, just as some working explanation of the universe is necessary — however absurd — to the happiness of every individual who seeks to do his duty in the world and face the problems of life. The simile seemed to me at the time an exact parallel.

I at once set the pitch melting, and presently the Swede joined me at the work, though under the best conditions in the world the canoe could not be safe for traveling till the following day. I drew his attention casually to the hollows in the sand.

"Yes," he said, "I know. They're all over the island. But *you* can explain them, no doubt!"

"Wind, of course," I answered without hesitation. "Have you never watched those little whirlwinds in the street that twist and twirl everything into a circle? This sand's loose enough to yield, that's all."

He made no reply, and we worked on in silence for a bit. I watched him surreptitiously all the time, and I had an idea he was watching me. He seemed, too, to be always listening attentively to something I could not hear, or perhaps for something that he expected to hear, for he kept turning about and staring into the bushes, and up into the sky, and out across the water where it was visible through the openings among the willows. Sometimes he even put his hand to his ear and held it there for several minutes. He said nothing to me, however, about it, and I asked no questions. And meanwhile, as he mended that torn canoe with the skill and address of a red Indian, I was glad to notice his absorption in the work, for there was a vague dread in my heart that he would speak of the changed aspect of the willows. And, if he had noticed that, my imagination could no longer be held a sufficient explanation of it.

At length, after a long pause, he began to talk.

"Queer thing," he added in a hurried sort of voice, as though he wanted to say something and get it over. "Queer thing. I mean, about that otter last night."

I had expected something so totally different that he caught me with surprise, and I looked up sharply.

"Shows how lonely this place is. Otters are awfully shy things —"

"I don't mean that, of course," he interrupted. "I mean — do you think — did you think it really was an otter?"

"What else, in the name of Heaven, what else?"

"You know, I saw it before you did, and at first it seemed — so *much* bigger than an otter."

"The sunset as you looked up-stream magnified it, or something," I replied.

He looked at me absently a moment, as though his mind were busy with other thoughts.

"It had such extraordinary yellow eyes," he went on half to himself.

"That was the sun too," I laughed, a trifle boisterously. "I suppose you'll wonder next if that fellow in the boat —"

I suddenly decided not to finish the sentence. He was in the act again of listening, turning his head to the wind, and something in the expression of his face made me halt. The subject dropped, and we went on with our caulking.

Apparently he had not noticed my unfinished sentence. Five minutes later, however, he looked at me across the canoe, the smoking pitch in his hand, his face exceedingly grave.

"I *did* rather wonder, if you want to know," he said slowly, "what that thing in the boat was. I remember thinking at the time it was not a man. The whole business seemed to rise quite suddenly out of the water."

I laughed again boisterously in his face, but this time there was impatience, and a strain of anger too, in my feeling.

"Look here now," I cried, "this place is quite queer enough without going out of our way to imagine things! That boat was an ordinary boat, and the man in it was an ordinary man, and they were both going down-stream as fast as they could lick. And that otter *was* an otter, so don't let's play the fool about it!"

He looked steadily at me with the same grave expression. He was not in the least annoyed. I took courage from his silence.

"And, for Heaven's sake," I went on, "don't keep pretending you hear things, because it only gives me the jumps, and there's nothing to hear but the river and this cursed old thundering wind."

"You *fool!*" he answered in a low, shocked voice, "you utter fool. That's just the way all victims talk. As if you didn't understand just as well as I do!" he sneered with scorn in his voice, and a sort of resignation. "The best thing you can do is to keep quiet and try to hold your mind as firm as possible. This feeble attempt at self-deception only makes the truth harder when you're forced to meet it."

My little effort was over, and I found nothing more to say, for I knew quite well his words were true, and that I was the fool, not he. Up to a certain stage in the adventure he kept ahead of me easily, and I think I felt annoyed to be out of it, to be thus proved less psychic, less sensitive than himself to these extraordinary happenings, and half ignorant all the time of what was going on under my very nose. *He knew* from the very beginning, apparently. But at the moment I wholly missed the point of his words about the necessity of there being a victim, and that we ourselves were destined to satisfy the want. I dropped all pretence thenceforward, but thenceforward likewise my fear increased steadily to the climax.

"But you're quite right about one thing," he added, before the subject passed, "and that is that we're wiser not to talk about it, or even to think about it, because what one *thinks* finds expression in words, and what one *says*, happens."

That afternoon, while the canoe dried and hardened, we spent trying to fish, testing the leak, collecting wood, and watching the enormous flood of rising water. Masses of driftwood swept near our shores sometimes, and we fished for them with long willow branches. The island grew perceptibly smaller as the banks were torn away with great gulps and splashes. The weather kept brilliantly fine till about four o'clock, and then for the first time for three days the wind showed signs of abating. Clouds began to gather in the south-west, spreading thence slowly over the sky.

This lessening of the wind came as a great relief, for the incessant roaring, banging, and thundering had irritated our nerves. Yet the silence that came about five o'clock with its sudden cessation was in a manner quite as oppressive. The booming of the river had everything in its own way then; it filled the air with deep murmurs, more musical than the wind noises, but infinitely more monotonous. The wind held many notes, rising, falling, always beating out some sort of great elemental tune; whereas the river's song lay between three notes at most — dull pedal notes, that held a lugubrious quality foreign to the wind, and somehow seemed to me, in my then nervous state, to sound wonderfully well the music of doom.

It was extraordinary, too, how the withdrawal suddenly of bright sunlight took everything out of the landscape that made for cheerfulness; and since this particular landscape had already managed to convey the suggestion of something sinister, the change of course was all the more unwelcome and noticeable. For me, I know, the darkening outlook became distinctly more alarming, and I found myself more than once calculating how soon after sunset the full moon would get up in the east, and whether the gathering clouds would greatly interfere with her lighting of the little island.

With this general hush of the wind — though it still indulged in occasional brief gusts — the river seemed to me to grow blacker, the willows to stand more densely together. The latter, too, kept up a sort of independent movement of their own, rustling among themselves when no wind stirred, and shaking oddly from the roots upwards. When common objects in this way become charged with the suggestion of horror, they stimulate the imagination far more than things of unusual appearance; and these bushes, crowding huddled about us, assumed for me in the darkness a bizarre *grotesquerie* of appearance that lent to them somehow the aspect of purposeful and living creatures. Their very ordinariness, I felt, masked what was malignant and hostile to us. The forces of the region drew nearer with the coming of night. They were focusing upon our island, and more particularly upon ourselves. For thus, somehow, in the terms of the imagination, did my really indescribable sensations in this extraordinary place present themselves.

I had slept a good deal in the early afternoon, and had thus recovered somewhat from the exhaustion of a disturbed night, but this only served apparently to render me more susceptible than before to the obsessing spell of the haunting. I fought against it, laughing at my feelings as absurd and childish, with very obvious physiological explanations, yet, in spite of every effort, they gained in strength upon me so that I dreaded the night as a child lost in a forest must dread the approach of darkness.

The canoe we had carefully covered with a waterproof sheet during the day, and the one remaining paddle had been securely tied by the Swede to the base of a tree, lest the wind should rob us of that too. From five o'clock onwards I busied myself with the stew-pot and preparations for dinner, it being my turn to cook that night. We had potatoes, onions, bits of bacon fat to add flavor, and a general thick residue from former stews at the bottom of the pot; with black bread broken up into it the result was most excellent, and it was followed by a stew of plums with sugar and a brew of strong tea with dried milk. A good pile of wood lay close at hand, and the absence of wind made my duties easy.

My companion sat lazily watching me, dividing his attentions between cleaning his pipe and giving useless advice — an admitted privilege of the off-duty man. He had been very quiet all the afternoon, engaged in re-caulking the canoe, strengthening the tent ropes, and fishing for driftwood while I slept. No more talk about undesirable things had passed between us, and I think his only remarks had to do with the gradual destruction of the island, which he declared was now fully a third smaller than when we first landed.

The pot had just begun to bubble when I heard his voice calling to me from the bank, where he had wandered away without my noticing. I ran up.

"Come and listen," he said, "and see what you make of it." He held his hand cupwise to his ear, as so often before.

"*Now* do you hear anything?" he asked, watching me curiously.

We stood there, listening attentively together. At first I heard only the deep note of the water and the hissings rising from its turbulent surface. The willows, for once, were motionless and silent. Then a sound began to reach my ears faintly, a peculiar sound — something like the humming of a distant gong. It seemed to come across to us in the darkness from the waste of swamps and willows opposite. It was repeated at regular intervals, but it was certainly neither the sound of a bell nor the hooting of a distant steamer. I can liken it to nothing so much as to the sound of an immense gong, suspended far up in the sky, repeating incessantly its muffled metallic note, soft and musical, as it was repeatedly struck. My heart quickened as I listened.

"I've heard it all day," said my companion. "While you slept this afternoon it came all round the island. I hunted it down, but could never get near enough to see — to localize it correctly. Sometimes it was overhead, and sometimes it seemed under the water. Once or twice, too, I could have sworn it was not outside at all, but *within myself* — you know — the way a sound in the fourth dimension is supposed to come."

I was too much puzzled to pay much attention to his words. I listened carefully, striving to associate it with any known familiar sound I could think of, but without success. It changed in the direction, too, coming nearer, and then sinking utterly away into remote distance. I cannot say that it was ominous in quality, because to me it seemed distinctly musical, yet I must admit it set going a distressing feeling that made me wish I had never heard it.

"The wind blowing in those sand-funnels," I said, determined to find an explanation, "or the bushes rubbing together after the storm perhaps."

"It comes off the whole swamp," my friend answered. "It comes from everywhere at once." He ignored my explanations. "It comes from the willow bushes somehow — "

"But now the wind has dropped," I objected. "The willows can hardly make a noise by themselves, can they?"

His answer frightened me, first because I had dreaded it, and secondly, because I knew intuitively it was true.

"It is *because* the wind has dropped we now hear it. It was drowned before. It is the cry, I believe, of the — "

I dashed back to my fire, warned by the sound of bubbling that the stew was in danger, but determined at the same time to escape further conversation. I was resolute, if possible, to avoid the exchanging of views. I dreaded, too, that he would begin about the gods, or the elemental forces, or something else disquieting, and I wanted to keep myself well in hand for what might happen later. There was another night to be faced before we escaped from this distressing place, and there was no knowing yet what it might bring forth.

"Come and cut up bread for the pot," I called to him, vigorously stirring the appetizing mixture. That stew-pot held sanity for us both, and the thought made me laugh.

He came over slowly and took the provision sack from the tree, fumbling in its mysterious depths, and then emptying the entire contents upon the ground-sheet at his feet.

"Hurry up!" I cried; "it's boiling."

The Swede burst out into a roar of laughter that startled me. It was forced laughter, not artificial exactly, but mirthless.

"There's nothing here!" he shouted, holding his sides.

"Bread, I mean."

"It's gone. There is no bread. They've taken it!"

I dropped the long spoon and ran up. Everything the sack had contained lay upon the ground-sheet, but there was no loaf.

The whole dead weight of my growing fear fell upon me and shook me. Then I burst out laughing too. It was the only thing to do: and the sound of my laughter also made me understand his. The stain of psychical pressure caused it — this explosion of unnatural laughter in both of us; it was an effort of repressed forces to seek relief; it was a temporary safety-valve. And with both of us it ceased quite suddenly.

"How criminally stupid of me!" I cried, still determined to be consistent and find an explanation. "I clean forgot to buy a loaf at Pressburg. That chattering woman put everything out of my head, and I must have left it lying on the counter or — "

"The oatmeal, too, is much less than it was this morning," the Swede interrupted.

Why in the world need he draw attention to it? I thought angrily.

"There's enough for tomorrow," I said, stirring vigorously, "and we can get lots more at Komorn or Gran. In twenty-four hours we shall be miles from here."

"I hope so — to God," he muttered, putting the things back into the sack, "unless we're claimed first as victims for the sacrifice," he added with a foolish laugh. He dragged the sack into the tent, for safety's sake, I suppose, and I heard him mumbling to himself, but so indistinctly that it seemed quite natural for me to ignore his words.

Our meal was beyond question a gloomy one, and we ate it almost in silence, avoiding one another's eyes, and keeping the fire bright. Then we washed up and prepared for the night, and, once smoking, our minds unoccupied with any definite duties, the apprehension I had felt all day long became more and more acute. It was not then active fear, I think, but the very vagueness of its origin distressed me far more that if I had been able to ticket and face it squarely. The curious sound I have likened to the note of a gong became now almost incessant, and filled the stillness of the night with a faint, continuous ringing rather than a series of distinct notes. At one time it was behind and at another time in front of us. Sometimes I fancied it came from the bushes on our left, and then again from the clumps on our right. More often it hovered directly overhead like the whirring of wings. It was really everywhere at once, behind, in front, at our sides and over our heads, completely surrounding us. The sound really defies description. But nothing within my knowledge is like that ceaseless muffled humming rising off the deserted world of swamps and willows.

We sat smoking in comparative silence, the strain growing every minute greater. The worst feature of the situation seemed to me that we did not know what to expect, and could therefore make no sort of preparation by way of defense. We could anticipate nothing. My explanations made in the sunshine, moreover, now came to haunt me with their foolish and wholly unsatisfactory nature, and it was more and more clear to us that some kind of plain talk with my companion was inevitable, whether I liked it or not. After all, we had to spend the night together, and to sleep in the same tent side by side. I saw that I could not get along much longer without the support of his mind, and for that, of course, plain talk was imperative. As long as possible, however, I postponed this little climax, and tried to ignore or laugh at the occasional sentences he flung into the emptiness.

Some of these sentences, moreover, were confoundedly disquieting to me, coming as they did to corroborate much that I felt myself; corroboration, too — which made it so much more convincing — from a totally different point of view. He composed such curious sentences, and hurled them at me in such an inconsequential sort of way, as though his main line of thought was secret to himself, and these fragments were mere bits he found it impossible to digest. He got rid of them by uttering them. Speech relieved him. It was like being sick.

"There are things about us, I'm sure, that make for disorder, disintegration, destruction, our destruction," he said once, while the fire blazed between us. "We've strayed out of a safe line somewhere."

And, another time, when the gong sounds had come nearer, ringing much louder than before, and directly over our heads, he said as though talking to himself:

"I don't think a gramophone would show any record of that. The sound doesn't come to me by the ears at all. The vibrations reach me in another manner altogether, and seem to be within me, which is precisely how a fourth dimensional sound might be supposed to make itself heard."

I purposely made no reply to this, but I sat up a little closer to the fire and peered about me into the darkness. The clouds were massed all over the sky, and no trace of moonlight came through. Very still, too, everything was, so that the river and the frogs had things all their own way.

"It has that about it," he went on, "which is utterly out of common experience. It is *unknown*. Only one thing describes it really; it is a non-human sound; I mean a sound outside humanity."

Having rid himself of this indigestible morsel, he lay

quiet for a time, but he had so admirably expressed my own feeling that it was a relief to have the thought out, and to have confined it by the limitation of words from dangerous wandering to and fro in the mind.

The solitude of that Danube camping-place, can I ever forget it? The feeling of being utterly alone on an empty planet! My thoughts ran incessantly upon cities and the haunts of men. I would have given my soul, as the saying is, for the "feel" of those Bavarian villages we had passed through by the score; for the normal, human commonplaces; peasants drinking beer, tables beneath the trees, hot sunshine, and a ruined castle on the rocks behind the red-roofed church. Even the tourists would have been welcome.

Yet what I felt of dread was no ordinary ghostly fear. It was infinitely greater, stranger, and seemed to arise from some dim ancestral sense of terror more profoundly disturbing than anything I had known or dreamed of. We had "strayed," as the Swede put it, into some region or some set of conditions where the risks were great, yet unintelligible to us; where the frontiers of some unknown world lay close about us. It was a spot held by the dwellers in some outer space, a sort of peep-hole whence they could spy upon the earth, themselves unseen, a point where the veil between had worn a little thin. As the final result of too long a sojourn here, we should be carried over the border and deprived of what we called "our lives," yet by mental, not physical, processes. In that sense, as he said, we should be the victims of our adventure — a sacrifice.

It took us in different fashion, each according to the

measure of his sensitiveness and powers of resistance. I translated it vaguely into a personification of the mightily disturbed elements, investing them with the horror of a deliberate and malefic purpose, resentful of our audacious intrusion into their breeding-place; whereas my friend threw it into the unoriginal form at first of a trespass on some ancient shrine, some place where the old gods still held sway, where the emotional forces of former worshippers still clung, and the ancestral portion of him yielded to the old pagan spell.

At any rate, here was a place unpolluted by men, kept clean by the winds from coarsening human influences, a place where spiritual agencies were within reach and aggressive. Never, before or since, have I been so attacked by indescribable suggestions of a "beyond region," of another scheme of life, another revolution not parallel to the human. And in the end our minds would succumb under the weight of the awful spell, and we should be drawn across the frontier into *their* world.

Small things testified to the amazing influence of the place, and now in the silence round the fire they allowed themselves to be noted by the mind. The very atmosphere had proved itself a magnifying medium to distort every indication: the otter rolling in the current, the hurrying boatman making signs, the shifting willows, one and all had been robbed of its natural character, and revealed in something of its other aspect — as it existed across the border to that other region. And this changed aspect I felt was now not merely to me, but to the race. The whole experience whose verge we touched was unknown to humanity at all. It was a new order of experience, and, in the true sense of the word, *unearthly*.

"It's the deliberate, calculating purpose that reduces one's courage to zero," the Swede said suddenly, as if he had been actually following my thoughts. "Otherwise imagination might count for much. But the paddle, the canoe, the lessening food — "

"Haven't I explained all that once?" I interrupted viciously.

"You have," he answered dryly; "you have indeed."

He made other remarks too, as usual, about what he called the "plain determination to provide a victim"; but, having now arranged my thoughts better, I recognized that this was simply the cry of his frightened soul against the knowledge that he was being attacked in a vital part, and that he would be somehow taken or destroyed. The situation called for a courage and calmness of reasoning that neither of us could compass, and I have never before been so clearly conscious of two persons in me — the one that explained everything, and the other that laughed at such foolish explanations, yet was horribly afraid.

Meanwhile, in the pitchy night the fire died down and the wood pile grew small. Neither of us moved to replenish the stock, and the darkness consequently came up very close to our faces. A few feet beyond the circle of firelight it was inky black. Occasionally a stray puff of wind set the willows shivering about us, but apart from this not very welcome sound a deep and depressing silence reigned, broken only by the gurgling of the river and the humming in the air overhead.

We both missed, I think, the shouting company of the winds.

At length, at a moment when a stray puff prolonged itself as though the wind were about to rise again, I reached the point for me of saturation, the point where it was absolutely necessary to find relief in plain speech, or else to betray myself by some hysterical extravagance that must have been far worse in its effect upon both of us. I kicked the fire into a blaze, and turned to my companion abruptly. He looked up with a start.

"I can't disguise it any longer," I said; "I don't like this place, and the darkness, and the noises, and the awful feelings I get. There's something here that beats me utterly. I'm in a blue funk, and that's the plain truth. If the other shore was — different, I swear I'd be inclined to swim for it!"

The Swede's face turned very white beneath the deep tan of sun and wind. He stared straight at me and answered quietly, but his voice betrayed his huge excitement by its unnatural calmness. For the moment, at any rate, he was the strong man of the two. He was more phlegmatic, for one thing.

"It's not a physical condition we can escape from by running away," he replied, in the tone of a doctor diagnosing some grave disease; "we must sit tight and wait. There are forces close here that could kill a herd of elephants in a second as easily as you or I could squash a fly. Our only chance is to keep perfectly still. Our insignificance perhaps may save us."

I put a dozen questions into my expression of face, but

found no words. It was precisely like listening to an accurate description of a disease whose symptoms had puzzled me.

"I mean that so far, although aware of our disturbing presence, they have not *found* us — not 'located' us, as the Americans say," he went on. "They're blundering about like men hunting for a leak of gas. The paddle and canoe and provisions prove that. I think they *feel* us, but cannot actually see us. We must keep our minds quiet — it's our minds they feel. We must control our thoughts, or it's all up with us."

"Death, you mean?" I stammered, icy with the horror of his suggestion.

"Worse — by far," he said. "Death, according to one's belief, means either annihilation or release from the limitations of the senses, but it involves no change of character. *You* don't suddenly alter just because the body's gone. But this means a radical alteration, a complete change, a horrible loss of oneself by substitution — far worse than death, and not even annihilation. We happen to have camped in a spot where their region touches ours, where the veil between has worn thin" — horrors! he was using my very own phrase, my actual words — "so that they are aware of our being in their neighborhood."

"But *who* are aware?" I asked.

I forgot the shaking of the willows in the windless calm, the humming overhead, everything except that I was waiting for an answer that I dreaded more than I can possibly explain.

He lowered his voice at once to reply, leaning forward a little over the fire, an indefinable change in his face that made me avoid his eyes and look down upon the ground.

"All my life," he said, "I have been strangely, vividly conscious of another region — not far removed from our own world in one sense, yet wholly different in kind — where great things go on unceasingly, where immense and terrible personalities hurry by, intent on vast purposes compared to which earthly affairs, the rise and fall of nations, the destinies of empires, the fate of armies and continents, are all as dust in the balance; vast purposes, I mean, that deal directly with the soul, and not indirectly with mere expressions of the soul — "

"I suggest just now — " I began, seeking to stop him, feeling as though I was face to face with a madman. But he instantly overbore me with his torrent that *had* to come.

"You think," he said, "it is the spirit of the elements, and I thought perhaps it was the old gods. But I tell you now it is — *neither.* These would be comprehensible entities, for they have relations with men, depending upon them for worship or sacrifice, whereas these beings who are now about us have absolutely nothing to do with mankind, and it is mere chance that their space happens just at this spot to touch our own."

The mere conception, which his words somehow made so convincing, as I listened to them there in the dark stillness of that lonely island, set me shaking a little all over. I found it impossible to control my movements.

"And what do you propose?" I began again.

"A sacrifice, a victim, might save us by distracting them until we could get away," he went on, "just as the wolves stop to devour the dogs and give the sleigh another start.

But — I see no chance of any other victim now."

I stared blankly at him. The gleam in his eye was dreadful. Presently he continued.

"It's the willows, of course. The willows *mask* the others, but the others are feeling about for us. If we let our minds betray our fear, we're lost, lost utterly." He looked at me with an expression so calm, so determined, so sincere, that I no longer had any doubts as to his sanity. He was as sane as any man ever was. "If we can hold out through the night," he added, "we may get off in the daylight unnoticed, or rather, *undiscovered*."

"But you really think a sacrifice would — "

That gong-like humming came down very close over our heads as I spoke, but it was my friend's scared face that really stopped my mouth.

"Hush!" he whispered, holding up his hand. "Do not mention them more than you can help. Do not refer to them *by name*. To name is to reveal; it is the inevitable clue, and our only hope lies in ignoring them, in order that they may ignore us."

"Even in thought?" He was extraordinarily agitated.

"Especially in thought. Our thoughts make spirals in their world. We must keep them *out of our minds* at all costs if possible."

I raked the fire together to prevent the darkness having everything its own way. I never longed for the sun as I longed for it then in the awful blackness of that summer night.

"Were you awake all last night?" he went on suddenly.

"I slept badly a little after dawn," I replied evasively,

trying to follow his instructions, which I knew instinctively were true, "but the wind, of course —"

"I know. But the wind won't account for all the noises."

"Then you heard it too?"

"The multiplying countless little footsteps I heard," he said, adding, after a moment's hesitation, "and that other sound —"

"You mean above the tent, and the pressing down upon us of something tremendous, gigantic?"

He nodded significantly.

"It was like the beginning of a sort of inner suffocation?" I said.

"Partly, yes. It seemed to me that the weight of the atmosphere had been altered — had increased enormously, so that we should have been crushed."

"And *that*," I went on, determined to have it all out, pointing upwards where the gong-like note hummed ceaselessly, rising and falling like wind. "What do you make of that?"

"It's their sound," he whispered gravely. "It's the sound of their world, the humming in their region. The division here is so thin that it leaks through somehow. But, if you listen carefully, you'll find it's not above so much as around us. It's in the willows. It's the willows themselves humming, because here the willows have been made symbols of the forces that are against us."

I could not follow exactly what he meant by this, yet the thought and idea in my mind were beyond question the thought and idea in his. I realized what he realized, only with less power of analysis than his. It was on the tip of my tongue to tell him at last about my hallucination of the ascending figures and the moving bushes, when he suddenly thrust his face again close into mine across the firelight and began to speak in a very earnest whisper. He amazed me by his calmness and pluck, his apparent control of the situation. This man I had for years deemed unimaginative, stolid!

"Now listen," he said. "The only thing for us to do is to go on as though nothing had happened, follow our usual habits, go to bed, and so forth; pretend we feel nothing and notice nothing. It is a question wholly of the mind, and the less we think about them the better our chance of escape. Above all, don't *think*, for what you think happens!"

"All right," I managed to reply, simply breathless with his words and the strangeness of it all; "all right, I'll try, but tell me one more thing first. Tell me what you make of those hollows in the ground all about us, those sand-funnels?"

"No!" he cried, forgetting to whisper in his excitement. "I dare not, simply dare not, put the thought into words. If you have not guessed I am glad. Don't try to. *They* have put it into my mind; try your hardest to prevent their putting it into yours."

He sank his voice again to a whisper before he finished, and I did not press him to explain. There was already just about as much horror in me as I could hold. The conversation came to an end, and we smoked our pipes busily in silence.

Then something happened, something unimportant apparently, as the way is when the nerves are in a very great state of tension, and this small thing for a brief space gave me an entirely different point of view. I chanced to look down at my sand-shoe — the sort we used for the canoe — and something to do with the hole at the toe suddenly recalled to me the London shop where I had bought them, the difficulty the man had in fitting me, and other details of the uninteresting but practical operation. At once, in its train, followed a wholesome view of the modern skeptical world I was accustomed to move in at home. I thought of roast beef, and ale, motor-cars, policemen, brass bands, and a dozen other things that proclaimed the soul of ordinariness or utility. The effect was immediate and astonishing even to myself. Psychologically, I suppose, it was simply a sudden and violent reaction after the strain of living in an atmosphere of things that to the normal consciousness must seem impossible and incredible. But, whatever the cause, it momentarily lifted the spell from my heart, and left me for the short space of a minute feeling free and utterly unafraid. I looked up at my friend opposite.

"You damned old pagan!" I cried, laughing aloud in his face. "You imaginative idiot! You superstitious idolater! You — "

I stopped in the middle, seized anew by the old horror. I tried to smother the sound of my voice as something sacrilegious. The Swede, of course, heard it too — the strange cry overhead in the darkness — and that sudden drop in the air as though something had come nearer.

He had turned ashen white under the tan. He stood bolt upright in front of the fire, stiff as a rod, staring at me.

"After that," he said in a sort of helpless, frantic way, "we must go! We can't stay now; we must strike camp this very instant and go on — down the river."

He was talking, I saw, quite wildly, his words dictated by abject terror — the terror he had resisted so long, but which had caught him at last.

"In the dark?" I exclaimed, shaking with fear after my hysterical outburst, but still realizing our position better than he did. "Sheer madness! The river's in flood, and we've only got a single paddle. Besides, we only go deeper into their country! There's nothing ahead for fifty miles but willows, willows, willows!"

He sat down again in a state of semi-collapse. The positions, by one of those kaleidoscopic changes nature loves, were suddenly reversed, and the control of our forces passed over into my hands. His mind at last had reached the point where it was beginning to weaken.

"What on earth possessed you to do such a thing?" he whispered with the awe of genuine terror in his voice and face.

I crossed round to his side of the fire. I took both his hands in mine, kneeling down beside him and looking straight into his frightened eyes.

"We'll make one more blaze," I said firmly, "and then turn in for the night. At sunrise we'll be off full speed for Komorn. Now, pull yourself together a bit, and remember your own advice about *not thinking fear*!"

He said no more, and I saw that he would agree and obey. In some measure, too, it was a sort of relief to get up and make an excursion into the darkness for more wood.

We kept close together, almost touching, groping among the bushes and along the bank. The humming overhead never ceased, but seemed to me to grow louder as we increased our distance from the fire. It was shivery work!

We were grubbing away in the middle of a thickish clump of willows where some driftwood from a former flood had caught high among the branches, when my body was seized in a grip that made me half drop upon the sand. It was the Swede. He had fallen against me, and was clutching me for support. I heard his breath coming and going in short gasps.

"Look! By my soul!" he whispered, and for the first time in my experience I knew what it was to hear tears of terror in a human voice. He was pointing to the fire, some fifty feet away. I followed the direction of his finger, and I swear my heart missed a beat.

There, in front of the dim glow, *something was moving*.

I saw it through a veil that hung before my eyes like the gauze drop-curtain used at the back of a theater — hazily a little. It was neither a human figure nor an animal. To me it gave the strange impression of being as large as several animals grouped together, like horses, two or three, moving slowly. The Swede, too, got a similar result, though expressing it differently, for he thought it was shaped and sized like a clump of willow bushes, rounded at the top, and moving all over upon its surface — "coiling upon itself like smoke," he said afterwards.

"I watched it settle downwards through the bushes," he sobbed at me. "Look, by God! It's coming this way! Oh, oh!" — he gave a kind of whistling cry. *"They've found us."*

I gave one terrified glance, which just enabled me to see that the shadowy form was swinging towards us through the bushes, and then I collapsed backwards with a crash into the branches. These failed, of course, to support my weight, so that with the Swede on top of me we fell in a struggling heap upon the sand. I really hardly knew what was happening. I was conscious only of a sort of enveloping sensation of icy fear that plucked the nerves out of their fleshly covering, twisted them this way and that, and replaced them quivering. My eyes were tightly shut; something in my throat choked me; a feeling that my consciousness was expanding, extending out into space, swiftly gave way to another feeling that I was losing it altogether, and about to die.

An acute spasm of pain passed through me, and I was aware that the Swede had hold of me in such a way that he hurt me abominably. It was the way he caught at me in falling.

But it was the pain, he declared afterwards, that saved me; it caused me to *forget them* and think of something else at the very instant when they were about to find me. It concealed my mind from them at the moment of discovery, yet just in time to evade their terrible seizing of me. He himself, he says, actually swooned at the same moment, and that was what saved him.

I only know that at a later date, how long or short is impossible to say, I found myself scrambling up out of the slippery network of willow branches, and saw my companion standing in front of me holding out a hand to assist me. I stared at him in a dazed way, rubbing the arm he had twisted for me. Nothing came to me to say, somehow.

"I lost consciousness for a moment or two," I heard him say. "That's what saved me. It made me stop thinking about them."

"You nearly broke my arm in two," I said, uttering my only connected thought at the moment. A numbness came over me.

"That's what saved *you!*" he replied. "Between us, we've managed to set them off on a false tack somewhere. The humming has ceased. It's gone — for the moment at any rate!"

A wave of hysterical laughter seized me again, and this time spread to my friend too — great healing gusts of shaking laughter that brought a tremendous sense of relief in their train. We made our way back to the fire and put the wood on so that it blazed at once. Then we saw that the tent had fallen over and lay in a tangled heap upon the ground.

We picked it up, and during the process tripped more than once and caught our feet in sand.

"It's those sand-funnels," exclaimed the Swede, when the tent was up again and the firelight lit up the ground for several yards about us. "And look at the size of them!"

All round the tent and about the fireplace where we had seen the moving shadows there were deep funnel-shaped hollows in the sand, exactly similar to the ones we had already found over the island, only far bigger and deeper, beautifully formed, and wide enough in some instances to admit the whole of my foot and leg.

Neither of us said a word. We both knew that sleep

was the safest thing we could do, and to bed we went accordingly without further delay, having first thrown sand on the fire and taken the provision sack and the paddle inside the tent with us. The canoe, too, we propped in such a way at the end of the tent that our feet touched it, and the least motion would disturb and wake us.

In case of emergency, too, we again went to bed in our clothes, ready for a sudden start.

V.

It was my firm intention to lie awake all night and watch, but the exhaustion of nerves and body decreed otherwise, and sleep after a while came over me with a welcome blanket of oblivion. The fact that my companion also slept quickened its approach. At first he fidgeted and constantly sat up, asking me if I "heard this" or "heard that." He tossed about on his cork mattress, and said the tent was moving and the river had risen over the point of the island, but each time I went out to look I returned with the report that all was well, and finally he grew calmer and lay still. Then at length his breathing became regular and I heard unmistakable sounds of snoring — the first and only time in my life when snoring has been a welcome and calming influence. This, I remember, was the last thought in my mind before dozing off.

A difficulty in breathing woke me, and I found the blanket over my face. But something else besides the blanket was pressing upon me, and my first thought was that my companion had rolled off his mattress on to my own in his sleep. I called to him and sat up, and at the same moment it came to me that the tent was *surrounded*. That sound of multitudinous soft pattering was again audible outside, filling the night with horror.

I called again to him, louder than before. He did not answer, but I missed the sound of his snoring, and also noticed that the flap of the tent was down. This was the unpardonable sin. I crawled out in the darkness to hook it back securely, and it was then for the first time I realized positively that the Swede was not here. He had gone.

I dashed out in a mad run, seized by a dreadful agitation, and the moment I was out I plunged into a sort of torrent of humming that surrounded me completely and came out of every quarter of the heavens at once. It was that same familiar humming — gone mad! A swarm of great invisible bees might have been about me in the air. The sound seemed to thicken the very atmosphere, and I felt that my lungs worked with difficulty.

But my friend was in danger, and I could not hesitate.

The dawn was just about to break, and a faint whitish light spread upwards over the clouds from a thin strip of clear horizon. No wind stirred. I could just make out the bushes and river beyond, and the pale sandy patches. In my excitement I ran frantically to and fro about the island, calling him by name, shouting at the top of my voice the

first words that came into my head. But the willows smothered my voice, and the humming muffled it, so that the
sound only traveled a few feet round me. I plunged among
the bushes, tripping headlong, tumbling over roots, and
scraping my face as I tore this way and that among the
preventing branches.

Then, quite unexpectedly, I came out upon the island's
point and saw a dark figure outlined between the water
and the sky. It was the Swede. And already he had one
foot in the river! A moment more and he would have taken
the plunge.

I threw myself upon him, flinging my arms about his
waist and dragging him shorewards with all my strength.
Of course he struggled furiously, making a noise all the
time just like that cursed humming, and using the most
outlandish phrases in his anger about "going *inside* to
Them," and "taking the way of the water and the wind,"
and God only knows what more besides, that I tried in
vain to recall afterwards, but which turned me sick with
horror and amazement as I listened. But in the end I
managed to get him into the comparative safety of the
tent, and flung him breathless and cursing upon the
mattress where I held him until the fit had passed.

I think the suddenness with which it all went and he
grew calm, coinciding as it did with the equally abrupt
cessation of the humming and pattering outside — I think
this was almost the strangest part of the whole business
perhaps. For he had just opened his eyes and turned his
tired face up to me so that the dawn threw a pale light
upon it through the doorway, and said, for all the world

just like a frightened child:

"My life, old man — it's my life I owe you. But it's all over now anyhow. They've found a victim in our place!"

Then he dropped back upon his blankets and went to sleep literally under my eyes. He simply collapsed, and began to snore again as healthily as though nothing had happened and he had never tried to offer his own life as a sacrifice by drowning. And when the sunlight woke him three hours later — hours of ceaseless vigil for me — it became so clear to me that he remembered absolutely nothing of what he had attempted to do, that I deemed it wise to hold my peace and ask no dangerous questions.

He woke naturally and easily, as I have said, when the sun was already high in a windless hot sky, and he at once got up and set about the preparation of the fire for breakfast. I followed him anxiously at bathing, but he did not attempt to plunge in, merely dipping his head and making some remark about the extra coldness of the water.

"River's falling at last," he said, "and I'm glad of it."

"The humming has stopped too," I said.

He looked up at me quietly with his normal expression. Evidently he remembered everything except his own attempt at suicide.

"Everything has stopped," he said, "because — "

He hesitated. But I knew some reference to that remark he had made just before he fainted was in his mind, and I was determined to know it.

"Because 'They've found another victim'?" I said, forcing a little laugh.

"Exactly," he answered, "exactly! I feel as positive of it

as though — as though — I feel quite safe again, I mean," he finished.

He began to look curiously about him. The sunlight lay in hot patches on the sand. There was no wind. The willows were motionless. He slowly rose to feet.

"Come," he said; "I think if we look, we shall find it."

He started off on a run, and I followed him. He kept to the banks, poking with a stick among the sandy bays and caves and little back-waters, myself always close on his heels.

"Ah!" he exclaimed presently, "ah!"

The tone of his voice somehow brought back to me a vivid sense of the horror of the last twenty-four hours, and I hurried up to join him. He was pointing with his stick at a large black object that lay half in the water and half on the sand. It appeared to be caught by some twisted willow roots so that the river could not sweep it away. A few hours before the spot must have been under water.

"See," he said quietly, "the victim that made our escape possible!"

And when I peered across his shoulder I saw that his stick rested on the body of a man. He turned it over. It was the corpse of a peasant, and the face was hidden in the sand. Clearly the man had been drowned, but a few hours before, and his body must have been swept down upon our island somewhere about the hour of the dawn — *at the very time the fit had passed.*

"We must give it a decent burial, you know."

"I suppose so," I replied. I shuddered a little in spite of myself, for there was something about the appearance of that poor drowned man that turned me cold.

The Swede glanced up sharply at me, an undecipherable expression on his face, and began clambering down the bank. I followed him more leisurely. The current, I noticed, had torn away much of the clothing from the body, so that the neck and part of the chest lay bare.

Halfway down the bank my companion suddenly stopped and held up his hand in warning; but either my foot slipped, or I had gained too much momentum to bring myself quickly to a halt, for I bumped into him and sent him forward with a sort of leap to save himself. We tumbled together on to the hard sand so that our feet splashed into the water. And, before anything could be done, we had collided a little heavily against the corpse.

The Swede uttered a sharp cry. And I sprang back as if I had been shot.

At the moment we touched the body there rose from its surface the loud sound of humming — the sound of several hummings — which passed with a vast commotion as of winged things in the air about us and disappeared upwards into the sky, growing fainter and fainter till they finally ceased in the distance. It was exactly as though we had disturbed some living yet invisible creatures at work.

My companion clutched me, and I think I clutched him, but before either of us had time properly to recover from the unexpected shock, we saw that a movement of the current was turning the corpse round so that it became released from the grip of the willow roots. A moment later it had turned completely over, the dead face uppermost, staring at the sky. It lay on the edge of the main stream.

In another moment it would be swept away.

The Swede started to save it, shouting again something I did not catch about a "proper burial" — and then abruptly dropped upon his knees on the sand and covered his eyes with his hands. I was beside him in an instant.

I saw what he had seen.

For just as the body swung round to the current the face and the exposed chest turned full towards us, and showed plainly how the skin and flesh were indented with small hollows, beautifully formed, and exactly similar in shape and kind to the sand-funnels that we had found all over the island.

"Their mark!" I heard my companion mutter under his breath. "Their awful mark!"

And when I turned my eyes again from his ghastly face to the river, the current had done its work, and the body had been swept away into mid-stream and was already beyond our reach and almost out of sight, turning over and over on the waves like an otter.

The INSANITY *of* JONES.
-A Study in Reincarnation-

I.

Adventures come to the adventurous, and mysterious things fall in the way of those who, with
wonder and imagination, are on the watch for
them; but the majority of people go past the doors that are
half ajar, thinking them closed, and fail to notice the faint
stirrings of the great curtain that hangs ever in the form
of appearances between them and the world of causes
behind.

For only to the few whose inner senses have been

quickened, perchance by some strange suffering in the depths, or by a natural temperament bequeathed from a remote past, comes the knowledge, not too welcome, that this greater world lies ever at their elbow, and that any moment a chance combination of moods and forces may invite them to cross the shifting frontier.

Some, however, are born with this awful certainty in their hearts, and are called to no apprenticeship, and to this select company Jones undoubtedly belonged.

All his life he had realised that his senses brought to him merely a more or less interesting set of sham appearances; that space, as men measure it, was utterly misleading; that time, as the clock ticked it in a succession of minutes, was arbitrary nonsense; and, in fact, that all his sensory perceptions were but a clumsy representation of *real* things behind the curtain — things he was for ever trying to get at, and that sometimes he actually did get at.

He had always been tremblingly aware that he stood on the borderland of another region, a region where time and space were merely forms of thought, where ancient memories lay open to the sight, and where the forces behind each human life stood plainly revealed and he could see the hidden springs at the very heart of the world. Moreover, the fact that he was a clerk in a fire insurance office, and did his work with strict attention, never allowed him to forget for one moment that, just beyond the dingy brick walls where the hundred men scribbled with pointed pens beneath the electric lamps, there existed this glorious region where the important part of himself dwelt and moved and had its being. For in this region he pictured himself playing the part of a spectator to his ordinary workaday life, watching, like a king, the stream of events, but untouched in his own soul by the dirt, the noise, and the vulgar commotion of the outer world.

And this was no poetic dream merely. Jones was not playing prettily with idealism to amuse himself. It was a living, working belief. So convinced was he that the external world was the result of a vast deception practised upon him by the gross senses, that when he stared at a great building like St. Paul's he felt it would not very much surprise him to see it suddenly quiver like a shape of jelly and then melt utterly away, while in its place stood all at once revealed the mass of colour, or the great intricate vibrations, or the splendid sound — the spiritual idea — which it represented in stone.

For something in this way it was that his mind worked.

Yet, to all appearances, and in the satisfaction of all business claims, Jones was normal and unenterprising. He felt nothing but contempt for the wave of modern psychism. He hardly knew the meaning of such words as "clairvoyance" and "clairaudience." He had never felt the least desire to join the Theosophical Society and to speculate in theories of astral-plane life, or elementals. He attended no meetings of the Psychical Research Society, and knew no anxiety as to whether his "aura" was black or blue; nor was he conscious of the slightest wish to mix in with the revival of cheap occultism which proves so attractive to weak minds of mystical tendencies and unleashed imaginations.

There were certain things he *knew*, but none he cared to argue about; and he shrank instinctively from attempting to put names to the contents of this other region, knowing well that such names could only limit and define things that, according to any standards in use in the ordinary world, were simply undefinable and illusive.

So that, although this was the way his mind worked, there was clearly a very strong leaven of common sense in Jones. In a word, the man the world and the office knew as Jones *was* Jones. The name summed him up and labelled him correctly — John Enderby Jones.

Among the things that he *knew*, and therefore never cared to speak or speculate about, one was that he plainly saw himself as the inheritor of a long series of past lives, the net result of painful evolution, always as himself, of course, but in numerous different bodies each determined by the behaviour of the preceding one. The present John Jones was the last result to date of all the previous thinking, feeling, and doing of John Jones in earlier bodies and in other centuries. He pretended to no details, nor claimed distinguished ancestry, for he realised his past must have been utterly commonplace and insignificant to have produced his present; but he was just as sure he had been at this weary game for ages as that he breathed, and it never occurred to him to argue, to doubt, or to ask questions. And one result of this belief was that his thoughts dwelt upon the past rather than upon the future; that he read much history, and felt specially drawn to certain periods whose spirit he understood instinctively as though he had lived in them; and that he found all religions uninteresting because, almost without exception, they start from the present and speculate ahead as to what men shall become, instead of looking back and speculating why men have got here as they are.

In the insurance office he did his work exceedingly well, but without much personal ambition. Men and women he regarded as the impersonal instruments for inflicting upon him the pain or pleasure he had earned by his past workings, for chance had no place in his scheme of things at all; and while he recognised that the practical world could not get along unless every man did his work thoroughly and conscientiously, he took no interest in the accumulation of fame or money for himself, and simply, therefore, did his plain duty, with indifference as to results.

In common with others who lead a strictly impersonal life, he possessed the quality of utter bravery, and was always ready to face any combination of circumstances, no matter how terrible, because he saw in them the just working-out of past causes he had himself set in motion which could not be dodged or modified. And whereas the majority of people had little meaning for him, either by way of attraction or repulsion, the moment he met some one with whom he felt his past had been *vitally* interwoven his whole inner being leapt up instantly and shouted the fact in his face, and he regulated his life with the utmost skill and caution, like a sentry on watch for an enemy whose feet could already be heard approaching.

Thus, while the great majority of men and women left him uninfluenced — since he regarded them as so many souls merely passing with him along the great stream of evolution — there were, here and there, individuals with whom he recognised that his smallest intercourse was of the gravest importance. These were persons with whom he knew in every fibre of his being he had accounts to settle, pleasant or otherwise, arising out of dealings in past lives; and into his relations with these few, therefore, he concentrated as it were the efforts that most people spread over their intercourse with a far greater number. By what means he picked out these few individuals only those conversant with the startling processes of the subconscious memory may say, but the point was that Jones believed the main purpose, if not quite the entire purpose, of his present incarnation lay in his faithful and thorough settling of these accounts, and that if he sought to evade the least detail of such settling, no matter how unpleasant, he would have lived in vain, and would return to his next incarnation with this added duty to perform. For according to his beliefs there was no Chance, and could be no ultimate shirking, and to avoid a problem was merely to waste time and lose opportunities for development.

And there was one individual with whom Jones had long understood clearly he had a very large account to settle, and towards the accomplishment of which all the main currents of his being seemed to bear him with unswerving purpose. For, when he first entered the insurance office as a junior clerk ten years before, and through a glass door had caught sight of this man seated in an inner room, one of his sudden overwhelming flashes of intuitive memory had burst up into him from the depths, and he had seen, as in a flame of blinding light, a symbolical picture of the future rising out of a dreadful past, and he had, without any act of definite volition, marked down this man for a real account to be settled.

"With *that* man I shall have much to do," he said to himself, as he noted the big face look up and meet his eye through the glass. "There is something I cannot shirk — a vital relation out of the past of both of us."

And he went to his desk trembling a little, and with shaking knees, as though the memory of some terrible pain had suddenly laid its icy hand upon his heart and touched the scar of a great horror. It was a moment of genuine terror when their eyes had met through the glass door, and he was conscious of an inward shrinking and loathing that seized upon him with great violence and convinced him in a single second that the settling of this account would be almost, perhaps, more than he could manage.

The vision passed as swiftly as it came, dropping back again into the submerged region of his consciousness; but he never forgot it, and the whole of his life thereafter became a sort of natural though undeliberate preparation for the fulfilment of the great duty when the time should be ripe.

In those days — ten years ago — this man was the Assistant Manager, but had since been promoted as Manager to one of the company's local branches; and soon afterwards Jones had likewise found himself transferred to this same branch. A little later, again, the branch at Liverpool, one of the most important, had been in peril owing to misman- agement and defalcation, and the man had gone to take charge of it, and again, by mere chance apparently, Jones had been promoted to the same place. And this pursuit of the Assistant Manager had continued for several years, often, too, in the most curious fashion; and though Jones had never exchanged a single word with him, or been so

much as noticed indeed by the great man, the clerk understood perfectly well that these moves in the game were all
part of a definite purpose. Never for one moment did he
doubt that the Invisibles behind the veil were slowly and
surely arranging the details of it all so as to lead up suitably
to the climax demanded by justice, a climax in which
himself and the Manager would play the leading *rôles*.

"It is inevitable," he said to himself, "and I feel it may
be terrible; but when the moment comes I shall be ready,
and I pray God that I may face it properly and act like a
man."

Moreover, as the years passed, and nothing happened,
he felt the horror closing in upon him with steady increase,
for the fact was Jones hated and loathed the Manager with
an intensity of feeling he had never before experienced
towards any human being. He shrank from his presence,
and from the glance of his eyes, as though he remembered
to have suffered nameless cruelties at his hands; and he
slowly began to realise, moreover, that the matter to be
settled between them was one of very ancient standing,
and that the nature of the settlement was a discharge of
accumulated punishment which would probably be very
dreadful in the manner of its fulfilment.

When, therefore, the chief cashier one day informed
him that the man was to be in London again — this time
as General Manager of the head office — and said that he
was charged to find a private secretary for him from among
the best clerks, and further intimated that the selection
had fallen upon himself, Jones accepted the promotion
quietly, fatalistically, yet with a degree of inward loathing

hardly to be described. For he saw in this merely another move in the evolution of the inevitable Nemesis which he simply dared not seek to frustrate by any personal consideration; and at the same time he was conscious of a certain feeling of relief that the suspense of waiting might soon be mitigated. A secret sense of satisfaction, therefore, accompanied the unpleasant change, and Jones was able to hold himself perfectly well in hand when it was carried into effect and he was formally introduced as private secretary to the General Manager.

Now the Manager was a large, fat man, with a very red face and bags beneath his eyes. Being short-sighted, he wore glasses that seemed to magnify his eyes, which were always a little bloodshot. In hot weather a sort of thin slime covered his cheeks, for he perspired easily. His head was almost entirely bald, and over his turn-down collar his great neck folded in two distinct reddish collops of flesh. His hands were big and his fingers almost massive in thickness.

He was an excellent business man, of sane judgment and firm will, without enough imagination to confuse his course of action by showing him possible alternatives; and his integrity and ability caused him to be held in universal respect by the world of business and finance. In the important regions of a man's character, however, and at heart, he was coarse, brutal almost to savagery, without consideration for others, and as a result often cruelly unjust to his helpless subordinates.

In moments of temper, which were not infrequent, his face turned a dull purple, while the top of his bald head shone by contrast like white marble, and the bags under his eyes swelled till it seemed they would presently explode with a pop. And at these times he presented a distinctly repulsive appearance.

But to a private secretary like Jones, who did his duty regardless of whether his employer was beast or angel, and whose mainspring was principle and not emotion, this made little difference. Within the narrow limits in which any one could satisfy such a man, he pleased the General Manager; and more than once his piercing intuitive faculty, amounting almost to clairvoyance, assisted the chief in a fashion that served to bring the two closer together than might otherwise have been the case, and caused the man to respect in his assistant a power of which he possessed not even the germ himself. It was a curious relationship that grew up between the two, and the cashier, who enjoyed the credit of having made the selection, profited by it indirectly as much as any one else.

So for some time the work of the office continued normally and very prosperously. John Enderby Jones received a good salary, and in the outward appearance of the two chief characters in this history there was little change noticeable, except that the Manager grew fatter and redder, and the secretary observed that his own hair was beginning to show rather greyish at the temples.

There were, however, two changes in progress, and they both had to do with Jones, and are important to mention.

One was that he began to dream evilly. In the region of deep sleep, where the possibility of significant dreaming first develops itself, he was tormented more and more with vivid scenes and pictures in which a tall thin man, dark and sinister of countenance, and with bad eyes, was closely associated with himself. Only the setting was that of a past age, with costumes of centuries gone by, and the scenes had to do with dreadful cruelties that could not belong to modern life as he knew it.

The other change was also significant, but is not so easy to describe, for he had in fact become aware that some new portion of himself, hitherto unawakened, had stirred slowly into life out of the very depths of his consciousness. This new part of himself amounted almost to another personality, and he never observed its least manifestation without a strange thrill at his heart.

For he understood that it had begun to watch the Manager!

II.

It was the habit of Jones, since he was compelled to work among conditions that were utterly distasteful, to withdraw his mind wholly from business once the day was over. During office hours he kept the strictest possible watch upon himself, and turned the key on all inner dreams, lest any sudden uprush from the deeps should interfere with his duty. But, once the working day was over, the gates flew open, and he began to enjoy himself.

He read no modern books on the subjects that interested him, and, as already said, he followed no course of training, nor belonged to any society that dabbled with half-told mysteries; but, once released from the office desk in the Manager's room, he simply and naturally entered the other region, because he was an old inhabitant, a rightful denizen, and because he belonged there. It was, in fact, really a case of dual personality; and a carefully drawn agreement existed between Jones-of-the-fire-insurance-office and Jones-of-the-mysteries, by the terms of which, under heavy penalties, neither region claimed him out of hours.

For the moment he reached his rooms under the roof in Bloomsbury, and had changed his city coat to another, the iron doors of the office clanged far behind him, and in front, before his very eyes, rolled up the beautiful gates of ivory, and he entered into the places of flowers and singing and wonderful veiled forms. Sometimes he quite lost touch with the outer world, forgetting to eat his dinner or go to bed, and lay in a state of trance, his consciousness working far out of the body. And on other occasions he walked the streets on air, half-way between the two regions, unable to distinguish between incarnate and discarnate forms, and not very far, probably, beyond the strata where poets, saints, and the greatest artists have moved and thought and found their inspiration. But this was only when some insistent bodily claim prevented his full release, and more often than not he was entirely independent of his physical portion and free of the real region, without let or hindrance.

One evening he reached home utterly exhausted after the burden of the day's work. The Manager had been more than usually brutal, unjust, ill-tempered, and Jones had been almost persuaded out of his settled policy of contempt into answering back. Everything seemed to have gone amiss, and the man's coarse, underbred nature had been in the ascendant all day long: he had thumped the desk with his great fists, abused, found fault unreasonably, uttered outrageous things, and behaved generally as he actually was — beneath the thin veneer of acquired business varnish. He had done and said everything to wound all that was woundable in an ordinary secretary, and though Jones fortunately dwelt in a region from which he looked down upon such a man as he might look down on the blundering of a savage animal, the strain had nevertheless told severely upon him, and he reached home wondering for the first time in his life whether there was perhaps a point beyond which he would be unable to restrain himself any longer.

For something out of the usual had happened. At the close of a passage of great stress between the two, every nerve in the secretary's body tingling from undeserved abuse, the Manager had suddenly turned full upon him, in the corner of the private room where the safes stood, in such a way that the glare of his red eyes, magnified by the glasses, looked straight into his own. And at this very second that other personality in Jones — the one that was ever *watching* — rose up swiftly from the deeps within and held a mirror to his face.

A moment of flame and vision rushed over him, and for one single second — one merciless second of clear sight — he saw the Manager as the tall dark man of his evil dreams, and the knowledge that he had suffered at his hands some awful injury in the past crashed through his mind like the report of a cannon.

It all flashed upon him and was gone, changing him from fire to ice, and then back again to fire; and he left the office with the certain conviction in his heart that the time for his final settlement with the man, the time for the inevitable retribution, was at last drawing very near.

According to his invariable custom, however, he succeeded in putting the memory of all this unpleasantness out of his mind with the changing of his office coat, and after dozing a little in his leather chair before the fire, he started out as usual for dinner in the Soho French restaurant, and began to dream himself away into the region of flowers and singing, and to commune with the Invisibles that were the very sources of his real life and being.

For it was in this way that his mind worked, and the habits of years had crystallised into rigid lines along which it was now necessary and inevitable for him to act.

At the door of the little restaurant he stopped short, a half-remembered appointment in his mind. He had made an engagement with some one, but where, or with whom, had entirely slipped his memory. He thought it was for dinner, or else to meet just after dinner, and for a second it came back to him that it had something to do with the office, but, whatever it was, he was quite unable to recall it, and a reference to his pocket engagement book showed only a blank page. Evidently he had even omitted to enter it; and after standing a moment vainly trying to recall either the time, place, or person, he went in and sat down.

But though the details had escaped him, his subconscious memory seemed to know all about it, for he experienced a sudden sinking of the heart, accompanied by a sense of foreboding anticipation, and felt that beneath his exhaustion there lay a centre of tremendous excitement. The emotion caused by the engagement was at work, and would presently cause the actual details of the appointment to reappear.

Inside the restaurant the feeling increased, instead of passing: some one was waiting for him somewhere — some one whom he had definitely arranged to meet. He was expected by a person that very night and just about that very time. But by whom? Where? A curious inner trembling came over him, and he made a strong effort to hold himself in hand and to be ready for anything that might come.

And then suddenly came the knowledge that the place of appointment was this very restaurant, and, further, that the person he had promised to meet was already here, waiting somewhere quite close beside him.

He looked up nervously and began to examine the faces round him. The majority of the diners were Frenchmen, chattering loudly with much gesticulation and laughter; and there was a fair sprinkling of clerks like himself who came because the prices were low and the food good, but there was no single face that he recognised until his glance fell upon the occupant of the corner seat opposite, generally filled by himself.

"There's the man who's waiting for me!" thought Jones instantly.

He knew it at once. The man, he saw, was sitting well back into the corner, with a thick overcoat buttoned tightly up to the chin. His skin was very white, and a heavy black beard grew far up over his cheeks. At first the secretary took him for a stranger, but when he looked up and their eyes met, a sense of familiarity flashed across him, and for a second or two Jones imagined he was staring at a man he had known years before. For, barring the beard, it was the face of an elderly clerk who had occupied the next desk to his own when he first entered the service of the insurance company, and had shown him the most painstaking kindness and sympathy in the early difficulties of his work. But a moment later the illusion passed, for he remembered that Thorpe had been dead at least five years. The similarity of the eyes was obviously a mere suggestive trick of memory.

The two men stared at one another for several seconds, and then Jones began to act *instinctively*, and because he had to. He crossed over and took the vacant seat at the other's table, facing him; for he felt it was somehow imperative to explain why he was late, and how it was he had almost forgotten the engagement altogether.

No honest excuse, however, came to his assistance, though his mind had begun to work furiously.

"Yes, you *are* late," said the man quietly, before he could find a single word to utter. "But it doesn't matter. Also, you had forgotten the appointment, but that makes no difference either."

"I knew — that there was an engagement," Jones stammered, passing his hand over his forehead; "but somehow — "

"You will recall it presently," continued the other in a gentle voice, and smiling a little. "It was in deep sleep last night we arranged this, and the unpleasant occurrences of today have for the moment obliterated it."

A faint memory stirred within him as the man spoke, and a grove of trees with moving forms hovered before his eyes and then vanished again, while for an instant the stranger seemed to be capable of self-distortion and to have assumed vast proportions, with wonderful flaming eyes.

"Oh!" he gasped. "It was there — in the other region?"

"Of course," said the other, with a smile that illumined his whole face. "You will remember presently, all in good time, and meanwhile you have no cause to feel afraid."

There was a wonderful soothing quality in the man's voice, like the whispering of a great wind, and the clerk felt calmer at once. They sat a little while longer, but he could not remember that they talked much or ate anything. He only recalled afterwards that the head waiter came up and whispered something in his ear, and that he glanced round and saw the other people were looking at him curiously, some of them laughing, and that his companion then got up and led the way out of the restaurant.

They walked hurriedly through the streets, neither of them speaking; and Jones was so intent upon getting back the whole history of the affair from the region of deep sleep, that he barely noticed the way they took. Yet it was clear he knew where they were bound for just as well as his companion, for he crossed the streets often ahead of him, diving down alleys without hesitation, and the other followed always without correction.

The pavements were very full, and the usual night crowds of London were surging to and fro in the glare of the shop lights, but somehow no one impeded their rapid movements, and they seemed to pass through the people as if they were smoke. And, as they went, the pedestrians and traffic grew less and less, and they soon passed the Mansion House and the deserted space in front of the Royal Exchange, and so on down Fenchurch Street and within sight of the Tower of London, rising dim and shadowy in the smoky air.

Jones remembered all this perfectly well, and thought it was his intense preoccupation that made the distance seem so short. But it was when the Tower was left behind and they turned northwards that he began to notice how altered everything was, and saw that they were in a neighbourhood where houses were suddenly scarce, and lanes and fields beginning, and that their only light was the stars overhead. And, as the deeper consciousness more and more asserted itself to the exclusion of the surface happenings of his mere body during the day, the sense of exhaustion vanished, and he realised that he was moving somewhere in the region of causes behind the veil, beyond the gross deceptions of the senses, and released from the clumsy spell of space and time.

Without great surprise, therefore, he turned and saw that his companion had altered, had shed his overcoat and black hat, and was moving beside him absolutely *without sound*. For a brief second he saw him, tall as a tree, extending through space like a great shadow, misty and wavering of outline, followed by a sound like wings in the darkness; but, when he stopped, fear clutching at his heart, the other resumed his former proportions, and Jones could plainly see his normal outline against the green field behind.

Then the secretary saw him fumbling at his neck, and at the same moment the black beard came away from the face in his hand.

"Then you *are* Thorpe!" he gasped, yet somehow without overwhelming surprise.

They stood facing one another in the lonely lane, trees meeting overhead and hiding the stars, and a sound of mournful sighing among the branches.

"I am Thorpe," was the answer in a voice that almost seemed part of the wind. "And I have come out of our far past to help you, for my debt to you is large, and in this life I had but small opportunity to repay."

Jones thought quickly of the man's kindness to him in the office, and a great wave of feeling surged through him as he began to remember dimly the friend by whose side he had already climbed, perhaps through vast ages of his soul's evolution.

"To help me *now?*" he whispered.

"You will understand me when you enter into your real memory and recall how great a debt I have to pay for old faithful kindnesses of long ago," sighed the other in a voice like falling wind.

"Between us, though, there can be no question of *debt*," Jones heard himself saying, and remembered the reply that floated to him on the air and the smile that lightened for a moment the stern eyes facing him.

"Not of debt, indeed, but of privilege."

Jones felt his heart leap out towards this man, this old friend, tried by centuries and still faithful. He made a movement to seize his hand. But the other shifted like a thing of mist, and for a moment the clerk's head swam and his eyes seemed to fail.

"Then you are *dead?*" he said under his breath with a slight shiver.

"Five years ago I left the body you knew," replied Thorpe. "I tried to help you then instinctively, not fully recognising you. But now I can accomplish far more."

With an awful sense of foreboding and dread in his heart, the secretary was beginning to understand.

"It has to do with — with — ?"

"Your past dealings with the Manager," came the answer, as the wind rose louder among the branches overhead and carried off the remainder of the sentence into the air.

Jones's memory, which was just beginning to stir among the deepest layers of all, shut down suddenly with a snap, and he followed his companion over fields and down sweet-smelling lanes where the air was fragrant and cool, till they came to a large house, standing gaunt and lonely in the shadows at the edge of a wood. It was wrapped in utter stillness, with windows heavily draped in black, and the clerk, as he looked, felt such an overpowering wave of sadness invade him that his eyes began to burn and smart, and he was conscious of a desire to shed tears.

The key made a harsh noise as it turned in the lock, and when the door swung open into a lofty hall they heard a confused sound of rustling and whispering, as of a great throng of people pressing forward to meet them. The air seemed full of swaying movement, and Jones was certain he saw hands held aloft and dim faces claiming recognition, while in his heart, already oppressed by the approaching burden of vast accumulated memories, he was aware of the *uncoiling of something* that had been asleep for ages.

As they advanced he heard the doors close with a muffled thunder behind them, and saw that the shadows seemed to retreat and shrink away towards the interior of the house, carrying the hands and faces with them. He heard the wind singing round the walls and over the roof, and its wailing voice mingled with the sound of deep, collective breathing that filled the house like the murmur of a sea; and as they walked up the broad staircase and through the vaulted rooms, where pillars rose like the stems of trees, he knew that the building was crowded, row upon row, with the thronging memories of his own long past.

"This is the *House of the Past*," whispered Thorpe beside him, as they moved silently from room to room; "the house of *your* past. It is full from cellar to roof with the memories of what you have done, thought, and felt from the earliest stages of your evolution until now.

"The house climbs up almost to the clouds, and stretches back into the heart of the wood you saw outside, but the remoter halls are filled with the ghosts of ages ago too many to count, and even if we were able to waken them you could not remember them now. Some day, though, they will come and claim you, and you must know them, and answer their questions, for they can never rest till they have exhausted themselves again through you, and justice has been perfectly worked out.

"But now follow me closely, and you shall see the particular memory for which I am permitted to be your guide, so that you may know and understand a great force in your present life, and may use the sword of justice, or rise to the level of a great forgiveness, according to your degree of power."

Icy thrills ran through the trembling clerk, and as he walked slowly beside his companion he heard from the vaults below, as well as from more distant regions of the vast building, the stirring and sighing of the serried ranks of sleepers, sounding in the still air like a chord swept from unseen strings stretched somewhere among the very foundations of the house.

Stealthily, picking their way among the great pillars, they moved up the sweeping staircase and through several dark corridors and halls, and presently stopped outside a small door in an archway where the shadows were very deep.

"Remain close by my side, and remember to utter no cry," whispered the voice of his guide, and as the clerk turned to reply he saw his face was stern to whiteness and even shone a little in the darkness.

The room they entered seemed at first to be pitchy black, but gradually the secretary perceived a faint reddish glow against the farther end, and thought he saw figures moving silently to and fro.

"Now watch!" whispered Thorpe, as they pressed close to the wall near the door and waited. "But remember to keep absolute silence. It is a torture scene."

Jones felt utterly afraid, and would have turned to fly if he dared, for an indescribable terror seized him and his knees shook; but some power that made escape impossible held him remorselessly there, and with eyes glued on the spots of light he crouched against the wall and waited.

The figures began to move more swiftly, each in its own dim light that shed no radiance beyond itself, and he heard a soft clanking of chains and the voice of a man groaning in pain. Then came the sound of a door closing, and thereafter Jones saw but one figure, the figure of an old man, naked entirely, and fastened with chains to an iron framework on the floor. His memory gave a sudden leap of fear as he looked, for the features and white beard were familiar, and he recalled them as though of yesterday.

The other figures had disappeared, and the old man became the centre of the terrible picture. Slowly, with ghastly groans; as the heat below him increased into a steady glow, the aged body rose in a curve of agony, resting on the iron frame only where the chains held wrists and ankles fast. Cries and gasps filled the air, and Jones felt exactly as though they came from his own throat, and as if the chains were burning into his own wrists and ankles, and the heat scorching the skin and flesh upon his own back. He began to writhe and twist himself.

"Spain!" whispered the voice at his side, "and four hundred years ago."

"And the purpose?" gasped the perspiring clerk, though he knew quite well what the answer must be.

"To extort the name of a friend, to his death and betrayal," came the reply through the darkness.

A sliding panel opened with a little rattle in the wall immediately above the rack, and a face, framed in the same red glow, appeared and looked down upon the dying victim. Jones was only just able to choke a scream, for he recognised the tall dark man of his dreams. With horrible, gloating eyes he gazed down upon the writhing form of the old man, and his lips moved as in speaking, though no words were actually audible.

"He asks again for the name," explained the other, as the clerk struggled with the intense hatred and loathing that threatened every moment to result in screams and action. His ankles and wrists pained him so that he could scarcely keep still, but a merciless power held him to the scene.

He saw the old man, with a fierce cry, raise his tortured head and spit up into the face at the panel, and then the shutter slid back again, and a moment later the increased glow beneath the body, accompanied by awful writhing, told of the application of further heat. There came the odour of burning flesh; the white beard curled and burned to a crisp; the body fell back limp upon the red-hot iron, and then shot up again in fresh agony; cry after cry, the most awful in the world, rang out with deadened sound between the four walls; and again the panel slid back creaking, and revealed the dreadful face of the torturer.

Again the name was asked for, and again it was refused; and this time, after the closing of the panel, a door opened, and the tall thin man with the evil face came slowly into the chamber. His features were savage with rage and disappointment, and in the dull red glow that fell upon them he looked like a very prince of devils. In his hand he held a pointed iron at white heat.

"Now the murder!" came from Thorpe in a whisper that sounded as if it was outside the building and far away.

Jones knew quite well what was coming, but was unable even to close his eyes. He felt all the fearful pains himself just as though he were actually the sufferer; but now, as he stared, he felt something more besides; and when the tall man deliberately approached the rack and plunged the heated iron first into one eye and then into the other, he heard the faint fizzing of it, and felt his own eyes burst in frightful pain from his head. At the same moment, unable longer to control himself, he uttered a wild shriek and dashed forward to seize the torturer and tear him to a thousand pieces. Instantly, in a flash, the entire scene vanished; darkness rushed in to fill the room, and he felt himself lifted off his feet by some force like a great wind and borne swiftly away into space.

W hen he recovered his senses he was standing just outside the house and the figure of Thorpe was beside him in the gloom. The great doors were in the act of closing behind him, but before they shut he fancied he caught a glimpse of an immense veiled figure standing upon the threshold, with flaming eyes, and in his hand a bright weapon like a shining sword of fire.

"Come quickly now — all is over!" Thorpe whispered.

"And the dark man — ?" gasped the clerk, as he moved swiftly by the other's side.

"In this present life is the Manager of the company."

"And the victim?"

"Was yourself!"

"And the friend he — *I* refused to betray?"

"I was that friend," answered Thorpe, his voice with every moment sounding more and more like the cry of the wind. "You gave your life in agony to save mine."

"And again, in this life, we have all three been together?"

"Yes. Such forces are not soon or easily exhausted, and

justice is not satisfied till all have reaped what they sowed."

Jones had an odd feeling that he was slipping away into some other state of consciousness. Thorpe began to seem unreal. Presently he would be unable to ask more questions. He felt utterly sick and faint with it all, and his strength was ebbing.

"Oh, quick!" he cried, "now tell me more. Why did I see this? What must I do?"

The wind swept across the field on their right and entered the wood beyond with a great roar, and the air round him seemed filled with voices and the rushing of hurried movement.

"To the ends of justice," answered the other, as though speaking out of the centre of the wind and from a distance, "which sometimes is entrusted to the hands of those who suffered and were strong. One wrong cannot be put right by another wrong, but your life has been so worthy that the opportunity is given to —"

The voice grew fainter and fainter, already it was far overhead with the rushing wind.

"You may punish or —"

Here Jones lost sight of Thorpe's figure altogether, for he seemed to have vanished and melted away into the wood behind him. His voice sounded far across the trees, very weak, and ever rising.

"Or if you can rise to the level of a great forgiveness —"

The voice became inaudible. . . . The wind came crying out of the wood again.

J ones shivered and stared about him. He shook himself violently and rubbed his eyes. The room was dark, the fire was out; he felt cold and stiff. He got up out of his armchair, still trembling, and lit the gas. Outside the wind was howling, and when he looked at his watch he saw that it was very late and he must go to bed.

He had not even changed his office coat; he must have fallen asleep in the chair as soon as he came in, and he had slept for several hours. Certainly he had eaten no dinner, for he felt ravenous.

III.

Next day, and for several weeks thereafter, the business of the office went on as usual, and Jones did his work well and behaved outwardly with perfect propriety. No more visions troubled him, and his relations with the Manager became, if anything, somewhat smoother and easier.

True, the man *looked* a little different, because the clerk kept seeing him with his inner and outer eye promiscuously, so that one moment he was broad and red-faced, and the next he was tall, thin, and dark, enveloped, as it were, in a sort of black atmosphere tinged with red. While at times a confusion of the two sights took place, and Jones saw the two faces mingled in a composite countenance that was very horrible indeed to contemplate. But, beyond this occasional change in the outward appearance of the Manager, there was nothing that the secretary noticed as the result of his vision, and business went on more or less as before, and perhaps even with a little less friction.

But in the rooms under the roof in Bloomsbury it was different, for there it was perfectly clear to Jones that Thorpe had come to take up his abode with him. He never saw him, but he knew all the time he was there. Every night on returning from his work he was greeted by the well-known whisper, "Be ready when I give the sign!" and often in the night he woke up suddenly out of deep sleep and was aware that Thorpe had that minute moved away from his bed and was standing waiting and watching somewhere in the darkness of the room. Often he followed him down the stairs, though the dim gas jet on the landings never revealed his outline; and sometimes he did not come into the room at all, but hovered outside the window, peering through the dirty panes, or sending his whisper into the chamber in the whistling of the wind.

For Thorpe had come to stay, and Jones knew that he would not get rid of him until he had fulfilled the ends of justice and accomplished the purpose for which he was waiting.

Meanwhile, as the days passed, he went through a tremendous struggle with himself, and came to the perfectly honest decision that the "level of a great forgiveness" was impossible for him, and that he must therefore accept the alternative and use the secret knowledge placed in his hands — and execute justice. And once this decision was arrived at, he noticed that Thorpe no longer left him alone during the day as before, but now accompanied him to the office and stayed more or less at his side all through business hours as well. His whisper made itself heard in the streets and in the train, and even in the Manager's room where he worked; sometimes warning, sometimes urging, but never for a moment suggesting the abandonment of the main purpose, and more than once so plainly audible that the clerk felt certain others must have heard it as well as himself.

The obsession was complete. He felt he was always under Thorpe's eye day and night, and he knew he must acquit himself like a man when the moment came, or prove a failure in his own sight as well in the sight of the other.

And now that his mind was made up, nothing could prevent the carrying out of the sentence. He bought a pistol, and spent his Saturday afternoons practising at a target in lonely places along the Essex shore, marking out in the sand the exact measurements of the Manager's room. Sundays he occupied in like fashion, putting up at an inn overnight for the purpose, spending the money that usually went into the savings bank on travelling expenses and cartridges. Everything was done very thoroughly, for there must be no possibility of failure; and at the end of several weeks he had become so expert with his six-shooter that at a distance of 25 feet, which was the greatest length of the Manager's room, he could pick the inside out of a halfpenny nine times out of a dozen, and leave a clean, unbroken rim.

There was not the slightest desire to delay. He had thought the matter over from every point of view his mind could reach, and his purpose was inflexible. Indeed, he felt proud to think that he had been chosen as the instrument of justice in the infliction of so well-deserved and so terrible a punishment. Vengeance may have had some part in his decision, but he could not help that, for he still felt at times the hot chains burning his wrists and ankles with fierce agony through to the bone. He remembered the hideous pain of his slowly roasting back, and the point when he thought death must intervene to end his suffering, but instead new powers of endurance had surged up in him, and awful further stretches of pain had opened up, and unconsciousness seemed farther off than ever. Then at last the hot irons in his eyes. . . . It all came back to him, and caused him to break out in icy perspiration at the mere thought of it. . . the vile face at the panel. . . the expression of the dark face. . . . His fingers worked. His blood boiled. It was utterly impossible to keep the idea of vengeance altogether out of his mind.

Several times he was temporarily baulked of his prey. Odd things happened to stop him when he was on the point of action. The first day, for instance, the Manager fainted from the heat. Another time when he had decided to do the deed, the Manager did not come down to the office at all. And a third time, when his hand was actually in his hip pocket, he suddenly heard Thorpe's horrid whisper telling him to wait, and turning, he saw that the head cashier had entered the room noiselessly without his noticing it. Thorpe evidently knew what he was about, and did not intend to let the clerk bungle the matter.

He fancied, moreover, that the head cashier was watching him. He was always meeting him in unexpected corners and places, and the cashier never seemed to have an adequate excuse for being there. His movements seemed suddenly of particular interest to others in the office as well, for clerks were always being sent to ask him unnecessary questions, and there was apparently a general design to keep him under a sort of surveillance, so that he was never much alone with the Manager in the private room where they worked. And once the cashier had even gone so far as to suggest that he could take his holiday earlier than usual if he liked, as the work had been very arduous of late and the heat exceedingly trying.

He noticed, too, that he was sometimes followed by a certain individual in the streets, a careless-looking sort of man, who never came face to face with him, or actually ran into him, but who was always in his train or omnibus, and whose eye he often caught observing him over the top of his newspaper, and who on one occasion was even waiting at the door of his lodgings when he came out to dine.

There were other indications too, of various sorts, that led him to think something was at work to defeat his purpose, and that he must act at once before these hostile forces could prevent.

And so the end came very swiftly, and was thoroughly approved by Thorpe.

It was towards the close of July, and one of the hottest days London had ever known, for the City was like an oven, and the particles of dust seemed to burn the throats of the unfortunate toilers in street and office. The portly Manager, who suffered cruelly owing to his size, came down perspiring and gasping with the heat. He carried a light-coloured umbrella to protect his head.

"He'll want something more than that, though!" Jones laughed quietly to himself when he saw him enter.

The pistol was safely in his hip pocket, every one of its six chambers loaded.

The Manager saw the smile on his face, and gave him a long steady look as he sat down to his desk in the corner. A few minutes later he touched the bell for the head cashier — a single ring — and then asked Jones to fetch some papers from another safe in the room upstairs.

A deep inner trembling seized the secretary as he noticed these precautions, for he saw that the hostile forces were at work against him, and yet he felt he could delay no longer and must act that very morning, interference or no interference. However, he went obediently up in the lift to the next floor, and while fumbling with the combination of the safe, known only to himself, the cashier, and the Manager, he again heard Thorpe's horrid whisper just behind him:

"You must do it today! You must do it today!"

He came down again with the papers, and found the Manager alone. The room was like a furnace, and a wave of dead heated air met him in the face as he went in. The moment he passed the doorway he realised that he had been the subject of conversation between the head cashier and his enemy. They had been discussing him. Perhaps an inkling of his secret had somehow got into their minds. They had been watching him for days past. They had become suspicious.

Clearly, he must act now, or let the opportunity slip by

perhaps for ever. He heard Thorpe's voice in his ear, but this time it was no mere whisper, but a plain human voice, speaking out loud.

"Now!" it said. "Do it now!"

The room was empty. Only the Manager and himself were in it.

Jones turned from his desk where he had been standing, and locked the door leading into the main office. He saw the army of clerks scribbling in their shirt-sleeves, for the upper half of the door was of glass. He had perfect control of himself, and his heart was beating steadily.

The Manager, hearing the key turn in the lock, looked up sharply.

"What's that you're doing?" he asked quickly.

"Only locking the door, sir," replied the secretary in a quite even voice.

"Why? Who told you to — ?"

"The voice of Justice, sir," replied Jones, looking steadily into the hated face.

The Manager looked black for a moment, and stared angrily across the room at him. Then suddenly his expression changed as he stared, and he tried to smile. It was meant to be a kind smile evidently, but it only succeeded in being frightened.

"That is a good idea in this weather," he said lightly, "but it would be much better to lock it on the *outside*, wouldn't it, Mr. Jones?"

"I think not, sir. You might escape me then. Now you can't."

Jones took his pistol out and pointed it at the other's

face. Down the barrel he saw the features of the tall dark man, evil and sinister. Then the outline trembled a little and the face of the Manager slipped back into its place. It was white as death, and shining with perspiration.

"You tortured me to death four hundred years ago," said the clerk in the same steady voice, "and now the dispensers of justice have chosen me to punish you."

The Manager's face turned to flame, and then back to chalk again. He made a quick movement towards the telephone bell, stretching out a hand to reach it, but at the same moment Jones pulled the trigger and the wrist was shattered, splashing the wall behind with blood.

"That's *one* place where the chains burnt," he said quietly to himself. His hand was absolutely steady, and he felt that he was a hero.

The Manager was on his feet, with a scream of pain, supporting himself with his right hand on the desk in front of him, but Jones pressed the trigger again, and a bullet flew into the other wrist, so that the big man, deprived of support, fell forward with a crash on to the desk.

"You damned madman!" shrieked the Manager. "Drop that pistol!"

"That's *another* place," was all Jones said, still taking careful aim for another shot.

The big man, screaming and blundering, scrambled beneath the desk, making frantic efforts to hide, but the secretary took a step forward and fired two shots in quick succession into his projecting legs, hitting first one ankle and then the other, and smashing them horribly.

"Two more places where the chains burnt," he said,

going a little nearer.

The Manager, still shrieking, tried desperately to squeeze his bulk behind the shelter of the opening beneath the desk, but he was far too large, and his bald head protruded through on the other side. Jones caught him by the scruff of his great neck and dragged him yelping out on to the carpet. He was covered with blood, and flopped helplessly upon his broken wrists.

"Be quick now!" cried the voice of Thorpe.

There was a tremendous commotion and banging at the door, and Jones gripped his pistol tightly. Something seemed to crash through his brain, clearing it for a second, so that he thought he saw beside him a great veiled figure, with drawn sword and flaming eyes, and sternly approving attitude.

"Remember the eyes! Remember the eyes!" hissed Thorpe in the air above him.

Jones felt like a god, with a god's power. Vengeance disappeared from his mind. He was acting impersonally as an instrument in the hands of the Invisibles who dispense justice and balance accounts. He bent down and put the barrel close into the other's face, smiling a little as he saw the childish efforts of the arms to cover his head. Then he pulled the trigger, and a bullet went straight into the right eye, blackening the skin. Moving the pistol two inches the other way, he sent another bullet crashing into the left eye. Then he stood upright over his victim with a deep sigh of satisfaction.

The Manager wriggled convulsively for the space of a single second, and then lay still in death.

There was not a moment to lose, for the door was already broken in and violent hands were at his neck. Jones put the pistol to his temple and once more pressed the trigger with his finger.

But this time there was no report. Only a little dead click answered the pressure, for the secretary had forgotten that the pistol had only six chambers, and that he had used them all. He threw the useless weapon on to the floor, laughing a little out loud, and turned, without a struggle, to give himself up.

"I *had* to do it," he said quietly, while they tied him. "It was simply my duty! And now I am ready to face the consequences, and Thorpe will be proud of me. For justice has been done and the gods are satisfied."

He made not the slightest resistance, and when the two policemen marched him off through the crowd of shuddering little clerks in the office, he again saw the veiled figure moving majestically in front of him, making slow sweeping circles with the flaming sword, to keep back the host of faces that were thronging in upon him from the Other Region.

The DANCE *of* DEATH.

Browne went to the dance feeling genuinely depressed, for the doctor had just warned him that his heart was weak and that he must be exceedingly careful in the matter of exertion.

"Dancing?" he asked, with that assumed lightness some natures affect in the face of a severe shock — the plucky instinct to conceal pain.

"Well — in moderation, perhaps," hummed the doctor. "Not *wildly!*" he added, with a smile that betrayed something more than mere professional sympathy.

At any other time Browne would probably have laughed, but the doctor's serious manner put a touch of ice on the springs of laughter. At the age of twenty-six one hardly realises death; life is still endless; and it is only old people who have "hearts" and such-like afflictions. So it was that the professional dictum came as a real shock; and with it too, as a sudden revelation, came that little widening of sympathy for others that is part of every deep experience as the years roll up and pass.

At first he thought of sending an excuse. He went about carefully, making the 'buses stop dead before he got out, and going very slowly up steps. Then gradually he grew more accustomed to the burden of his dread secret: the commonplace events of the day; the hated drudgery of the office, where he was an underpaid clerk; the contact with other men who bore similar afflictions with assumed indifference; the faultfinding of the manager, making him fearful of his position — all this helped to reduce the sense of first alarm, and, instead of sending an excuse, he went to the dance, as we have seen, feeling deeply depressed, and moving all the time as if he carried in his side a brittle glass globe that the least jarring might break into a thousand pieces.

The spontaneous jollity natural to a boy and girl dance served, however, to emphasise vividly the contrast of his own mood, and to make him very conscious again of his little hidden source of pain. But, though he would gladly have availed himself of a sympathetic ear among the many there whom he knew intimately, he nevertheless exercised the restraint natural to his character, and avoided any reference to the matter that bulked so largely in his consciousness. Once or twice he was tempted, but a prevision of the probable conversation that would ensue stopped him always in time: "Oh, I *am* so sorry, Mr. Browne, and you mustn't dance *too* hard, you know," and then his careless laugh as he remarked that it didn't matter a bit, and his little joke as he whirled his partner off for another spin.

He knew, of course, there was nothing very sensational about being told that one's heart was weak.

Even the doctor had smiled a little; and he now recalled more than one acquaintance who had the same trouble and made light of it. Yet it sounded in Browne's life a note of profound and sinister gloom. It snatched beyond his reach at one fell swoop all that he most loved and enjoyed, destroying a thousand dreams, and painting the future a dull drab colour without hope. He was an idealist at heart, hating the sordid routine of the life he led as a business underling. His dreams were of the open air, of mountains, forests, and great plains, of the sea, and of the lonely places of the world. Wind and rain spoke intimately to his soul, and the storms of heaven, as he heard them raging at night round his high room in Bloomsbury, stirred savage yearnings that haunted him for days afterwards with the voices of the desert. Sometimes during the lunch hour, when he escaped temporarily from the artificial light and close air of his high office stool, to see the white clouds sailing by overhead, and to hear the wind singing in the wires, it set such a fever in his blood that for the remainder of the afternoon he found it impossible to concentrate on his work, and thus exasperated the loud-voiced manager almost to madness.

Having no expectations, and absolutely no practical business ability, he was fortunate, however, in having a "place" at all, and the hard fact that promotion was unlikely made him all the more careful to keep his dreams in their place, to do his work as well as possible, and to save what little he could.

His holidays were the only points of light in an otherwise dreary existence. And one day, when he should have saved enough, he looked forward vaguely to a life close to Nature, perhaps a shepherd on a hundred hills, a dweller in the woods, within sound of his beloved trees and waters, where the smell of the earth and camp fire would be ever in his nostrils, and the running stream always ready to bear his boat swiftly away into happiness.

And now the knowledge that he had a weak heart came to spoil everything. It shook his dream to the very foundations. It depressed him utterly. Any moment the blow might fall. It might catch him in the water, swimming, or half-way up the mountain, or midway in one of his lonely tramps, just when his enjoyment depended most upon his being reckless and forgetful of bodily limitations — that freedom of the spirit in the wilderness he so loved. He might even be forced to spend his holiday, to say nothing of the dream of the far future, in some farmhouse *"quietly,"* instead of gloriously in the untrodden wilds. The thought made him angry with pain. All day he was haunted and dismayed, and all day he heard the wind whispering among branches and the water lapping somewhere against sandy banks in the sun.

The dance was a small subscription affair, hastily arranged and happily informal. It took place in a large hall that was used in the daytime as a gymnasium, but the floor was good and the music more than good. Foils and helmets hung round the walls, and high up under the brown rafters were ropes, rings, and trapezes coiled away out of reach, their unsightliness further concealed by an array of brightly coloured flags. Only the light was not of the best, for the hall was very long, and the gallery at the far end loomed in a sort of twilight that was further deepened by the shadows of the flags overhead. But its benches afforded excellent sitting-out places, where strong light was not always an essential to happiness, and no one dreamed of finding fault.

At first he danced cautiously, but by degrees the spirit of the time and place relieved his depression and helped him to forget. He had probably exaggerated the importance of his malady.

Lots of other fellows, even as young as he was, had weak hearts and thought nothing of it. All the time, however, there was an undercurrent of sadness and disappointment not to be denied.

Something had gone out of life. A note of darkness had crept in. He found his partners dull, and they no doubt found him still duller.

Yet this dance, with nothing apparently to distinguish it from a hundred others, stood out in all his experience with an indelible red mark against it. It is a common trick of Nature — and a profoundly significant one — that, just when despair is deepest, she waves a wand before the weary eyes and does her best to waken an impossible hope. Her idea, presumably, being to keep her victim going actively to the very end of the chapter, lest through indifference he should lose something of the lesson she wishes to teach.

Thus it was that, midway in the dance, Browne's listless glance fell upon a certain girl whose appearance instantly galvanised him into a state of keenest possible desire. A flash of white light entered his heart and set him all on fire to know her. She attracted him tremendously. She was dressed in pale green, and always danced with the same man — a man about his own height and colouring, whose face, however, he never could properly see. They sat out together much of the time — always in the gallery where the shadows were deepest. The girl's face he saw clearly, and there was something about her that simply lifted him bodily out of himself and sent strange thrills of delight coursing over him like shocks of electricity. Several times their eyes met, and when this happened he could not tear his glance away. She fascinated him, and all the forces in his being merged into a single desire to be with her, to dance with her, speak with her, and to know her name. Especially he wondered who the man was she so favoured; he reminded him so oddly of himself. No one knows precisely what he himself looks like, but this tall dark figure, whose face he never could contrive to see, started the strange thought in him that it was his own *double*.

In vain he sought to compass an introduction to this girl. No one seemed to know her. Her dress, her hair, and a certain wondrous slim grace made him think of a young tree waving in the wind; of ivy leaves; of something that belonged to the life of the woods rather than to ordinary humanity. She possessed him, filling his thoughts with wild woodland dreams. Once, too, he was certain when their eyes met that she smiled at him, and the call was so well-nigh irresistible that he almost dropped his partner's arm to run after her.

But it seemed impossible to obtain an introduction from any one.

"Do you know who that girl is over there?" he asked one of his partners while sitting out a square dance, half exhausted with his exertions; "the one up there in the gallery?"

"In pink?"

"No, the one in green, I mean."

"Oh, next the wall-flower lady in red!"

"*In* the gallery, not *under* it," he explained impatiently.

"I can't see up there. It's so dark," returned the girl after a careful survey through glasses. "I don't think I see any one at all."

"It *is* rather dark," he remarked.

"Why? Do you know who she is?" she asked foolishly.

He did not like to insist. It seemed so rude to his partner. But this sort of thing happened once or twice. Evidently no one knew this girl in green, or else he described her so inaccurately that the people he asked looked at some one else instead.

"In that green sort of ivy-looking dress," he tried another.

"With the rose in her hair and the red nose? Or the one sitting out?"

After that he gave it up finally. His partners seemed to sniff a little when he asked. Evidently *la désirée* was not a popular maiden. Soon after, too, she disappeared and he lost sight of her. Yet the thought that she might have gone home made his heart sink into a sort of horrible blackness.

He lingered on much later than he intended in the hope of getting an introduction, but at last, when he had filled all his engagements, or nearly all, he made up his mind to slip out and go home. It was already late, and he had to be in the office — that hateful office — punctually at nine o'clock. He felt tired, awfully tired, more so than ever before at a dance. It was, of course, his weak heart. He still dawdled a little while, however, hoping for another glimpse of the sylph in green, hungering for a last look that he could carry home with him and perhaps mingle with his dreams. The mere thought of her filled him with pain and joy, and a sort of rarefied delight he had never known before. But he could not wait for ever, and it was already close upon two o'clock in the morning. His rooms were only a short distance down the street; he would light a cigarette and stroll home. No; he had forgotten for a moment; *without* a cigarette: the doctor had been very stern on that point.

He was in the act of turning his back on the whirl of dancing figures, when the flags at the far end of the room parted for an instant in the moving air, and his eye rested upon the gallery just visible among the shadows.

A great pain ran swiftly through his heart as he looked.

There were only two figures seated there: the tall dark man, who was his double, and the ivy girl in green. She was looking straight at him down the length of the room, and even at that distance he could see that she smiled.

He stopped short. The flags waved back again and hid the picture, but on the instant he made up his mind to act. There, among all this dreary crowd of dancing dolls, was some one he really wanted to know, to speak with, to touch — some one who drew him beyond all he had ever known, and made his soul cry aloud. The room was filled with automatic lay-figures, but here was some one *alive*. He must know her. It was impossible to go home without speech, utterly impossible.

A fresh stab of pain, worse than the first, gave him momentary pause. He leant against the wall for an instant just under the clock, where the hands pointed to two, waiting for the swooning blackness to go. Then he passed on, disregarding it utterly. It supplied him, in truth, with the extra little impetus he needed to set the will into vigorous action, for it reminded him forcibly of what *might* happen. His time might be short; he had known few enough of the good things of life; he would seize what he could. He had no introduction, but — to the devil with the conventions. The risk was nothing. To meet her eyes at close quarters, to hear her voice, to know something of the perfume of that hair and dress — what was the risk of a snub compared to that? He slid down the side of the long room, dodging the dancers as best he could. The tall man, he noted, had left the gallery, but the girl sat on alone. He made his way quickly up the wooden steps, light as air, trembling with anticipation. His heart beat like a quick padded hammer, and the blood played a tambourine in his ears. It was odd he did not meet the tall man on the stairs, but doubtless there was another exit from the gallery that he had not observed. He topped the stairs and turned the corner. By Jove, she was still there, a few feet in front of him, sitting with her arms upon the railing, peering down upon the dancers below. His eyes swam for a moment, and something clutched at the very roots of his being.

But he did not hesitate. He went up quite close past the empty seats, meaning to ask naturally and simply if he might beg for the pleasure of a dance. Then, when he was within a few feet of her side, the girl suddenly turned and faced him, and the words died away on his lips. They seemed absolutely foolish and inadequate.

"Yes, I am ready," she said quietly, looking straight into his eyes; "but what a long time you were in coming. Was it such a great effort to *leave?*"

The form of the question struck him as odd, but he was too happy to pause. He became transfigured with joy. The sound of her voice instantly drowned all the clatter of the ball-room, and seemed to him the only thing in the whole world. It did not break on the consonants like most human speech. It f lowed smoothly; it was the sound of wind among branches, of water running over pebbles. It swept into him and caught him away, so that for a moment he saw his beloved woods and hills and seas. The stars were somewhere in it too, and the murmur of the plains.

By the gods! Here was a girl he could speak with in the words of silence; she stretched every string in his soul and then played on them. His spirit expanded with life and happiness. She would listen gladly to all that concerned him. To her he could talk openly about his poor broken heart, for she would sympathise. Indeed, it was all he could do to prevent himself running forward at once with his arms outstretched to take her. There was a perfume of earth and woods about her.

"Oh, I am so *awfully* glad — " he began lamely, his eyes on her face. Then, remembering something of earthly manners, he added:

"My name — er — is — "

Something unusual — something indescribable — in her gesture stopped him. She had moved to give him space at her side.

"Your name!" she laughed, drawing her green skirts with a soft rustle like leaves along the bench to make room; "but you need no name *now*, you know!"

Oh, the wonder of it! She understood him. He sat down with a feeling that he had been flying in a free wind and was resting among the tops of trees. The room faded out temporarily.

"But my name, if you like to know, is Issidy," she said, still smiling.

"Miss Issidy," he stammered, making another attempt at the forms of worldly politeness.

"Not *Miss* Issidy," she laughed aloud merrily. It surely was the sound of wind in poplars. "Issidy is my first name; so if you call me anything, you must call me that."

The name was pure music in his ears, but though he blundered about in his memory to find his own, it had utterly vanished; for the life of him he could not recollect what his friends called him.

He stared a moment, vaguely wondering, almost beside

himself with delight. No other girls he had known — ye heavens above! There were no longer any other girls! He had never known any other girl than this one. Here was his universe, framed in a green dress, with a voice of sea and wind, eyes like the sun, and movements of bending grasses. All else was mere shadow and fantasy. For the first time in his existence he was alive, *and knew that he was alive.*

"I was sure you would come to me," she was saying. "You couldn't help yourself." Her eyes were always on his face.

"I was afraid at first — "

"But your thoughts," she interrupted softly, "your thoughts were up here with me all the time."

"You knew that!" he cried, delighted.

"I felt them," she replied simply. "They — you kept me company, for I have been alone here all the evening. I know no one else here — *yet.*"

Her words amazed him. He was just going to ask who the tall dark man was, when he saw that she was rising to her feet and that she wanted to dance.

"But my heart — " he stammered.

"It won't hurt your poor heart to dance with *me*, you know," she laughed. "You may trust me. I shall know how to take care of it."

Browne felt simply ecstatic; it was too wonderful to be true; it was impossible — this meeting in London, at an ordinary dull dance, in the twentieth century. He would wake up presently from a dream of silver and gold. Yet he felt even then that she was drawing his arm about her waist for the dance, and with that first magical touch he almost lost consciousness and passed with her into a state of pure spirit.

It puzzled him for a moment how they reached the floor so quickly and found themselves among the whirling couples. He had no recollection of coming down the stairs. But meanwhile he was dancing on wings, and the girl in green beside him seemed to fly too, and as he pressed her to his heart he found it impossible to think of anything else in the world but that — that and his astounding happiness.

And the music was within them, rather than without; indeed they seemed to make their own music out of their swift whirling movements, for it never ceased and he never grew tired. His heart had ceased to pain him. Other curious things happened, too, but he hardly noticed them; or, rather, they no longer seemed strange. In that crowded ball-room they never once touched other people. His partner required no steering. She made no sound. Then suddenly he realised that his own feet made no sound either. They skimmed the floor with noiseless feet like spirits dancing.

No one else appeared to take the least notice of them. Most of the faces seemed, indeed, strange to him now, as though he had not seen them before, but once or twice he could have sworn that he passed couples who were dancing almost as happily and lightly as themselves, couples he had known in past years, couples who were *dead*.

Gradually the room emptied of its original comers, and others filled their places, silently, with airy graceful movements and happy faces, till the whole floor at length was covered with the soundless feet and whirling forms of those who had already left the world. And, as the artificial light faded away, there came in its place a soft white light that filled the room with beauty and made all the faces look radiant. And, once, as they skimmed past a mirror, he saw that the girl beside him was not there — that he seemed to be dancing alone, clasping no one; yet when he glanced down, there was her magical face at his shoulder and he felt her little form pressing up against him.

Such dancing, too, he had never even dreamed about, for it was like swinging with the treetops in the winds.

Then they danced farther out, ever swifter and swifter, past the shadows beneath the gallery, under the motionless hanging flags — and out into the night. The walls were behind them. They were off their feet and the wind was in their hair. They were rising, rising, rising towards the stars.

He felt the cool air of the open sky on his cheeks, and when he looked down, as they cleared the summit of the dark-lying hills, he saw that Issidy had melted away into himself and they had become one being. And he knew then that his heart would never pain him again on earth, or cause him to fear for any of his beloved dreams.

But the manager of the "hateful office" only knew two days later why Browne had not turned up to his desk, nor sent any word to explain his absence. He read it in the paper — how he had dropped down dead at a dance, suddenly stricken by heart disease. It happened just before two o'clock in the morning.

"Well," thought the manager, "he's no loss to us anyhow. He had no real business instincts. Smith will do his work much better — and for less money too."

The OLD MAN *of* VISIONS.

I.

The image of Teufelsdröckh, sitting in his watch-tower "alone with the stars," leaped into my mind the moment I saw him; and the curious expression of his eyes proclaimed at once that here was a being who allowed the world of small effects to pass him by, while he himself dwelt among the eternal verities. It was only necessary to catch a glimpse of the bent grey figure, so slight yet so tremendous, to realise that he carried staff and wallet, and was travelling alone in a spiritual region, uncharted, and full of wonder, difficulty, and fearful joy.

The inner eye perceived this quite as clearly as the outer

was aware of his Hebraic ancestry; but along what winding rivers, through what haunted woods, by the shores of what singing seas he pressed forward towards the mountains of his goal, no one could guess from a mere inspection of that wonderful old face.

To have stumbled upon such a figure in the casual way I did seemed incredible to me even at the time, yet I at once caught something of the uplifting airs that followed this inhabitant of a finer world, and I spent days — and considered them well spent — trying to get into conversation with him, so that I might know something more than the thin disguise of his holding a reader's ticket for the Museum Library.

To reach the stage of intimacy where actual speech is a hindrance to close understanding, one need not in some cases have spoken at all, thus by merely setting my mind, and above all, my imagination, into tune with his, and by steeping myself so much in his atmosphere that I absorbed and then gave back to him with my own stamp the forces he exhaled, it was at length possible to persuade those vast-seeing eyes to turn in my direction; and our glances having once met, I simply rose when he rose, and followed him out of the little smoky restaurant so closely up the street that our clothes brushed, and I thought I could even catch the sound of his breathing.

Whether, having already weighed me, he accepted the office, or whether he was grateful for the arm to lean upon, with his many years' burden, I do not know; but the sympathy between us was such that, without a single word, we walked up that foggy London street to the door of his lodging in Bloomsbury, while I noticed that at the touch of his arm the noise of the town seemed to turn into deep singing, and even the hurrying passers-by seemed bent upon noble purposes; and though he barely reached to my shoulder, and his grey beard almost touched my glove as I bent my arm to hold his own, there was something immense about his figure that sent him with towering stature above me and filled my thoughts with enchanting dreams of grandeur and high beauty.

But it was only when the door had closed on him with a little rush of wind, and I was walking home alone, that I fully realised the shock of my return to earth; and on reaching my own rooms I shook with laughter to think I had walked a mile and a half with a complete stranger without uttering a single syllable. Then the laughter suddenly hushed as I caught my face in the glass with the expression of the soul still lingering about the eyes and forehead, and for a brief moment my heart leaped to a sort of noble fever in the blood, leaving me with the smart of the soul's wings stirring beneath the body's crushing weight. And when it passed I found myself dwelling upon the only words he had spoken when I left him at the door:

"I am the Old Man of Visions, and I am *at your service*."

I think he never had a name — at least, it never passed his lips, and perhaps lay buried with so much else of the past that he clearly deemed unimportant. To me, at any rate, he became simply the Old Man of Visions, and to the little waiting-maid and the old landlady he was known simply as "Mister" — Mister, neither more nor less. The impenetrable veil that hung over his past never lifted for any vital revelations of his personal history, though he evidently knew all countries of the world, and had absorbed into his heart and brain the experience of all possible types of human nature; and there was an air about him not so much of "Ask me no questions" as "Do not ask me, for I cannot answer you *in words.*"

He could satisfy, but not in mere language; he would reveal, but by the wonderful words of silence only; for he was the Old Man of Visions, and visions need no words, being swift and of the spirit.

Moreover, the landlady — poor, dusty, faded woman — the landlady stood in awe, and disliked being probed for information in a passage-way down which he might any moment tread, for she could only tell me, "He just came in one night, years ago, and he's been here ever since!" And more than that I never knew. "Just came in — one night — years ago." This adequately explained him, for where he came *from*, or was journeying *to*, was something quite beyond the scope of ordinary limited language.

I pictured him suddenly turning aside from the stream of unimportant events, quietly stepping out of the world of straining, fighting, and shouting, and moving to take his rightful place among the forces of the still, spiritual region where he belonged by virtue of long pain and difficult attainment. For he was unconnected with any conceivable network of relations, friends, or family, and his terrible aloofness could not be disturbed by any one unless with his permission and by his express wish. Nor could he be imagined as "belonging" to any definite set of souls. He was apart from the world — and above it.

But it was only when I began to creep a little nearer to him, and our strange, silent intimacy passed from mental to spiritual, that I began really to understand more of this wonderful Old Man of Visions.

Steeped in the tragedy, and convulsed with laughter at the comedy, of life, he yet lived there in his high attic wrapped in silence as in a golden cloud; and so seldom did he actually speak to me that each time the sound of his voice, that had something elemental in it — something of winds and waters — thrilled me with the power of the first time. He lived, like Teufelsdröckh, "alone with the stars," and it seemed impossible, more and more, to link him on anywhere into practical dealings with ordinary men and women. Life somehow seemed to pass *below* him. Yet the small, selfish spirit of the recluse was far from him, and he was tenderly and deeply responsive to pain and suffering, and more particularly to genuine yearning for the far things of beauty. The unsatisfied longings of others could move him at once to tears.

"My relations with men are perfect," he said one night as we neared his dwelling. "I give them all sympathy out of my stores of knowledge and experience, and they give to me what kindness I need. My outer shell lies within impenetrable solitude, for only so can my inner life move freely along the paths and terraces that are thronged with the beings to whom I belong." And when I asked him how he maintained such deep sympathy with humanity, and had yet absolved himself apparently from action as from speech, he stopped against an area railing and turned his great eyes on to my face, as though their fires could communicate his thought without the husk of words:

"I have peered too profoundly into life and beyond it," he murmured, " to wish to express in language what I *know*. Action is not for all, always; and I am in touch with the cisterns of thought that lie behind action. I ponder the mysteries. What I may solve is not lost for lack either of speech or action, for the true mystic is ever the true man of action, and my thought will reach others as soon as they are ready for it in the same way that it reached you. All who strongly yearn must, sooner or later, find me and be comforted."

His eyes shifted from my face towards the stars, softly shining above the dark Museum roof, and a moment later he had disappeared into the hall-way of his house.

"An old poet who has strayed afield and lost his way," I mused; but through the door where he had just vanished the words came back to me as from a great distance: " A priest, rather, who has begun to find his way."

For a space I stood, pondering on his face and words: — that mercilessly intelligent look of the Hebrew woven in with the expression of the sadness of a whole race, yet touched with the glory of the spirit; and his utterance — that he had passed through all the traditions and no longer needed a formal, limited creed to hold to. I forget how I reached my own door several miles away, but it seemed to me that I flew.

In this way, and by unregistered degrees, we came to know each other better, and he accepted me and took me into his life. Always wrapped in the great calm of his delightful silence, he taught me more, and told me more, than could ever lie within the confines of mere words; and in moments of need, no matter when or where, I always knew exactly how to find him, reaching him in a few seconds by some swift way that disdained the means of ordinary locomotion.

Then at last one day he gave me the key of his house. And the first time I found my way into his eyry, and realised that it was a haven I could always fly to when the yearnings of the heart and soul struggled vainly for recompense, the full meaning and importance of the Old Man of Vision became finally clear to me.

II.

The room, high up creaky, darkened stairs in the ancient house, was bare and fireless, looking through a single patched window across a tumbled sea of roofs and chimneys; yet there was that in it which instantly proclaimed it a little holy place out of the world, a temple in which some one with spiritual vitality had worshipped, prayed, wept, and sung.

It was dusty and unswept, yet it was utterly *unsoiled*; and the Old Man of Visions who lived there, for all his shabby and stained garments, his uncombed beard and broken shoes, stood within its door revealed in his real self, moving in a sort of divine whiteness, iridescent, shining. And here, in this attic (lampless and unswept), high up under the old roofs of Bloomsbury, the window scarred with rain and the corners dropping cobwebs, I heard his

255

silver whisper issue from the shadows:

"Here you may satisfy your soul's desire and may commune with the Invisibles; only, to find the Invisibles, you must first be able to lose yourself."

Ah! through that stained window-pane, the sight leaping at a single bound from black roofs up to the stars, what pictures, dreams, and visions the Old Man has summoned to my eyes! Distances, measureless and impossible hitherto, became easy, and from the oppression of dead bricks and the market-place he transported me in a moment to the slopes of the Mountains of Dream; leading me to little places near the summits where the pines grew thinly and the stars were visible through their branches, fading into the rose of dawn; where the winds tasted of the desert, and the voices of the wilderness fled upward with a sound of wings and falling streams. At his word houses melted away, and the green waves of all the seas flowed into their places; forests waved themselves into the coastline of dull streets; and the power of the old earth, with all her smells and flowers and wild life, thrilled down among the dead roofs and caught me away into freedom among the sunshine of meadows and the music of sweet pipings. And with the divine deliverance came the crying of sea-gulls, the glimmer of reedy tarns, the whispering of wind among grasses, and the healing scorch of a real sun upon the skin.

And poetry such as was never known or heard before clothed all he uttered, yet even then took no form in actual words, for it was of the substance of aspiration and yearning, voicing adequately all the busy, high-born dreams that haunt the soul yet never live in the uttered line. He breathed it about him in the air so that it filled my being. It was part of him — beyond words; and it sang my own longings, and sang them perfectly so that I was satisfied; for my own mood never failed to touch him instantly and to waken the right response. In its essence it was spiritual — the mystic poetry of heaven; still, the love of humanity informed it, for star-fire and heart's blood were about equally mingled there, while the mystery of unattainable beauty moved through it like a white flame.

With other dreams and longings, too, it was the same; and all the most beautiful ideas that ever haunted a soul undowered with expression here floated with satisfied eyes and smiling lips before one — floated in silence, unencumbered, unlimited, unrestrained by words.

In this dim room, never made ugly by artificial light, but always shadowy in a kind of gentle dusk, the Old Man of Visions had only to lead me to the window to bring peace. Music, that rendered the soul fluid, as it poured across the old roofs into the room, was summoned by him at need; and when one's wings beat sometimes against the prison walls and the yearning for escape oppressed the heart, I have heard the little room rush and fill with the sound of trees, wind among grasses, whispering branches, and lapping waters. The very odours of space and mountain-side came too, and the looming of noble hills seemed visible overhead against the stars, as though the ceiling had suddenly become transparent.

For the Old Man of Visions had the power of instantly satisfying an ideal when once that ideal created a yearning

that could tear and burn its way out with sufficient force
to set the will a-moving.

III.

B ut as the time passed and I came to depend more and more upon the intimacy with my strange old friend, new light fell upon the nature and possibilities of our connection. I discovered, for instance, that though I held the key to his dwelling, and was familiar with the way, he was nevertheless not always available. Two things, in different fashion, rendered him inaccessible, or mute; and, for the first, I gradually learned that when life was prosperous, and the body singing loud, I could not find my way to his house. No amount of wandering, calculation, or persevering effort enabled me even to find the street again. With any burst of worldly success, however fleeting, the Old Man of Visions somehow slipped away into remote shadows and became unreal and misty. A merely passing desire to be with him, to seek his inspiration by a glimpse through that magic window-pane, resulted only in vain and tiresome pacing to and fro along ugly streets that produced weariness and depression; and after these periods it became, I noticed, less and less easy to discover the house, to fit the key in the door, or, having gained access to the temple, to the visions I *thought* I craved for.

Often, in this way, have I searched in vain for days, but only succeeded in losing myself in the murky purlieus of a quite strange Bloomsbury; stopping outside numberless counterfeit doors, and struggling vainly with locks that knew nothing of my little shining key.

But, on the other hand, pain, loneliness, sorrow — the merest whisper of spiritual affliction — and, lo, in a single moment the difficult geography became plain, and without hesitation, when I was unhappy or distressed, I found the way to his house as by a bird's instinctive flight, and the key slipped into the lock as though it loved it and was returning home.

The other cause to render him inaccessible, though not so determined — since it never concealed the way to the house — was even more distressing, for it depended wholly on myself; and I came to know how the least ugly action, involving a depreciation of ideals, so confused the mind that, when I got into the house, with difficulty, and found him in the little room after much searching, he was able to do or say scarcely anything at all for me. The mirror facing the door then gave back, I saw, no proper reflection of his person, but only a faded and wavering shadow with dim eyes and stooping, indistinct outline, and I even fancied

I could see the pattern of the wall and shape of the furniture *through* his body, as though he had grown semi-transparent.

"You must not expect yearnings to weigh," came his whisper, like wind far overhead, "unless you lend to them your own substance; and *your own* substance you cannot both keep and lend. If you would know the Invisibles, forget yourself."

And later, as the years slipped away one after another into the mists, and the frontier between the real and the unreal began to shift amazingly with his teachings, it became more and more clear to me that he belonged to a permanent region that, with all the changes in the world's history, has itself never altered in any essential particular. This immemorial Old Man of Visions, as I grew to think of him, had existed always; he was old as the sea and coeval with the stars; and he dwelt beyond time and space, reaching out a hand to all those who, weary of the shadows and illusions of practical life, really call to him with their heart of hearts. To me, indeed, the touch of sorrow was always near enough to prevent his becoming often inaccessible, and after a while even his voice became so *living* that I sometimes heard it calling to me in the street and in the fields.

Oh, wonderful Old Man of Visions! Happy the days of disaster, since they taught me how to know you, the Unraveller of Problems, the Destroyer of Doubts, who bore me ever away with soft flight down the long, long vistas of the heart and soul!

And his loneliness in that temple attic under the stars,

his loneliness, too, had a meaning I did not fail to understand later, and why he was always available for me and
seemed to belong to no other.

"To every one who finds me," he said, with the strange
smile that wrapped his whole being and not his face alone,
"to every one I am the same, and yet different. I am not
really ever alone. The whole world, nay" — his voice rose
to a singing cry — "the whole universe lies in this room, or
just beyond that window-pane; for here past and future
meet and all real dreams find completeness. But remember,"
he added — and there was a sound as of soft wind and rain
in the room with his voice — "no true dream can ever be
shared, and should you seek to explain me to another you
must lose me beyond recall. You have never asked my name,
nor must you ever tell it. Each must find me in his own
way."

Yet one day, for all my knowledge and his warnings, I
felt so sure of my intimacy with this immemorial being,
that I spoke of him to a friend who was, I had thought, so
much a part of myself that it seemed no betrayal. And my
friend, who went to search and found nothing, returned
with the fool's laughter on his face, and swore that no street
or number existed, for he had looked in vain, and had
repeatedly *asked the way*.

And, from that day to this, the Old Man of Visions
has neither called to me nor let his place be found; the
streets are strange and empty, and I have even lost the little
shining key.

MAY DAY EVE.

I.

I t was in the spring when I at last found time from the hospital work to visit my friend, the old folk-lorist, in his country isolation, and I rather chuckled to myself, because in my bag I was taking down a book that utterly refuted all his tiresome pet theories of magic and the powers of the soul.

These theories were many and various, and had often troubled me. In the first place, I scorned them for professional reasons, and, in the second, because I had never been able to argue quite well enough to convince or to shake his faith, in even the smallest details, and any scientific knowledge I brought to bear only fed him with confirmatory data. To find such a book, therefore, and to know that it was safely in my bag, wrapped up in brown paper and addressed to him, was a deep and satisfactory joy, and I speculated a good deal during the journey how he would deal with the overwhelming arguments it contained against the existence of any important region outside the world of sensory perceptions.

Speculative, too, I was whether his visionary habits and absorbing experiments would permit him to remember my arrival at all, and I was accordingly relieved to hear from the solitary porter that the "professor" had sent a "veeckle" to meet me, and that I was thus free to send my bag and walk the four miles to the house across the hills.

It was a calm, windless evening, just after sunset, the air warm and scented, and delightfully still. The train, already sinking into distance, carried away with it the noise of crowds and cities and the last suggestions of the stressful life behind me, and from the little station on the moorland I stepped at once into the world of silent, growing things, tinkling sheepbells, shepherds, and wild, desolate spaces.

My path lay diagonally across the turfy hills. It slanted a mile or so to the summit, wandered vaguely another two miles among gorse-bushes along the crest, passed Tom Bassett's cottage by the pines, and then dropped sharply down on the other side through rather thin woods to the ancient house where the old folk-lorist lived and dreamed himself into his impossible world of theory and fantasy. I fell to thinking busily about him during the first part of the ascent, and convinced myself, as usual, that, but for his generosity to the poor, and his benign aspect, the peasantry must undoubtedly have regarded him as a wizard who speculated in souls and had dark dealings with the world of faery.

The path I knew tolerably well. I had already walked it once before — a winter's day some years ago — and from the cottage onward felt sure of my way; but for the first mile or so there were so many cross cattle-tracks, and the light had become so dim that I felt it wise to inquire more particularly. And this I was fortunately able to do of a man who with astonishing suddenness rose from the grass where he had been lying behind a clump of bushes, and passed a few yards in front of me at a high pace downhill toward the darkening valley.

He was in such a state of hurry that I called out loudly to him, fearing to be too late, but on hearing my voice he turned sharply, and seemed to arrive almost at once beside me. In a single instant he was standing there, quite close, looking, with a smile and a certain expression of curiosity, I thought, into my face. I remember thinking that his features, pale and wholly untanned, were rather wonderful for a countryman, and that the eyes were those of a foreigner; his great swiftness, too, gave me a distinct sensation — something almost of a start — though I knew my vision was at fault at the best of times, and of course especially so in the deceptive twilight of the open hillside.

Moreover — as the way often is with such instructions — the words did not stay in my mind very clearly after he had uttered them, and the rapid, panther-like movements of the man as he quickly vanished down the hill again left me with little more than a sweeping gesture indicating the line I was to follow. No doubt his sudden rising from behind the gorse-bush, his curious swiftness, and the way he peered into my face, and even touched me on the shoulder, all combined to distract my attention somewhat from the actual words he used; and the fact that I was travelling at a wrong angle, and should have come out a mile too far to the right, helped to complete my feeling that his gesture, pointing the way, was sufficient.

On the crest of the ridge, panting a little with the unwonted exertion, I lay down to rest a moment on the grass beside a flaming yellow gorse-bush. There was still a good hour before I should be looked for at the house; the grass was very soft, the peace and silence soothing. I lingered, and lit a cigarette. And it was just then, I think, that my subconscious memory gave back the words, the actual words, the man had spoken, and the heavy significance of the personal pronoun, as he had emphasised it in his odd foreign voice, touched me with a sense of vague amusement: "The safest way *for you* now," he had said, as though I was so obviously a townsman and might be in danger on the lonely hills after dark. And the quick way he had reached my side, and then slipped off again like a shadow down the steep slope, completed a definite little picture in my mind. Then other thoughts and memories rose up and formed a series of pictures, following each other in rapid succession, and forming a chain of reflections undirected by the will and without purpose or meaning. I fell, that is, into a pleasant reverie.

Below me, and infinitely far away, it seemed, the valley

lay silent under a veil of blue evening haze, the lower end losing itself among darkening hills whose peaks rose here and there like giant plumes that would surely nod their great heads and call to one another once the final shadows were down. The village lay, a misty patch, in which lights already twinkled. A sound of rooks faintly cawing, of sea-gulls crying far up in the sky, and of dogs barking at a great distance rose up out of the general murmur of evening voices. Odours of farm and field and open spaces stole to my nostrils, and everything contributed to the feeling that I lay on the top of the world, nothing between me and the stars, and that all the huge, free things of the earth — hills, valleys, woods, and sloping fields — lay breathing deeply about me.

A few sea-gulls — in daytime hereabouts they fill the air — still circled and wheeled within range of sight, uttering from time to time sharp, petulant cries; and far in the distance there was just visible a shadowy line that showed where the sea lay.

Then, as I lay gazing dreamily into this still pool of shadows at my feet, something rose up, something sheet-like, vast, imponderable, off the whole surface of the mapped-out country, moved with incredible swiftness down the valley, and in a single instant climbed the hill where I lay and swept by me, yet without hurry, and in a sense without speed. Veils in this way rose one after another, filling the cups between the hills, shrouding alike fields, village, and hillside as they passed, and settled down some-where into the gloom behind me over the ridge, or slipped off like vapour into the sky.

Whether it was actually mist rising from the surface of the fast-cooling ground, or merely the earth giving up her heat to the night, I could not determine. The coming of the darkness is ever a series of mysteries. I only know that this indescribable vast stirring of the landscape seemed to me as though the earth were unfolding immense sable wings from her sides, and lifting them for silent, gigantic strokes so that she might fly more swiftly from the sun into the night. The darkness, at any rate, did drop down over everything very soon afterward, and I rose up hastily to follow my pathway, realising with a degree of wonder strangely new to me the magic of twilight, the blue open depths into the valley below, and the pale yellow heights of the watery sky above.

I walked rapidly, a sense of chilliness about me, and soon lost sight of the valley altogether as I got upon the ridge proper of these lonely and desolate hills.

It could not have been more than fifteen minutes that I lay there in reverie, yet the weather, I at once noticed, had changed very abruptly, for mist was seething here and there about me, rising somewhere from smaller valleys in the hills beyond, and obscuring the path, while overhead there was plainly a sound of wind tearing past, far up, with a sound of high shouting. A moment before it had been the stillness of a warm spring night, yet now everything had changed; wet mist coated me, raindrops smartly stung my face, and a gusty wind, descending out of cool heights, began to strike and buffet me, so that I buttoned my coat and pressed my hat more firmly upon my head.

The change was really this — and it came to me for the

first time in my life with the power of a real conviction — that everything about me seemed to have become suddenly *alive*.

It came oddly upon me — prosaic, matter-of-fact, materialistic doctor that I was — this realisation that the world about me had somehow stirred into life; oddly, I say, because Nature to me had always been merely a more or less definite arrangement of measurement, weight, and colour, and this new presentation of it was utterly foreign to my temperament. A valley to me was always a valley; a hill, merely a hill; a field, so many acres of flat surface, grass or ploughed, drained well or drained ill; whereas now, with startling vividness, came the strange, haunting idea that after all they could be something more than valley, hill, and field; that what I had hitherto perceived by these names were only the veils of something that lay concealed within, something alive. In a word, that the poetic sense I had always rather sneered at, in others, or explained away with some shallow physiological label, had apparently suddenly opened up in myself without any obvious cause.

And, the more I puzzled over it, the more I began to realise that its genesis dated from those few minutes of reverie lying under the gorse-bush (reverie, a thing I had never before in all my life indulged in!); or, now that I came to reflect more accurately, from my brief interview with that wild-eyed, swift-moving, shadowy man of whom I had first inquired the way.

I recalled my singular fancy that veils were lifting off the surface of the hills and fields, and a tremor of excitement accompanied the memory. Such a thing had never before been possible to my practical intelligence, and it made me feel suspicious — suspicious about myself. I stood still a moment — I looked about me into the gathering mist, above me to the vanishing stars, below me to the hidden valley, and then sent an urgent summons to my individuality, as I had always known it, to arrest and chase these undesirable fancies.

But I called in vain. No answer came. Anxiously, hurriedly, confusedly, too, I searched for my normal self, but could not find it; and this failure to respond induced in me a sense of uneasiness that touched very nearly upon the borders of alarm.

I pushed on faster and faster along the turfy track among the gorse-bushes with a dread that I might lose the way altogether, and a sudden desire to reach home as soon as might be. Then, without warning, I emerged unexpectedly into clear air again, and the vapour swept past me in a rushing wall and rose into the sky. Anew I saw the lights of the village behind me in the depths, here and there a line of smoke rising against the pale yellow sky, and stars overhead peering down through thin wispy clouds that stretched their wind-signs across the night.

After all, it had been nothing but a stray bit of sea-fog driving up from the coast, for the other side of the hills, I remembered, dipped their chalk cliffs straight into the sea, and strange lost winds must often come a-wandering this way with the sharp changes of temperature about sunset. None the less, it was disconcerting to know that mist and storm lay hiding within possible reach, and I walked on smartly for a sight of Tom Bassett's cottage and the lights of the Manor House in the valley a short mile beyond.

The clearing of the air, however, lasted but a very brief while, and vapour was soon rising about me as before, hiding the path and making bushes and stone walls look like running shadows. It came, driven apparently, by little independent winds up the many side gullies, and it was very cold, touching my skin like a wet sheet. Curious great shapes, too, it assumed as the wind worked to and fro through it: forms of men and animals; grotesque, giant outlines; ever shifting and running along the ground with silent feet, or leaping into the air with sharp cries as the gusts twisted them inwardly and lent them voice. More and more I pushed my pace, and more and more darkness and vapour obliterated the landscape. The going was not otherwise difficult, and here and there cowslips glimmered in patches of dancing yellow, while the springy turf made it easy to keep up speed; yet in the gloom I frequently tripped and plunged into prickly gorse near the ground, so that from shin to knee was soon a-tingle with sharp pain. Odd puffs and spits of rain stung my face, and the periods of utter stillness were always followed by little shouting gusts of wind, each time from a new direction. Troubled is perhaps too strong a word, but flustered I certainly was; and though I recognised that it was due to my being in an environment so remote from the town life I was accustomed to, I found it impossible to stifle altogether the feeling of malaise that had crept into my heart, and I looked about with increasing eagerness for the lighted windows of Bassett's cottage.

More and more, little pin-pricks of distress and

confusion accumulated, adding to my realisation of being away from streets and shop-windows, and things I could classify and deal with. The mist, too, distorted as well as concealed, played tricks with sounds as well as with sights. And, once or twice, when I stumbled upon some crouching sheep, they got up without the customary alarm and hurry of sheep, and moved off slowly into the darkness, but in such a singular way that I could almost have sworn they were not sheep at all, but human beings crawling on all-fours, looking back and grimacing at me over their shoulders as they went. On these occasions — for there were more than one — I never could get close enough to feel their woolly wet backs, as I should have liked to do; and the sound of their tinkling bells came faintly through the mist, sometimes from one direction, sometimes from another, sometimes all round me as though a whole flock surrounded me; and I found it impossible to analyse or explain the idea I received that they were *not* sheep-bells at all, but something quite different.

But mist and darkness, and a certain confusion of the senses caused by the excitement of an utterly strange environment, can account for a great deal. I pushed on quickly. The conviction that I had strayed from the route grew, nevertheless, for occasionally there was a great commotion of seagulls about me, as though I had disturbed them in their sleeping-places. The air filled with their plaintive cries, and I heard the rushing of multitudinous wings, sometimes very close to my head, but always invisible owing to the mist. And once, above the swishing of the wet wind through the gorse-bushes, I was sure I caught the faint thunder of the sea and the distant crashing of waves rolling up some steep-throated gully in the cliffs. I went cautiously after this, and altered my course a little away from the direction of the sound.

Yet, increasingly all the time, it came to me how the cries of the sea-birds sounded like laughter, and how the everlasting wind blew and drove about me with a purpose, and how the low bushes persistently took the shape of stooping people, moving stealthily past me, and how the mist more and more resembled huge protean figures escorting me across the desolate hills, silently, with immense footsteps. For the inanimate world now touched my awakened poetic sense in a manner hitherto unguided, and became fraught with the pregnant messages of a dimly concealed life. I readily understood, for the first time, how easily a superstitious peasantry might people their world, and how even an educated mind might favour an atmosphere of legend. I stumbled along, looking anxiously for the lights of the cottage.

Suddenly, as a shape of writhing mist whirled past, I received so direct a stroke of wind that it was palpably a blow in the face. Something swept by with a shrill cry into the darkness. It was impossible to prevent jumping to one side and raising an arm by way of protection, and I was only just quick enough to catch a glimpse of the sea-gull as it raced past, with suddenly altered flight, beating its powerful wings over my head. Its white body looked enormous as the mist swallowed it. At the same moment a gust tore my hat from my head and flung the flap of my coat across my eyes. But I was well-trained by this time, and made a quick dash after the retreating black object, only to find on overtaking it that I held a prickly branch of gorse. The wind combed my hair viciously. Then, out of a corner of my eye, I saw my hat still rolling, and grabbed swiftly at it; but just as I closed on it, the real hat passed in front of me, turning over in the wind like a ball, and I instantly released my first capture to chase it. Before it was within reach, another one shot between my feet so that I stepped on it. The grass seemed covered with moving hats, yet each one, when I seized it, turned into a piece of wood, or a tiny gorse-bush, or a black rabbit hole, till my hands were scored with prickles and running blood. In the darkness, I reflected, all objects looked alike, as though by general conspiracy.

I straightened up and took a long breath, mopping the blood with my handkerchief. Then something tapped at my feet, and on looking down, there was the hat within easy reach, and I stooped down and put it on my head again. Of course, there were a dozen ways of explaining my confusion and stupidity, and I walked along wondering which to select. My eyesight, for one thing — and under such conditions why seek further? It was nothing, after all, and the dizziness was a momentary effect caused by the effort and stooping.

But for all that, I shouted aloud, on the chance that a wandering shepherd might hear me; and of course no answer came, for it was like calling in a padded room, and the mist suffocated my voice and killed its resonance.

It was really very discouraging: I was cold and wet and hungry; my legs and clothes torn by the gorse, my hands scratched and bleeding; the wind brought water to my eyes by its constant buffeting, and my skin was numb from contact with the chill mist. Fortunately I had matches, and after some difficulty, by crouching under a wall, I caught a swift glimpse of my watch, and saw that it was but little after eight o'clock. Supper I knew was at nine, and I was surely over halfway by this time. But here again was another instance of the way everything seemed in a conspiracy against me to appear otherwise than ordinary, for in the gleam of the match my watch-glass showed as the face of a little old gray man, uncommonly like the folk-lorist himself, peering up at me with an expression of whimsical laughter. My own reflection it could not possibly have been, for I am clean-shaven, and this face looked up at me through a running tangle of gray hair. Yet a second and third match revealed only the white surface with the thin black hands moving across it.

II.

A
nd it was at this point, I well remember, that I
reached what was for me the true heart of the
adventure, the little fragment of real experience
I learned from it and took back with me to my doctor's life
in London, and that has remained with me ever since, and
helped me to a new sympathetic insight into the intrica-
cies of certain curious mental cases I had never before
really understood.

For it was sufficiently obvious by now that a curious
change had been going forward in me for some time, dating,
so far as I could focus my thoughts sufficiently to analyse,
from the moment of my speech with that hurrying man of
shadow on the hillside. And the first deliberate manifestation of the change, now that I looked back, was surely
the awakening in my prosaic being of the "poetic thrill";

my sudden amazing appreciation of the world around me as something alive. From that moment the change in me had worked ahead subtly, swiftly. Yet, so natural had been the beginning of it, that although it was a radically new departure for my temperament, I was hardly aware at first of what had actually come about; and it was only now, after so many encounters, that I was forced at length to acknowledge it.

It came the more forcibly too, because my very commonplace ideas of beauty had hitherto always been associated with sunshine and crude effects; yet here this new revelation leaped to me out of wind and mist and desolation on a lonely hillside, out of night, darkness, and discomfort. New values rushed upon me from all sides. Everything had changed, and the very simplicity with which the new values presented themselves proved to me how profound the change, the readjustment, had been. In such trivial things the evidence had come that I was not aware of it until repetition forced my attention: the veils rising from valley and hill; the mountain tops as personalities that shout or murmur in the darkness; the crying of the sea birds and of the living, purposeful wind; above all, the feeling that Nature about me was instinct with a life differing from my own in degree rather than in kind; everything, from the conspiracy of the gorse-bushes to the disappearing hat, showed that a fundamental attitude of mind in me had changed — and changed, too, without my knowledge or consent.

Moreover, at the same time the deep sadness of beauty had entered my heart like a stroke; for all this mystery and loveliness, I realized poignantly was utterly independent and careless of me, as me; and that while I must pass, decay, grow old, these manifestations would remain for ever young and unalterably potent. And thus gradually had I become permeated with the recognition of a region hitherto unknown to me, and that I had always depreciated in others and especially, it now occurred to me, in my friend the old folk-lorist.

Here surely, I thought, was the beginning of conditions which, carried a little further, must become pathogenic. That the change was real and pregnant I had no doubt whatever. My consciousness was expanding and I had caught it in the very act. I had of course read much concerning the changes of personality, swift, kaleidoscopic — had come across something of it in my practice — and had listened to the folk-lorist holding forth like a man inspired upon ways and means of reaching concealed regions of the human consciousness, and opening it to the knowledge of things called magical, so that one became free of a larger universe. But it was only now for the first time, on these bare hills, in touch with the wind and the rain, that I realized in how simple a fashion the frontiers of consciousness could shift this way and that, or with what touch of genuine awe the certainty might come that one stood on the borderland of new, untried, perhaps dangerous, experiences.

At any rate, it did now come to me that my consciousness had shifted its frontiers very considerably, and that whatever might happen must seem not abnormal, but quite simple and inevitable, and of course utterly true. This very simplicity, however, doing no violence to my being, brought with it none the less a sense of dread and discomfort; and my dim awareness that unknown possibilities were about me in the night puzzled and distressed me perhaps more than I cared to admit.

III.

All this that takes so long to describe became apparent to me in a few seconds. What I had always despised ascended the throne.

But with the finding of Bassett's cottage, as a sign-post close to home, my former *sang-froid*, my stupidity, would doubtless return, and my relief was therefore considerable when at length a faint gleam of light appeared through the mist, against which the square dark shadow of the chimney-line pointed upwards. After all, I had not strayed so very far out of the way. Now I could definitely ascertain where I was wrong.

Quickening my pace, I scrambled over a broken stone wall, and almost ran across the open bit of grass to the door. One moment the black outline of the cottage was there in front of me, and the next, when I stood actually against it — there was nothing! I laughed to think how utterly I had been deceived. Yet not utterly, for as I groped back again over the wall, the cottage loomed up a little to the left, with its windows lighted and friendly, and I had only been mistaken in my angle of approach after all. Yet again, as I hurried to the door, the mist drove past and thickened a second time — and the cottage was not where I had seen it!

My confusion increased a lot after that. I scrambled about in all directions, rather foolishly hurried, and over countless stone walls it seemed, and completely dazed as to the true points of the compass. Then suddenly, just when a kind of despair came over me, the cottage stood there solidly before my eyes, and I found myself not two feet from the door. Was ever mist before so deceptive? And there, just behind it, I made out the row of pines like a dark wave breaking through the night. I sniffed the wet resinous odour with joy, and a genuine thrill ran through me as I saw the unmistakable yellow light of the windows. At last I was near home and my troubles would soon be over.

A cloud of birds rose with shrill cries off the roof and whirled into the darkness when I knocked with my stick on the door, and human voices, I was almost certain, mingled somewhere with them, though it was impossible to tell whether they were within the cottage or outside. It all sounded confusedly with a rush of air like a little whirl-wind, and I stood there rather alarmed at the clamour of my knocking. By way, too, of further proof that my imagination had awakened, the significance of that knocking at the door set something vibrating within me that most surely had never vibrated before, so that I suddenly realized with what atmosphere of mystical suggestion is the mere act of knocking surrounded — *knocking at a door* — both for him who knocks, wondering what shall be revealed on opening, and for him who stands within, waiting for the summons of the knocker. I only know that I hesitated a lot before making up my mind to knock a second time.

And, anyhow, what happened subsequently came in a sort of haze. Words and memory both fail me when I try to record it truthfully, so that even the faces are difficult to visualise again, the words almost impossible to hear.

Before I knew it the door was open and before I could frame the words of my first brief question, I was within the threshold, and the door was shut behind me.

I had expected the little dark and narrow hallway of a cottage, oppressive of air and odour, but instead I came straight into a room that was full of light and full of — people. And the air tasted like the air about a mountain-top.

To the end I never saw what produced the light, nor understood how so many men and women found space to move comfortably to and fro, and pass each other as they did, within the confines of those four walls. An uncomfortable sense of having intruded upon some private gathering was, I think, my first emotion; though how the poverty-stricken countryside could have produced such an assemblage puzzled me beyond belief. And my second emotion — if there was any division at all in the wave of wonder that fairly drenched me — was feeling a sort of glory in the presence of such an atmosphere of splendid and vital *youth*. Everything vibrated, quivered, shook about me, and I almost felt myself as an aged and decrepit man by comparison.

I know my heart gave a great fiery leap as I saw them, for the faces that met me were fine, vigourous, and comely, while burning everywhere through their ripe maturity shone the ardours of youth and a kind of deathless enthusiasm. Old, yet eternally young they were, as rivers and mountains count their years by thousands, yet remain ever youthful; and the first effect of all those pairs of eyes lifted to meet my own was to send a whirlwind of unknown thrills about my heart and make me catch my breath with mingled terror and delight. A fear of death, and at the same time a sensation of touching something vast and eternal that could never die, surged through me.

A deep hush followed my entrance as all turned to look at me. They stood, men and women, grouped about a table, and something about them — not their size alone — conveyed the impression of being *gigantic*, giving me strangely novel realisations of freedom, power, and immense existence more or less than human.

I can only record my thoughts and impressions as they came to me and as I dimly now remember them. I had expected to see old Tom Bassett crouching half asleep over a peat fire, a dim lamp on the table beside him, and instead this assembly of tall and splendid men and women stood there to greet me, and stood in silence. It was little wonder that at first the ready question died upon my lips, and I almost forgot the words of my own language.

"I thought this was Tom Bassett's cottage!" I managed to ask at length, and looked straight at the man nearest me across the table. He had wild hair falling about his shoulders and a face of clear beauty. His eyes, too, like all the rest, seemed shrouded by something veil-like that reminded me of the shadowy man of whom I had first inquired the way. They were *shaded*—and for some reason I was glad they were.

At the sound of my voice, unreal and thin, there was a general movement throughout the room, as though everyone changed places, passing each other like those shapes of fluid sort I had seen outside in the mist. But no answer came. It seemed to me that the mist even penetrated into the room about me and spread inwardly over my thoughts.

"Is this the way to the Manor House?" I asked again, louder, fighting my inward confusion and weakness. "Can *no one* tell me?"

Then apparently everyone began to answer at once, or rather, not to answer directly, but to speak to each other in such a way that I could easily overhear. The voices of the men were deep, and of the women wonderfully musical, with a slow rhythm like that of the sea, or of the wind through the pine-trees outside. But the unsatisfactory nature of what they said only helped to increase my sense of confusion and dismay.

"Yes," said one; "Tom Bassett *was* here for a while with the sheep, but his home was not here."

"He asks the way to a house when he does not even know the way to his own mind!" another voice said, sounding overhead it seemed.

"And could he recognise the signs if we told him?"

came in the singing tones of a woman's voice close behind me.

And then, with a noise more like running water, or wind in the wings of birds, than anything else I could liken it to, came several voices together:

"And what sort of way does he seek? The splendid way, or merely the easy?"

"Or the short way of fools!"

"But he must have *some* credentials, or he never could have got as far as this," came from another.

A laugh ran round the room at this, though what there was to laugh at I could not imagine. It sounded like wind rushing about the hills. I got the impression too that the roof was somehow open to the sky, for their laughter had such a spacious quality in it, and the air was so cool and fresh, and moving about in currents and waves.

"It was I who showed him the way," cried a voice belonging to someone who was looking straight into my face over the table. "It was the safest way for him once he had got so far — "

I looked up and met his eye, and the sentence remained unfinished. It was the hurrying, shadowy man of the hillside. He had the same shifting outline as the others now, and the same veiled and shaded eyes, and as I looked the sense of terror stirred and grew in me. I had come in to ask for help, but now I was only anxious to be free of them all and out again in the rain and darkness on the moor. Thoughts of escape filled my brain, and I searched quickly for the door through which I had entered. But nowhere could I discover it again. The walls were bare; not even the windows were visible. And the room seemed to fill and empty of these figures as the waves of the sea fill and empty a cavern, crowding one upon another, yet never occupying more space, or less. So the coming and going of these men and women always evaded me.

And my terror became simply a terror that the veils of their eyes might lift, and that they would look at me with their clear, naked sight. I became horribly aware of their eyes. It was not that I felt them evil, but that I feared the new depths in me their merciless and terrible insight would stir into life. My consciousness had expanded quite enough for one night! I must escape at all costs and claim my own self again, however limited. I must have sanity, even if with limitations, but sanity at any price.

But meanwhile, though I tried hard to find my voice again, there came nothing but a thin piping sound that was like reeds whistling where winds meet about a corner. My throat was contracted, and I could only produce the smallest and most ridiculous of noises. The power of movement, too, was far less than when I first came in, and every moment it became more difficult to use my muscles, so that I stood there, stiff and awkward, face to face with this assemblage of shifting, wonderful people.

"And now," continued the voice of the man who had last spoken, "and now the safest way for him will be through the other door, where he shall see that which he may more easily understand."

With a great effort I regained the power of movement, while at the same time a burst of anger and a determination to be done with it all and to overcome my dreadful confusion drove me forward.

He saw me coming, of course, and the others indeed opened up and made a way for me, shifting to one side or the other whenever I came too near them, and never allowing me to touch them. But at last, when I was close in front of the man, ready both to speak and act, he was no longer there. I never saw the actual change — but instead of a man it was a woman! And when I turned with amazement, I saw that the other occupants walking like figures in some ancient ceremony, were moving slowly toward the far end of the room. One by one, as they filed past, they raised their calm, passionless faces to mine, immensely vital, proud, austere, and then, without further word or gesture, they opened the door I had lost and disappeared through it one by one into the darkness of the night beyond. And as they went it seemed that the mist swallowed them up and a gust of wind caught them away, and the light also went with them, leaving me alone with the figure who had last spoken.

Moreover it was just here that a most disquieting thought flashed through my brain with unreasoning conviction, shaking my personality, as it were, to the foundations: viz., that I had hitherto been spending my life in the pursuit of false knowledge, in the mere classifying and labelling of effects, the analysis of results, scientific so called; whereas it was the folk-lorist, and such like, who with their dreams and prayers were all the time on the path of real knowledge, the trail of causes; that the one was merely adding to the mechanical comfort and safety of the body, ultimately degrading the highest part of man, and never advancing the type, while the other — but then I had never yet believed in a soul — and now was no time to begin, terror or no terror. Clearly, my thoughts were wandering.

IV.

I t was at this moment the sound of the purring first
reached me — deep, guttural purring — that made
me think at once of some large concealed animal. It
was precisely what I had heard many a time at the
Zoological Gardens, and I had visions of cows chewing
the cud, or horses munching hay in a stall outside the
cottage. It was certainly an animal sound, and one of
pleasure and contentment.

Semi-darkness filled the room. Only a very faint moonlight, struggling through the mist, came through the
window, and I moved back instinctively toward the support
of the wall against my back.

Somewhere, through openings, came the sound of the
night driving over the roof, and far above I had visions of
those everlasting winds streaming by with clouds as large

as continents on their wings. Something in me wanted to sing and shout, but something else in me at the same time was in a very vivid state of unreasoning terror. I felt immense, yet tiny, confident, yet timid; a part of huge, universal forces, yet an utterly small, personal, and very limited being.

In the corner of the room on my right stood the woman. Her face was hid by a mass of tumbling hair, that made me think of living grasses on a field in June. Thus her head was partially turned from me, and the moonlight, catching her outline, just revealed it against the wall like an impressionist picture. Strange hidden memories stirred in the depths of me, and for a moment I felt that I knew all about her. I stared about me quickly, nervously, trying to take in everything at once. Then the purring sound grew much louder and closer, and I forgot my notion that this woman was no stranger to me and that I knew her as well as I knew myself. That purring thing was in the room close beside me. Between us two, indeed, it was, for I now saw that her arm nearest to me was raised, and that she was pointing to the wall in front of us.

Following the direction of her hand, I saw that the wall was transparent, and that I could see through a portion of it into a small square space beyond, as though I was looking through gauze instead of bricks. This small inner space was lighted, and on stooping down I saw that it was a sort of cupboard or cell-like cage let into the wall. The thing that purred was there in the centre of it.

I looked closer. It was a being, apparently a *human* being, crouched down in its narrow cage, feeding. I saw the body stooping over a quantity of coarse-looking, piled-up substance that was evidently food. It was like a man huddled up. There it squatted, happy and contented, with the minimum of air, light, and space, dully satisfied with its prisoned cage behind the bars, utterly unconscious of the vast world about it, grunting with pleasure, purring like a great cat, scornfully ignorant of what might lie beyond. The cell, moreover, I saw was a perfect masterpiece of mechanical contrivance and inventive ingenuity — the very last word in comfort, safety and scientific skill. I was in the act of trying to fit in my memory some of the details of its construction and arrangement, when I made a chance noise, and at once became too agitated to note carefully what I saw. For at the noise the creature turned, and I saw that it *was* a human being — a man. I was aware of a face close against my own as it pressed forward, but a face with embryonic features impossible to describe and utterly loathsome, with eyes, ears, nose and skin, only just sufficiently alive and developed to transfer the minimum of gross sensation to the brain. The mouth, however, was large and thick-lipped, and the jaws were still moving in the act of slow mastication.

I shrank back, shuddering with mingled pity and disgust, and at the same moment the woman beside me called me softly *by my own name*. She had moved forward a little so that she stood quite close to me, full in the thin stream of moonlight that fell across the floor, and I was conscious of a swift transition from hell to heaven as my gaze passed from that embryonic visage to a countenance so refined, so majestic, so divinely sensitive in its strength, that it was like turning from the face of a devil to look upon the features of a goddess.

At the same instant I was aware that both beings — the creature and the woman — were moving rapidly toward me.

A pain like a sharp sword dived deep down into me and twisted horribly through my heart, for as I saw them coming I realized in one swift moment of terrible intuition that they had their life in me, that they were born of my own being, and were indeed *projections of myself.* They were portions of my consciousness projected outwardly into objectivity, and their degree of reality was just as great as that of any other part of me.

With a dreadful swiftness they rushed toward me, and in a single second had merged themselves into my own being; and I understood in some marvellous manner beyond the possibility of doubt that they were symbolic of my own soul: the dull animal part of me that had hitherto acknowledged nothing beyond its cage of minute sensations, and the higher part, almost out of reach, and in touch with the stars, that for the first time had feebly awakened into life during my journey over the hill.

V.

I forget altogether how it was that I escaped, whether by the window or the door. I only know I found myself a moment later making great speed over the moor, followed by screaming birds and shouting winds, straight on the track downhill toward the Manor House. Something must have guided me, for I went with the instinct of an animal, having no uncertainties as to turnings, and saw the welcome lights of windows before I had covered another mile. And all the way I felt as though a great sluice gate had been opened to let a flood of new perceptions rush like a sea over my inner being, so that I was half ashamed and half delighted, partly angry, yet partly happy.

Servants met me at the door, several of them, and I was aware at once of an atmosphere of commotion in the house. I arrived breathless and hatless, wet to the skin, my hands scratched and my boots caked with mud.

"We made sure you were lost, sir," I heard the old butler say, and I heard my own reply, faintly, like the voice of someone else:

"I thought so too."

A minute later I found myself in the study, with the old folk-lorist standing opposite. In his hands he held the book I had brought down for him in my bag, ready addressed. There was a curious smile on his face.

"It never occurred to me that you would dare to *walk* — to-night of all nights," he was saying.

I stared without a word. I was bursting with the desire to tell him something of what had happened and try to be patient with his explanations, but when I sought for words and sentences my story seemed suddenly flat and pointless, and the details of my adventure began to evaporate and melt away, and seemed hard to remember.

"I had an exciting walk," I stammered, still a little breathless from running. "The weather was all right when I started from the station."

"The weather is all right still," he said, "though you may have found some evening mist on the top of the hills. But it's not that I meant."

"What then?"

"I meant," he said, still laughing quizzically, "that you were a very brave man to walk to-night over the enchanted hills, because this is May Day eve, and on May Day eve, you know, *They* have power over the minds of men, and can put glamour upon the imagination — "

"Who — *'they?'* What do you mean?"

He put my book down on the table beside him and looked quietly for a moment into my eyes, and as he did so the memory of my adventure began to revive in detail, and I thought quickly of the shadowy man who had shown me the way first. What could it have been in the face of the old folk-lorist that made me think of this man? A dozen things ran like flashes through my excited mind, and while I attempted to seize them I heard the old man's voice continue. He seemed to be talking to himself as much as to me.

"The elemental beings you have always scoffed at, of course; they who operate ceaselessly behind the screen of appearances, and who fashion and mould the moods of the mind. And an extremist like you — for extremes are always dangerously weak — is their legitimate prey."

"Pshaw!" I interrupted him, knowing that my manner betrayed me hopelessly, and that he had guessed much. "Any man may have subjective experiences, I suppose — "

Then I broke off suddenly. The change in his face made me start; it had taken on for the moment so exactly the look of the man on the hillside. The eyes gazing so steadily into mine had shadows in them, I thought.

"Glamour!" he was saying, "all glamour! One of them must have come very close to you, or perhaps touched you." Then he asked sharply, "Did you meet anyone? Did you speak with anyone?"

"I came by Tom Bassett's cottage," I said. "I didn't feel quite sure of my way and I went in and asked."

"All glamour," he repeated to himself, and then aloud

to me, "and as for Bassett's cottage, it was burnt down three years ago, and nothing stands there now but broken, roofless walls — "

He stopped because I had seized him by the arm. In the shadows of the lamp-lit room behind him I thought I caught sight of dim forms moving past the book-shelves. But when my eye tried to focus them they faded and slipped away again into ceiling and walls. The details of the hill-top cottage, however, started into life again at the sight, and I seized my friend's arm to tell him. But instantly, when I tried, it all faded away again as though it had been a dream, and I could recall nothing intelligible to repeat to him.

He looked at me and laughed.

"They always obliterate the memory afterwards," he said gently, "so that little remains beyond a mood, or an emotion, to show how profoundly deep their touch has been. Though sometimes part of the change remains and becomes permanent — as I hope in your case it may."

Then, before I had time to answer, to swear, or to remonstrate, he stepped briskly past me and closed the door into the hall, and then drew me aside farther into the room. The change that I could not understand was still working in his face and eyes.

"If you have courage enough left to come with me," he said, speaking very seriously, "we will go out again and see more. Up till midnight, you know, there is still the opportunity, and with me perhaps you won't feel so — so — "

It was impossible somehow to refuse; everything combined to make me go. We had a little food and then went out into the hall, and he clapped a wide-awake on his gray hairs. I took a cloak and seized a walking-stick from the stand. I really hardly knew what I was doing. The new world I had awakened to seemed still a-quiver about me.

As we passed out on to the gravel drive the light from the hall windows fell upon his face, and I saw that the change I had been so long observing was nearing its completeness, for there breathed about him that keen, wonderful atmosphere of eternal youth I had felt upon the inmates of the cottage. He seemed to have gone back forty years; a veil was gathering over his eyes; and I could have sworn that somehow his stature had increased, and that he moved beside me with a vigour and power I had never seen in him before.

And as we began to climb the hill together in silence I saw that the stars were clear overhead and there was no mist, that the trees stood motionless without wind, and that beyond us on the summit of the hills there were lights dancing to and fro, appearing and disappearing like the inflection of stars in water.

MISS SLUMBUBBLE — *and* CLAUSTROPHOBIA

Miss Daphne Slumbubble was a nervous lady of uncertain age who invariably went abroad in the spring. It was her one annual holiday, and she slaved for it all the rest of the year, saving money by the many sad devices known only to those who find their incomes after forty "barely enough," and always hoping that something would one day happen to better her dreary condition of cheap tea, tin loaves, and weekly squabbles with the laundress.

This spring holiday was the only time she really *lived* in the whole year, and she half starved herself for months immediately after her return, so as to put by quickly enough money for the journey in the following year. Once those six pounds were safe she felt better. After that she only had to save so many sums of four francs, each four francs meaning another day in the little cheap *pension* she always went to on the flowery slopes of the Alps of Valais.

Miss Slumbubble was exceedingly conscious of the presence of men. They made her nervous and afraid. She thought in her heart that all men were untrustworthy, not excepting policemen and clergymen, for in her early youth she had been cruelly deceived by a man to whom she had unreservedly given her heart. He had suddenly gone away and left her without a word of explanation, and some months later had married another woman and allowed the announcement to appear in the papers. It is true that he had hardly once spoken to Daphne. But that was nothing.

For the way he looked at her, the way he walked about the room, the very way he avoided her at the tea-parties where she used to meet him at her rich sister's house — indeed, everything he did or left undone, brought convincing proof to her fluttering heart that he loved her secretly, and that he knew she loved him. His near presence disturbed her dreadfully, so much so that she invariably spilt her tea if he came even within scenting-distance of her; and once, when he crossed the room to offer her bread and butter, she was so certain the very way he held the plate interpreted his silent love, that she rose from her chair, looked straight into his eyes — and took the *whole plate* in a state of delicious confusion!

But all this was years ago, and she had long since learned to hold her grief in subjection and to prevent her life being too much embittered by the treachery — she felt it *was* treachery — of one man. She still, however, felt anxious and self-conscious in the presence of men, especially of silent, unmarried men, and to some extent it may be said that this fear haunted her life. It was shared, however, with other fears, probably all equally baseless. Thus, she lived in constant dread of fire, of railway accidents, of runaway cabs, and of being locked into a small, confined space. The former fears she shared, of course, with many other persons of both sexes, but the latter, the dread of confined spaces, was entirely due, no doubt, to a story she had heard in early youth to the effect that her father had once suffered from that singular nervous malady, *claustrophobia* (the fear of closed spaces), the terror of being caught in a confined place without possibility of escape.

Thus it was clear that Miss Daphne Slumbubble, this good, honest soul with jet flowers in her bonnet and rows of coloured photographs of Switzerland on her bedroom mantelpiece, led a life unnecessarily haunted.

The thought of the annual holiday, however, compensated for all else. In her lonely room behind Warwick Square she stewed through the dusty heat of summer, fought her way pluckily through the freezing winter fogs, and then, with the lengthening days, worked herself steadily into a fever heat of joyous anticipation as she counted the hours to the taking of her ticket in the first week of May. When the day came her happiness was so great that she wished for nothing else in the world. Even her name ceased to trouble her, for once on the other side of the Channel it sounded quite different on the lips of the foreigners, while in the little *pension* she was known as "Mlle. Daphné," and the mere sound brought music into her heart. The odious surname belonged to the sordid London life. It had nothing to do with the glorious days that Mlle. Daphné spent among the mountain tops.

The platform at Victoria was already crowded when she arrived a good hour before the train started, and got her tiny faded trunk weighed and labelled. She was so excited that she talked unnecessarily to any one who would listen — to any one in station uniform, that is. Already in fancy she saw the blue sky above the shining snow peaks, heard the tinkling cow-bells, and sniffed the odours of pinewood and sawmill. She imagined the cheerful *table d'hôte* room with its wooden floor and rows of chairs; the *diligence* winding up the hot white road far below; the fragrant *café complet* in her bedroom at 7:30 — and then the long mornings with sketch-book and poetry-book under the forest shade, the clouds trailing slowly across the great cliffs, and the air always humming with the echoes of falling water.

"And you feel sure the passage will be calm, do you?" she asked the porter for the third time, as she bustled to and fro by his side.

"Well, there ain't no wind 'ere, at any rate, Miss," he replied cheerfully, putting her small box on a barrow.

"Such a lot of people go by this train, don't they?" she piped.

"Oh, a tidy few. This is the season for foreign parts, I suppose."

"Yes, yes; and the trains on the other side will be very full, too, I dare say," she said, following him down the platform with quick, pattering footsteps, chirping all the way like a happy bird.

"Quite likely, Miss."

"I shall go in a 'Ladies only,' you know. I always do every year. I think it's safer, isn't it?"

"I'll see to it all for yer, Miss," replied the patient porter. "But the train ain't in yet, not for another 'arf hour or so."

"Oh, thank you; then I'll be here when it comes. 'Ladies only,' remember, and second class, and a corner seat facing the engine — no, *back* to the engine, I mean; and I *do* hope the Channel will be smooth. Do you think the wind — ?"

But the porter was out of hearing by this time, and Miss Slumbubble went wandering about the platform watching the people arrive, studying the blue and yellow advertisements of the *Côte d'azur*, and waggling her jet beads with delight — with passionate delight — as she thought of her own little village in the high Alps where the snow crept down to a few hundred feet above the church and the meadows were greener than any in the whole wide world.

"I've put yer wraps in a 'Lidies only,' Miss," said the porter at length, when the train came in, "and you've got the corner back to the engine all to yerself, an' quite comfortable. Thank you, Miss." He touched his cap and pocketed his sixpence, and the fussy little traveller went off to take up her position outside the carriage door for another half hour before the train started. She was always very nervous about trains; not only fearful of possible accidents to the engine and carriages, but of untoward happenings to the occupants of corridor-less compartments during long journeys without stops. The mere sight of a railway station, with its smoke and whistling and luggage, was sufficient to set her imagination in the direction of possible disaster.

The careful porter had piled all her belongings neatly in the corner for her: three newspapers, a magazine and a novel, a little bag to carry food in, two bananas and a Bath bun in paper, a bundle of wraps tied with a long strap, an umbrella, a bottle of Yanatas, an opera-glass (for the mountains), and a camera. She counted them all over, rearranged them a little differently, and then sighed a bit, partly from excitement, partly by way of protest at time delay.

A number of people came up and eyed the compartment critically and seemed on the point of getting in, but no one actually took possession. One lady put her umbrella in the corner, and then came tearing down the platform a few minutes later to take it away again, as though she had suddenly heard the train was not to start at all. There was much bustling to and fro, and a good deal of French was audible, and the sound of it thrilled Miss Daphne with happiness, for it was another delightful little anticipation of what was to come. Even the language sounded like a holiday, and brought with it a whiff of mountains and the subtle pleasures of sweet freedom.

Then a fat Frenchman arrived and inspected the carriage, and attempted to climb in. But she instantly pounced upon him in courageous dismay.

"Mais, c'est pour dames, m'sieur!" she cried, pronouncing it "dam."

"Oh, damn!" he exclaimed in English; "I didn't notice." And the rudeness of the man — it was the fur coat over his arm made her think he was French — set her all in a flutter, so that she jumped in and took her seat hurriedly, and spread her many parcels in a protective and prohibitive way about her.

For the tenth time she opened her black beaded bag and took out her purse and made sure her ticket was in it, and then counted over her belongings.

"I *do* hope," she murmured, "I do hope that stupid porter *has* put in my luggage all right, and that the Channel won't be rough. Porters *are* so stupid. One ought never to lose sight of them till the luggage is actually in. I think I'd better pay the extra fare and go first class on the boat if it is rough. I can carry all my own packages, I think."

At that moment the man came for tickets. She searched everywhere for her own, but could not find it.

"I'm certain I had it a moment ago," she said breathlessly, while the man stood waiting at the open door. "I know I had it — only this very minute. Dear me, what *can* I have done with it? Ah here it is!"

The man took so long examining the little tourist cover that she was afraid something must be wrong with it, and when at last he tore out a leaf and handed back the rest a sort of panic seized her.

"It's all right, isn't it, guard? I mean I'm all right, am I not?" she asked.

The guard closed the door and locked it.

"All right for Folkestone, ma'am," he said, and was gone.

There was much whistling and shouting and running up and down the platform, and the inspector was standing with his hand raised and the whistle at his lips, waiting to blow and looking cross. Suddenly her own porter flew past with an empty barrow. She dashed her head out of the window and hailed him.

"You're sure you put my luggage in aren't, you?" she cried. The man did not or would not hear, and as the train moved slowly off she bumped her head against an old lady standing on the platform who was looking the other way and waving to some one in a front carriage.

"Ooh!" cried Miss Slumbubble, straightening her bonnet, "you really should look where you're looking, madam!" — and then, realising she had said something foolish, she withdrew into the carriage and sank back in a fluster on the cushions.

"Oh!" she gasped again, "oh dear! I'm actually off at last. It's too good to be true. Oh, that horrid London!"

Then she counted her money over again, examined her ticket once more, and touched each of her many packages with a long finger in a cotton glove, saying, "*That's* there, and that, and that, and — *that!*" And then turning and pointing at herself she added, with a little happy laugh, "*and that!*"

The train gathered speed, and the dirty roofs and sea of ugly chimneys flew by as the dreary miles of depressing suburbs revealed themselves through the windows. She put all her parcels up in the rack and then took them all down again; and after a bit she put a few up — a carefully selected few that she would not need till Folkestone — and arranged the others, some upon the seat beside her, and some opposite. The paper bag of bananas she kept in her lap, where it grew warmer and warmer and more and more dishevelled in appearance.

"Actually off at last!" she murmured again, catching her breath a little in her joy. "Paris, Berne, Thun, Frutigen," she gave herself a little hug that made the jet beads rattle; "then the long *diligence* journey up those gorgeous mountains," she knew every inch of the way, "and a clear fifteen days at the *pension*, or even eighteen days, if I can get the cheaper room. Wheeeee! Can it be true? Can it be really true?" In her happiness she made sounds just like a bird.

She looked out of the window, where green fields had replaced the rows of streets. She opened her novel and tried to read. She played with the newspapers in a vain attempt to keep her eye on any one column. It was all in vain. A scene of wild beauty held her inner eye and made all else dull and uninteresting. The train sped on — slowly enough to her — yet every moment of the journey, every turn of the creaking wheels that brought her nearer, every little detail of the familiar route, became a source of keenest anticipatory happiness to her. She no longer cared about her name, or her silent and faithless lover of long ago, or of anything in the world but the fact that her absorbing little annual passion was now once again in a fair way to be gratified.

Then, quite suddenly, Miss Slumbubble realised her actual position, and felt afraid, unreasonably afraid. For the first time she became conscious that she was alone, alone in the compartment of an express train, and not even of a corridor express train.

Hitherto the excitement of getting off had occupied her mind to the exclusion of everything else, and if she had realised her solitude at all, she had realised it pleasurably. But now, in the first pause for breath as it were, when she had examined her packages, counted her money, glared at her ticket, and all the rest of it for the twentieth time, she leaned back in her seat and knew with a distinct shock that she was alone in a railway carriage on a comparatively long journey, alone for the first time in her life in a rattling, racing, shrieking train. She sat bolt upright and tried to collect herself a little.

Of all the emotions, that of fear is probably the least susceptible to the power of suggestion, certainly of *auto*-suggestion; and of vague fear that has no obvious cause this is especially true. With a fear of known origin one can argue, humour it, pacify, turn on the hose of ridicule — in a word, *suggest* that it depart; but with a fear that rises stealthily out of no comprehensible causes the mind finds itself at a complete loss. The mere assertion "I am not afraid" is as useless and empty as the subtler kind of suggestion that lies in affecting to ignore it altogether. Searching for the cause, moreover, tends to confuse the mind, and searching in vain, to terrify.

Miss Slumbubble pulled herself sharply together, and began to search for what made her afraid, but for a long time she searched in vain.

At first she searched externally: she thought perhaps it had something to do with one of her packages, and she placed them all out in a row on the seat in front of her and examined each in turn, bananas, camera, food bag, black bead bag, etc. etc. But she discovered nothing among them to cause alarm.

Then she searched internally: her thoughts, her rooms in London, her *pension*, her money, ticket, plans in general, her future, her past, her health, her religion, anything and everything among the events of her inner life she passed in review, yet found nothing that could have caused this sudden sense of being troubled and afraid.

Moreover, as she vainly searched, her fear increased. She got into a regular nervous flurry.

"I declare if I'm not all in a perspiration!" she exclaimed aloud, and shifted down the dirty cushions to another place, looking anxiously about her as she did so. She probed everywhere in her thoughts to find the reason of her fear, but could think of nothing. Yet in her soul there was a sense of growing distress.

She found her new seat no more comfortable than the one before it, and shifted in turn into all the corners of the carriage, and down the middle as well, till at last she had tried every possible part of it. In each place she felt less at ease than in the one before. She got up and looked into the empty racks, under the seats, beneath the heavy cushions, which she lifted with difficulty. Then she put all the packages back again into the rack, dropping several of them in her nervous hurry, and being obliged to kneel on the floor to recover them from under the seats. This made her breathless. Moreover, the dust got into her throat and made her cough. Her eyes smarted and she grew uncomfortably warm. Then, quite accidentally, she caught sight of her reflection in the coloured picture of Boulogne under the rack, and the appearance she presented added greatly to her dismay. She looked so unlike herself, and wore such an odd expression. It was almost like the face of another person altogether.

The sense of alarm, once wakened, is fed by anything and everything, from a buzzing fly to a dark cloud in the sky. The woman collapsed on to the seat behind her in a distressing fluster of nervous fear.

But Miss Daphne Slumbubble had pluck. She was not so easily dismayed after all. She had read somewhere that terror was sometimes dispersed by the loud and strong affirmation of one's own name. She believed much that she read, provided it was plainly and vigorously expressed, and she acted at once on this knowledge.

"I am Daphne Slumbubble!" she affirmed in a firm, confident tone of voice, sitting stiffly on the edge of the seat; "I am not afraid — of anything." She added the last two words as an afterthought. "I am Daphne Slumbubble, and I have paid for my ticket, and know where I am going, and my luggage is in the van, and I have all my smaller things here!" She enumerated them one by one; she omitted nothing.

Yet the sound of her own voice, and especially of her own name, added apparently to her distress. It sounded oddly, like a voice outside the carriage. Everything seemed suddenly to have become strange, and unfamiliar, and unfriendly. She moved across to the opposite corner and looked out of the window: trees, fields, and occasional country houses flew past in endless swift succession. The country looked charming; she saw rooks flying and farm-horses moving laboriously over the fields. What in the world was there to feel afraid of? What in the world made her so restless and fidgety and frightened? Once again she examined her packages, her ticket, her money. All was right.

Then she dashed across to the window and tried to open it. The sash stuck. She pulled and pulled in vain. The sash refused to yield. She ran to the other window, with a like result. Both were closed. Both refused to open. Her fear grew. She was locked in! The windows would not open. Something was wrong with the carriage. She suddenly recalled the way every one had examined it and refused to enter. There must be something the matter with the carriage — something she had omitted to observe. Terror ran like a flame through her. She trembled and was ready to cry.

She ran up and down between the cushioned seats like a bird in a cage, casting wild glances at the racks and under the seats and out of the windows. A sudden panic took her, and she tried to open the door. It was locked. She flew to the other door. That, too, was locked. Good Heavens, both were locked! She was locked in. She was a prisoner. She was caught in a closed space. The mountains were out of her reach — the free open woods — the wide fields, the scented winds of heaven. She was caught, hemmed in, celled, restricted like a prisoner in a dungeon. The thought maddened her. The feeling that she could not reach the open spaces of sky and forest, of field and blue horizon, struck straight into her soul and touched all that she held most dear. She screamed. She ran down between the cushioned seats and screamed aloud.

Of course, no one heard her. The thunder of the train

killed the feeble sound of her voice. Her voice was the cry of the imprisoned person.

Then quite suddenly she understood what it all meant. There was nothing wrong with the carriage, or with her parcels, or with the train. She sat down abruptly upon the dirty cushions and faced the position there and then. It had nothing to do with her past or her future, her ticket or her money, her religion or her health. It was something else entirely. She knew what it was, and the knowledge brought icy terror at once. She had at last labelled the source of her consternation, and the discovery increased rather than lessened her distress.

It was the fear of closed spaces. It was *claustrophobia!*

There could no longer be any doubt about it. She was shut in. She was enclosed in a narrow space from which she could not escape. The walls and floor and ceiling shut her in implacably. The doors were fastened; the windows were sealed, there was no escape.

"That porter *might* have told me!" she exclaimed inconsequently, mopping her face. Then the foolishness of the saying dawned upon her, and she thought her mind must be going. That was the effect of claustrophobia, she remembered: the mind went, and one said and did foolish things. Oh, to get out into a free open space, uncornered! Here she was trapped, horribly trapped.

"The guard man should never have locked me in — never!" she cried, and ran up and down between the seats, throwing her weight first against one door and then against the other. Of course, fortunately, neither of them yielded.

Thinking food might calm her, perhaps, she took down the banana bag and peeled the squashy overripe fruit, munching it with part of the Bath bun from the other bag, and sitting midway on the forward seat. Suddenly the right-hand window dropped with a bang and a rattle. It had only been stuck after all, and her efforts, aided by the shaking of the train, had completed its undoing, or rather its unclosing. Miss Slumbubble shrieked, and dropped her banana and bun.

But the shock passed in a moment when she saw what had happened, and that the window was open and the sweet air pouring in from the flying fields. She rushed up and put her head out. This was followed by her hand, for she meant to open the door from the outside if possible. Whatever happened, the one imperative thing was that she must get into open space. The handle turned easily enough, but the door was locked higher up and she could not make it budge. She put her head farther out, so that the wind tore the jet bonnet off her head and left it twirling in the dusty whirlwind on the line far behind, and this sensation of the air whistling past her ears and through her flying hair somehow or other managed to make her feel wilder than ever. In fact, she completely lost her head, and began to scream at the top of her voice:

"I'm locked in! I'm a prisoner! Help, help!" she yelled.

A window opened in the next compartment and a young man put his head out.

"What the deuce is the matter? Are you being murdered?" he shouted down the wind.

"I'm locked in! I'm locked in!" screamed the hatless

lady, wrestling furiously with the obdurate door handle.

"Don't open the door!" cried the young man anxiously.

"I can't, you idiot! I can't!"

"Wait a moment and I'll come to you. Don't try to get out. I'll climb along the foot-board. Keep calm, madam, keep calm. I'll save you."

He disappeared from view. Good Heavens! He meant to crawl out and come to her carriage by the window! A man, a *young* man, would shortly be in the compartment with her. Locked in, too! No, it was impossible. That was worse than the claustrophobia, and she could not endure such a thing for a moment.

The young man would certainly kill her and steal all her packages.

She ran once or twice frantically up and down the narrow floor. Then she looked out of the window. "Oh, bless my heart and soul!" she cried out, "he's out already!"

The young man, evidently thinking the lady was being assaulted, had climbed out of the window and was pluckily coming to her rescue. He was already on the foot-board, swinging by the brass bars on the side of the coach as the train rocked down the line at a fearful pace.

But Miss Slumbubble took a deep breath and a sudden determination. She did, in fact, the only thing left to her to do. She pulled the communication cord once, twice, three times, and then drew the window up with a sudden snap just before the young man's head appeared round the corner of the sash. Then, stepping backwards, she trod on the slippery banana bag and fell flat on her back upon the dirty floor between the seats.

The train slackened speed almost immediately and came to a stop. Miss Slumbubble still sat on the floor, staring in a dazed fashion at her toes. She realised the enormity of her offence, and was thoroughly frightened. She had actually pulled the cord! — the cord that is meant to be seen but not touched, the little chain that meant a £5 fine and all sorts of dire consequences.

She heard voices shouting and doors opening, and a moment later a key rattled near her head, and she saw the guard swinging up on to the steps of the carriage. The door was wide open, and the young man from the next compartment was explaining volubly what he seen and heard.

"I thought it was murder," he was saying.

But the guard pushed quickly into the carriage and lifted the panting and dishevelled lady on to the seat.

"Now, what's all this about? Was it you that pulled the cord, ma'am?" he asked somewhat roughly. "It's serious stoppin' a train like this, you know, a mail train."

Now Miss Daphne did not mean to tell a lie. It was not deliberate, that is to say. It seemed to slip out of its own accord as the most natural and obvious thing to say. For she was terrified at what she had done, and *had* to find a good excuse. Yet, how in the world could she describe to this stupid and hurried official all she had gone through? Moreover, he would be so certain to think she was merely drunk.

"It was a man," she said, falling back instinctively upon her natural enemy. "There's a man somewhere!" She glanced round at the racks and under the seats. The guard followed her eyes.

"I don't see no man," he declared; "all I know is you've stopped the mail train without any visible or reasonable cause. I'll be obliged with your name and address, ma'am, if you please," he added, taking a dirty note-book from his pocket and wetting the blunt pencil in his mouth.

"Let me get air — at once," she said. "I must have air first. Of course you shall have my name. The whole affair is disgraceful." She was getting her wits back. She moved to the door.

"That may be, ma'am," the man said, "but I've my duty to perform, and I must report the facts, and then get the train on as quick as possible. You must stay in the carriage, please. We've been waiting 'ere a bit too long already."

Miss Slumbubble met her fate calmly. She realised it was not fair to keep all the passengers waiting while she got a little fresh air. There was a brief confabulation between the two guards, which ended by the one who had first come taking his seat in her carriage, while the other blew his whistle and the train started off again and flew at great speed the remaining miles to Folkestone.

"Now I'll take the name and address, if you please, ma'am," he said politely. "*Daphny*, yes, thank you; Daphny without a hef, all right, thank you."

He wrote it all down laboriously while the hatless little lady sat opposite, indignant, excited, ready to be voluble the moment she could think what was best to say, and above all fearful that her holiday would be delayed, if not prevented altogether.

Presently the guard looked up at her and put his note-book away in an inner pocket. It was just after he had entered the number of the carriage.

"You see, ma'am," he explained with sudden suavity, "this communication cord is only for cases of real danger, and if I report this, as I should do, it means a 'eavy fine. You must 'ave just pulled it as a sort of hexperiment, didn't you?"

Something in the man's voice caught her ear; there was a change in it; his manner, too, had altered somehow. He suddenly seemed to have become apologetic. She was quick to notice the change, though she could not understand what caused it. It began, she fancied, from the moment he entered the number of the carriage in his notebook.

"It's the delay to the train I've got to explain," he continued, as if speaking to himself, "and I can't put it all on to the engine-driver — "

"Perhaps we shall make it up and there won't be any delay," ventured Miss Slumbubble, carefully smoothing her hair and rearranging the stray hairpins.

" — and I don't want to get no one into any kind of trouble, least of all myself," he continued, wholly ignoring the interruption. Then he turned round in his seat and stared hard at his companion with rather a worried, puzzled expression of countenance and a shrug of the shoulders that was distinctly apologetic. Plainly, she thought, he was preparing the way for a compromise — for a tip!

The train was slackening speed; already it was in the cutting where it reverses and is pushed backwards on to the pier. Miss Slumbubble was desperate. She had never tipped a man before in her life except for obvious and recognised services, and this seemed to her like compounding a felony, or some such dreadful thing. Yet so much was at stake: she might be detained at Folkestone for days before the matter came into court, to say nothing of a £5 fine, which meant that her holiday would be utterly stopped. The blue and white mountains swam into her field of vision, and she heard the wind in the pine forest.

"Perhaps you would give this to your wife," she said timidly, holding out a sovereign.

The guard looked at it and shook his head.

"I 'aven't got a wife, exackly," he said; "but it isn't money I want. What I want is to 'ush this little matter up as quietly as possible. I may lose my job over this — but if you'll agree to say nothing about it, I think I can square the driver and t'other guard."

"*I* won't say anything, *of course*," stammered the astonished lady. "But I don't think I quite understand — "

"You couldn't understand either till I tell you," he replied, looking greatly relieved; "but the fact is, I never noticed the carriage till I come to put the number down, and then I see it's the very one — the very same number — "

"What number?"

He stared at her for a moment without speaking. Then he appeared to take a great decision.

"Well, I'm in your 'ands anyhow, ma'am, and I may as well tell you the lot, and then we both 'elps the other out. It's this way, you see. You ain't the first to try and jump out of this carriage — not by a long ways. It's been done before by a good number — "

"Gracious!"

"But the first who did it was that German woman, Binckmann—"

"Binckmann, the woman who was found on the line last year, and the carriage door open?" cried Miss Slumbubble, aghast.

"That's her. This was the carriage she jumped from, and they tried to say it was murder, but couldn't find any one who could have done it, and then they said she must have been crazy. And since then this carriage was said to be 'aunted, because so many other people tried to do the same thing and throw theirselves out too, till the company changed the number—"

"To this number?" cried the excited spinster, pointing to the figures on the door.

"That's it, ma'am. And if you look you'll see this number don't follow on with the others. Even then the thing didn't stop, and we got orders to let no one in. That's where I made my mistake. I left the door unlocked, and they put you in. If this gets in the papers I'll be dismissed for sure. The company's awful strict about that."

"I'm terrified!" exclaimed Miss Slumbubble, "for that's exactly what I felt—"

"That you'd got to jump out, you mean?" asked the guard.

"Yes. The terror of being shut in."

"That's what the doctors said Binckmann had—the fear of being shut up in a tight place. They gave it some long name, but that's what it was: she couldn't abide being closed in. Now, here we are at the pier, ma'am, and, if you'll allow me, I'll help you to carry your little bits of luggage."

"Oh, thank you, guard, thank you," she said faintly, taking his proffered hand and getting out with infinite relief on to the platform.

"Tchivalry ain't dead yet, Miss," he replied gallantly, as he loaded himself up within her packages and led the way down to the steamer.

Ten minutes later the deep notes of the siren echoed across the pier, and the paddles began to churn the green sea. And Miss Daphne Slumbubble, hatless but undismayed, went abroad to flutter the remnants of her faded youth before the indifferent foreigners in the cheap *pension* among the Alps.

The WOMAN'S GHOST STORY

"Yes," she said, from her seat in the dark corner, "I'll tell you an experience if you care to listen. And, what's more, I'll tell it briefly, without trimmings — I mean without unessentials. That's a thing story-tellers never do, you know," she laughed. "They drag in all the unessentials and leave their listeners to disentangle; but I'll give you just the essentials, and you can make of it what you please. But on one condition : that at the end you ask no questions, because I can't explain it and have no wish to."

We agreed. We were all serious. After listening to a dozen prolix stories from people who merely wished to "talk" but had nothing to tell, we wanted "essentials."

"In those days," she began, feeling from the quality of our silence that we were with her, "in those days I was interested in psychic things, and had arranged to sit up alone in a haunted house in the middle of London. It was a cheap and dingy lodging-house in a mean street, unfurnished. I had already made a preliminary examination in daylight that afternoon, and the keys from the caretaker, who lived next door, were in my pocket. The story was a good one — satisfied me, at any rate, that it was worth investigating; and I won't weary you with details as to the woman's murder and all the tiresome elaboration as to *why* the place was *alive*. Enough that it was.

"I was a good deal bored, therefore, to see a man, whom I took to be the talkative old caretaker, waiting for me on the steps when I went in at 11 p.m., for I had sufficiently explained that I wished to be there alone for the night.

" 'I wished to show you *the* room,' he mumbled, and of course I couldn't exactly refuse, having tipped him for the temporary loan of a chair and table.

" 'Come in, then, and let's be quick,' I said.

"We went in, he shuffling after me through the unlighted hall up to the first floor where the murder had taken place, and I prepared myself to hear his inevitable account before turning him out with the half-crown his persistence had earned. After lighting the gas I sat down in the arm-chair he had provided — a faded, brown plush arm-chair — and turned for the first time to face him and get through with the performance as quickly as possible. And it was in that instant I got my first shock. The man was *not* the caretaker. It was not the old fool, Carey, I had interviewed earlier in the day and made my plans with. My heart gave a horrid jump.

" 'Now who are *you*, pray?' I said. 'You're not Carey, the man I arranged with this afternoon. Who are you?'

"I felt uncomfortable, as you may imagine. I was a 'psychical researcher' and a young woman of new tendencies, and proud of my liberty, but I did not care to find myself in an empty house with a stranger. Something of my confidence left me.

"Confidence with women, you know, is all humbug after a certain point. Or perhaps you don't know, for most of you are men. But anyhow my pluck ebbed in a quick rush, and I felt afraid.

" 'Who are you?' I repeated quickly and nervously. The fellow was well dressed, youngish and good-looking, but with a face of great sadness. I myself was barely thirty. I am giving you essentials, or I would not mention it. Out of quite ordinary things comes this story. I think that's why it has value.

" 'No, he said; 'I'm the man who was frightened to death.'

"His voice and his words ran through me like a knife, and I felt ready to drop. In my pocket was the book I had bought to make notes in. I felt the pencil sticking in the socket. I felt, too, the extra warm things I had put on to sit up in, as no bed or sofa was available — a hundred things dashed through my mind, foolishly and without sequence or meaning, as the way is when one is really frightened. Unessentials leaped up and puzzled me, and I thought of what the papers might say if it came out, and what my 'smart' brother-in-law would think, and whether it would be told that I had cigarettes in my pocket, and was a free-thinker.

" 'The man who was frightened to death!' I repeated aghast.

" 'That's me,' he said stupidly.

"I stared at him just as you would have done — any one of you men now listening to me — and felt my life ebbing and flowing like a sort of hot fluid.

"You needn't laugh! That's how I felt. Small things, you know, touch the mind with great earnestness when terror is there — *real terror*. But I might have been at a middle-class tea-party, for all the ideas I had: they were so ordinary!

" 'But I thought you were the caretaker I tipped this afternoon to let me sleep here!' I gasped. 'Did — did Carey send you to meet me?'

" 'No,' he replied in a voice that touched my boots somehow. 'I am the man who was frightened to death. And what is more, I am frightened *now!*'

" 'So am I,' I managed to utter, speaking instinctively. 'I'm simply terrified.'

" 'Yes,' he replied in that same odd voice that seemed to sound within me. 'But you are still in the flesh, and I — *am not!*'

"I felt the need for vigorous self-assertion. I stood up in that empty, unfurnished room, digging the nails into my palms and clenching my teeth. I was determined to assert my individuality and my courage as a new woman and a free soul.

"You mean to say you are not in the flesh!' I gasped. 'What in the world are you talking about?

"The silence of the night swallowed up my voice. For the first time I realised that darkness was over the city; that dust lay upon the stairs; that the floor above was untenanted and the floor below empty. I was alone in an unoccupied and haunted house, unprotected, and a woman. I chilled. I heard the wind round the house, and knew the stars were hidden. My thoughts rushed to policemen and omnibuses, and everything that was useful and comforting. I suddenly realised what a fool I was to come to such a house alone. I was icily afraid. I thought the end of my life had come. I was an utter fool to go in for psychical research when I had not the necessary nerve.

" 'Good God!' I gasped. 'If you're not Carey, the man I arranged with, who are you?'

"I was really stiff with terror. The man moved slowly towards me across the empty room. I held out my arm to stop him, getting up out of my chair at the same moment, and he came to a halt just opposite to me, a smile on his worn, sad face.

" 'I told you who I am,' he repeated quietly with a sigh, looking at me with the saddest eyes I have ever seen, 'and I am frightened *still*.'

"By this time I was convinced that I was entertaining either a rogue or a madman, and I cursed my stupidity in bringing the man in without having seen his face. My mind was quickly made up, and I knew what to do. Ghosts and psychic phenomena flew to the winds. If I angered the creature my life might pay the price. I must humour him till I got to the door, and then race for the street. I stood bolt upright and faced him. We were about of a height, and I was a strong, athletic woman who played hockey in winter and climbed Alps in summer. My hand itched for a stick, but I had none.

" 'Now, of course, I remember,' I said with a sort of stiff smile that was very hard to force. 'Now I remember your case and the wonderful way you behaved. . . .'

"The man stared at me stupidly, turning his head to watch me as I backed more and more quickly to the door. But when his face broke into a smile I could control myself no longer. I reached the door in a run, and shot out on to the landing. Like a fool, I turned the wrong way, and stumbled over the stairs leading to the next storey. But it was too late to change. The man was after me, I was sure, though no sound of footsteps came; and I dashed up the next flight, tearing my skirt and banging my ribs in the darkness, and rushed headlong into the first room I came to. Luckily the door stood ajar, and, still more fortunate, there was a key in the lock. In a second I had slammed the door, flung my whole weight against it, and turned the key.

"I was safe, but my heart was beating like a drum. A second later it seemed to stop altogether, for I saw that there was someone else in the room besides myself. A man's figure stood between me and the windows, where the street lamps gave just enough light to outline his shape against the glass. I'm a plucky woman, you know, for even then I didn't give up hope, but I may tell you that I have never felt so vilely frightened in all my born days. I had locked myself in with him!

"The man leaned against the window, watching me where I lay in a collapsed heap upon the floor. So there were two men in the house with me, I reflected. Perhaps other rooms were occupied too! What could it all mean? But, as I stared something changed in the room, or in me — hard to say which — and I realised my mistake, so that my fear, which had so far been physical, at once altered its character and became *psychical*. I became afraid in my soul instead of in my heart, and I knew immediately who this man was.

" 'How in the world did you get up here?' I stammered to him across the empty room, amazement momentarily stemming my fear.

" 'Now, let me tell you,' he began, in that odd far-away voice of his that went down my spine like a knife. 'I'm in different space, for one thing, and you'd find me in any room you went into; for according to your way of measuring, I'm *all over the house*. Space is a bodily condition, but I am out of the body, and am not affected by space. It's my condition that keeps me here. I want something to change my condition for me, for then I could get away. What I want is sympathy. Or, really, more than sympathy; I want affection — I want *love!*'

While he was speaking I gathered myself slowly upon my feet. I wanted to scream and cry and laugh all at once, but I only succeeded in sighing, for my emotion was exhausted and a numbness was coming over me. I felt for the matches in my pocket and made a movement towards the gas jet.

" 'I should be much happier if you didn't light the gas,'

he said at once, 'for the vibrations of your light hurt me a good deal. You need not be afraid that I shall injure you. I can't touch your body to begin with, for there's a great gulf fixed, you know; and really this half-light suits me best. Now, let me continue what I was trying to say before. You know, so many people have come to this house to see me, and most of them have seen me, and one and all have been terrified. If only, oh! if only some one would be *not* terrified, but kind and loving to me! Then, you see, I might be able to change my condition and get away.'

"His voice was so sad that I felt tears start somewhere at the back of my eyes; but fear kept all else in check, and I stood shaking and cold as I listened to him.

" 'Who are you then ? Of course Carey didn't send you, I know now,' I managed to utter. My thoughts scattered dreadfully and I could think of nothing to say. I was afraid of a stroke.

" 'I know nothing about Carey, or who he is,' continued the man quietly, 'and the name my body had I have forgotten, thank God ; but I am the man who was frightened to death in this house ten years ago, and I have been frightened ever since, and am frightened still; for the succession of cruel and curious people who come to this house to see the ghost, and thus keep alive its atmosphere of terror, only helps to render my condition worse. If only some one would be kind to me — *laugh*, speak gently and rationally with me, cry if they like, pity, comfort, soothe me — anything but come here in curiosity and tremble as you are now doing in that corner. Now, madam, won't you take pity on me?' His voice rose to a dreadful cry. 'Won't you step out into the middle of the room and try to love me a little?'

"A horrible laughter came gurgling up in my throat as I heard him, but the sense of pity was stronger than the laughter, and I found myself actually leaving the support of the wall and approaching the centre of the floor.

" 'By God!' he cried, at once straightening up against the window, 'you have done a kind act. That's the first attempt at sympathy that has been shown me since I died, and I feel better already. In life, you know, I was a misanthrope. Everything went wrong with me, and I came to hate my fellow men so much that I couldn't bear to see them even. Of course, like begets like, and this hate was returned. Finally I suffered from horrible delusions, and my room became haunted with demons that laughed and grimaced, and one night I ran into a whole cluster of them near the bed — and the fright stopped my heart and killed me. It's hate and remorse, as much as terror, that clogs me so thickly and keeps me here. If only some one could feel pity, and sympathy, and perhaps a little love for me, I could get away and be happy. When you came this afternoon to see over the house I watched you, and a little hope came to me for the first time. I saw you had courage, originality, resources — *love*. If only I could touch your heart, without frightening you, I knew I could perhaps tap that love you have stored up in your being there, and thus borrow the wings for my escape!'

"Now I must confess my heart began to ache a little, as fear left me and the man's words sank their sad meaning into me. Still, the whole affair was so incredible, and so touched with unholy quality, and the story of a woman's murder I had come to investigate had so obviously nothing to do with this thing, that I felt myself in a kind of wild dream that seemed likely to stop at any moment and leave me somewhere in bed after a nightmare.

"Moreover, his words possessed me to such an extent that I found it impossible to reflect upon anything else at all, or to consider adequately any ways and means of action or escape.

"I moved a little nearer to him in the gloom, horribly frightened, of course, but with the beginnings of a strange determination in my heart.

" 'You women,' he continued, his voice plainly thrilling at my approach, 'you wonderful women, to whom life often brings no opportunity of spending your great love, oh, if you only could know how many of *us* simply yearn for it! It would save our souls, if you but knew. Few might find the chance that you now have, but if you only spent your love freely, without definite object, just letting it flow openly for all who need, you would reach hundreds and thousands of souls like me, and *release us!* Oh, madam, I ask you again to feel with me, to be kind and gentle — and if you can to love me a little!'

"My heart did leap within me and this time the tears did come, for I could not restrain them. I laughed too, for the way he called me 'madam' sounded so odd, here in this empty room at midnight in a London street, but my laughter stopped dead and merged in a flood of weeping when I saw how my change of feeling affected him. He had left his place by the window and was kneeling on the floor at my feet, his hands stretched out towards me, and the first signs of a kind of glory about his head.

" 'Put your arms round me and kiss me, for the love of God!' he cried. 'Kiss me, oh, kiss me, and I shall be freed! You have done so much already — now do this!'

"I stuck there, hesitating, shaking, my determination on the verge of action, yet not quite able to compass it. But the terror had almost gone.

" 'Forget that I'm a man and you're a woman,' he continued in the most beseeching voice I ever heard. 'Forget that I'm a ghost, and come out boldly and press me to you with a great kiss, and let your love flow into me. Forget yourself just for one minute and do a brave thing! Oh, love me, *love me*, LOVE ME! and I shall be free!'

"The words, or the deep force they somehow released in the centre of my being, stirred me profoundly, and an emotion infinitely greater than fear surged up over me and carried me with it across the edge of action. Without hesitation I took two steps forward towards him where he knelt, and held out my arms. Pity and love were in my heart at that moment, genuine pity, I swear, and genuine love. I forgot myself and my little tremblings in a great desire to help another soul.

" 'I love you! poor, aching, unhappy thing! I love you,' I cried through hot tears; 'and I am not the least bit afraid in the world.'

"The man uttered a curious sound, like laughter, yet not laughter, and turned his face up to me.

The light from the street below fell on it, but there was another light, too, shining all round it that seemed to come from the eyes and skin. He rose to his feet and met me, and in that second I folded him to my breast and kissed him full on the lips again and again."

All our pipes had gone out, and not even a skirt rustled in that dark studio as the story-teller paused a moment to steady her voice, and put a hand softly up to her eyes before going on again.

"Now, what can I say, and how can I describe to you, all you sceptical men sitting there with pipes in your mouths, the amazing sensation I experienced of holding an intangible, impalpable thing so closely to my heart that it touched my body with equal pressure all the way down, and then melted away somewhere into my very being? For it was like seizing a rush of cool wind and feeling a touch of burning fire the moment it had struck its swift blow and passed on. A series of shocks ran all over and all through me; a momentary ecstasy of flaming sweetness and wonder thrilled down into me; my heart gave another great leap — and then I was alone.

"The room was empty. I turned on the gas and struck a match to prove it. All fear had left me, and something was singing round me in the air and in my heart like the joy of a spring morning in youth. Not all the devils or shadows or hauntings in the world could then have caused me a single tremor.

"I unlocked the door and went all over the dark house, even into kitchen and cellar and up among the ghostly attics. But the house was empty. Something had left it. I lingered a short hour, analysing, thinking, wondering — you can guess what and how, perhaps, but I won't detail, for I promised only essentials, remember — and then went out to sleep the remainder of the night in my own flat, locking the door behind me upon a house no longer haunted.

"But my uncle, Sir Henry, the owner of the house, required an account of my adventure, and of course I was in duty bound to give him some kind of a true story. Before I could begin, however, he held up his hand to stop me.

" 'First,' he said, 'I wish to tell you a little deception I ventured to practise on you. So many people have been to that house and seen the ghost that I came to think the story acted on their imaginations, and I wished to make a better test.

So I invented for their benefit another story, with the idea that if you did see anything I could be sure it was not due merely to an excited imagination.'

" 'Then what you told me about a woman having been murdered, and all that, was not the true story of the haunting?'

" 'It was not. The true story is that a cousin of mine went mad in that house, and killed himself in a fit of morbid terror following upon years of miserable hypochondriasis. It is his figure that investigators see.'

" 'That explains, then,' I gasped.

" 'Explains what?'

I thought of that poor struggling soul, longing all these years for escape, and determined to keep my story for the present to myself.

" 'Explains, I mean, why I did not see the ghost of the murdered woman,' I concluded.

" 'Precisely,' said Sir Henry, 'and why, if you had seen anything, it would have had value, inasmuch as it could not have been caused by the imagination working upon a story you already knew.' ”

www.ingramcontent.com/pod-product-compliance
Lightning Source LLC
Chambersburg PA
CBHW062015170626

46813CB00001B/170